Noble Blood

by

Linda J. Parisi

This is a work of fiction. Names, characters, places, and incidents are either the product of the author's imagination or are used fictitiously, and any resemblance to actual persons living or dead, business establishments, events, or locales, is entirely coincidental.

Noble Blood

Contact Information: info@thewildrosepress.com

Cover Art by *The Wild Rose Press*

The Wild Rose Press
PO Box 708
Adams Basin, NY 14410-0706
Visit us at www.thewildrosepress.com

Publishing History
First Black Rose Edition, 2008
Print ISBN 1-60154-488-X
ISBN 13: 9781601544889

Published in the United States of America

The Sun. Always the Sun. How could her eyes, as tired as they were, open of their own accord? How could her feet carry her, of their own volition, to the tiny deck outside her living room? How could her mind, normally sane and logical, accept his presence as he stepped behind her? What was this need that not only consented to the hands on her shoulders but actually welcomed them?

The Sun. Golden glorious rays. A soft warm caress. A lover's touch. That spark of anticipation deep inside her belly as the sky lightened. She'd never known so many shades of gray could blend into pale yellow then burst upon the horizon with bright white light.

Nor had she known that the white light would burst inside of her, ripple under her skin, tantalize and tease her every sense. Such power. From her muscles to her bones to her individual cells, they all cried out with anticipation. But none more than her core, that deepest part of her, the place that made her—her.

She wanted. Not just the energy she absorbed and drank in like a greedy infant. She wanted more. Not just the molten heat deep inside her belly. She wanted *him*.

The pressure of his fingers increased. If she turned, he'd know. Deep inside, she was certain he knew already. Her body betrayed her, circling to meet his gaze. She'd never realized there were rings of fire around his irises. She'd never realized his eyes were almost silver, brilliant like a flash of light against polished chrome.

She'd called him Elrond that first time they met, likening him to the Master of Imladris. A leader who was hard from battling the forces of evil but just. A leader who was weary from shouldering the responsibility of saving a world he would eventually leave.

Dedication

Sometimes, all you have to go on is belief in yourself and a dream. This book is dedicated to all those who believed in me while I made my dream come true.

Chapter One

Bitterness still lives here.

Tamara Duncan sensed a deep pain, an angry agony, all absorbed by the structure before her. Funny that she should feel this way about a routine estate sale.

Ivy run amok, peeling paint, boards of what had once been a stately New Jersey home near the shore now curled in disgust. What a sin to see an old house dying of neglect. No, that wasn't quite right. Dying of the hatred that had lived within.

"Tara. L...ook."

Tara swung around towards her assistant, Morgan, glad for the interruption. He was busy clearing some vines off a section of rusted metal fence. At first Tara couldn't tell what he'd found, then realized it was some sort of coat of arms attached to the fence. "Do you recognize the crest?"

He blinked. Once. Twice. "No."

Poor Morgan. Brilliant mind. Delayed relay switch. He picked up his camera and took several pictures of his find. Morgan would work for weeks without stopping until he knew every last detail on a project. And he was happy for the chance. Most everyone thought he was slow. Tara knew better. "Let's go inside."

She walked up the steps with a tiny trip of trepidation and a great deal of wonder at the cause. The house? She didn't think so. This was simply another estate, close to her own home, and she was just another buyer looking to turn a profit.

"Wa...tch yourself." Morgan had a tendency to hover, which sometimes annoyed, usually amused, and at times like these, made her incredibly grateful. She wasn't used to someone caring about her. The Sisters tried, God knows. But once an orphan, always an orphan.

Tara smiled, hiding the pain that always rankled, simmering there just below the surface. "I will." She reached out to open the door, grasped the handle, and jumped back as if she'd touched a live wire.

"Tara?" Morgan's puzzled tone matched her thoughts. What the hell was that? Static electricity? Considering the dampness in the air, she doubted it. She reached out again but this time all she felt was a strange vibration running through her arm.

Fanciful, she could hear Father Duncan tell her yet again. *You're bein' fanciful, child. Always thinkin' of things that aren't there, walkin' around with your head in the clouds. You'd best set your head on straight.*

"What?" she asked, shaking her head to set it straight as she could hear Father Duncan telling her to. "Oh," she said, pushing the door open and stepping inside.

Tara shivered. Usually old houses had that musty, unused, un-lived in smell. What hit her broadside was the sense of decay underneath. As if someone had willed themselves to die here. Beside her, Morgan shivered also. "You feel it too?" He nodded.

His excitement gone, Morgan simply looked frightened. "Let's go." Morgan rarely spoke with such urgency. He did now. “Bad place.”

Tara wasn’t sure. Fear came from the unknown, and for the life of her, she wasn’t afraid. Nervous. Excited. Not afraid. “Stay here.”

“No.” He took a few steps and shuddered again. “St...ay with you.”

“I’ll be fine.” Touched by his loyalty she suggested, “Why don’t you start on this floor? I’ll go upstairs.”

He swallowed as if girding himself to argue. She placed a gentle hand on his arm. His face lit up as it always did. She had that affect on him as if her very presence righted his world. But she also had the feeling he sensed she was all right and he calmed down. He nodded. “OK.”

Tara climbed to the second floor. The bedrooms seemed unremarkable. The furniture would probably make an antique dealer’s day once the pieces were restored. None of that interested her. Attics. Basements. They hid her livelihood. Hidden treasure waiting to be discovered and displayed on the shelves of her store, The Treasure Trove. What people wanted to buy never ceased to amaze her and she went to great lengths to supply the unusual. Like now.

What stories this place could tell. She thought of the tales as she made note of a few collectibles she would purchase. She was being fanciful again, but what the heck, as an adult her imagination was her livelihood.

Yet she couldn’t find an attic stair or a hidden panel. *Where are you? Come out, come out wherever you are.*

Tara found herself standing at the top of the staircase leading back to the lower floor. She placed her hand on the end cap of the rail. An unknown influence caused her to look down. She realized the knob was engraved with a strange sort of symbol that made no sense to her. As her fingers explored, the odd thrum increased through her fingertips. She pushed in with her thumb, and all of a sudden the floor panel behind her moved.

How clever, she thought. A staircase behind a staircase. And rather than a hidden attic, she'd found the hidden basement instead. "Morgan?" She heard his running footsteps. "Come look."

His face brightened in answer to her excitement. He walked up the steps but as soon as he reached the top, he froze. "Bad. Bad, bad, bad, bad, bad, bad…" He would have continued but Tara grabbed his arm. Her touch soothed him. As always.

"Morgan. Take it easy. You're all right. I'm here. Morgan? It's all right."

"Go. Now. Mu…st go now. Must go."

He started hopping from one foot to the other, agitated, as she'd never seen him before. She increased the pressure of her fingers on his arm. This time, the gesture didn't soothe. He was so frightened he wouldn't stop moving. Maybe if she talked to him. "Calm down, Morgan. Just go back down the stairs and wait for me."

"No," he cried, piercing her soul. "You come with me now."

Taken aback, Tara didn't know what to say. Morgan never spoke in full sentences. Half the time she only understood him because she sensed his intent. "Morgan. Stop this, right this second."

She'd never spoken to him in a stern tone before but at least she had his attention. "There is absolutely nothing wrong. Do you understand me?"

He stood stock still for a split second then broke out of her grasp, turning in half circles as if not knowing which way to go or what to do. That was when she realized how much he really cared about her. He was frightened, not only for himself but for her. Funny that the thought of having a brother would come at a time like this. But he was acting like one.

"Listen. I know you're scared, but I'm fine." She tried to soothe him by stroking the top of his arm. "Go downstairs and finish your pictures. Go on. I'll be all right."

Shaking her head after he left, Tara could only wonder at his reaction. Usually she was the one able to sense things, recognize hidden emotions in people. When you guard yourself it's easy to see the shields in others. But Morgan was truly frightened for her. Why?

She closed her eyes and tried to get a feel of the house again. A shell. An empty husk. No life, but more important, none of the feelings that plagued her earlier. Wood. Stone. Mortar. Brick. How could it go from something to literally nothing in such a short period of time and for no reason?

Tara approached the opening and pulled a flashlight out of her pocket. She didn't think she'd find an active wall switch.

The stairs were fairly steep and quite narrow. With her focus mainly on getting down them, she didn't catch the impact of the room until she stood almost in its center. "Wow."

Understated elegance. Opulence. Rich velvet, plush carpet. She flicked the flashlight at the ceiling and marveled at the chandelier over her head. A retreat? Someone's secret hideaway? Excitement bubbled through her. Forget the antique hunters, as she called them. *She* was going to have a field day. Hurricane lamps, paintings, mantelpieces, and a snuffbox. Genuine? She hoped so. Exactly the kinds of items she was looking for.

Turning, Tara made her way back to the stairs. In her excitement to tell Morgan all she'd found, she bumped into a table. The table began to tip and out of the corner of her eye she saw something start to fall. It seemed like a box of some sort. Instinctively she reached out to grasp it, and the instant she touched it, a needle of white-hot flame pierced through her brain.

She staggered; her only thought was to escape—the house, the pain—just to get away. She crawled up the steep stairs, wanting to clutch her head with her hands, but needing them to help her in her ascent. As she reached the landing, she collapsed, half-sliding, half-rolling down the main staircase. She landed on the floor with a heavy thud. “Morgan,” she tried to call out.

The world went black.

****

Morgan rocked back and forth on his knees; tears pouring down his cheeks. “I did what you told me to do, Master.”

Well done.

“She’s still alive, Master.”

Interesting.

“I didn’t want to hurt her, Master.”

You didn’t.

“Did I do good, Master?”

Yes, of course you did.

“Shall I bring her to you now, Master?”

No. Leave her. Bring the box to me.

“Yes, Master.”

Use the cloth I gave you.

“Yes, Master.”

Now you will continue the plan.

“Yes, Master. I hear and obey.”

****

Nicholai Valentin strode through the casino, his mind closed to the Las Vegas din, glitz, and glitter. Nothing more than smoke and mirrors. Alexi played a dangerous game with an existence based on deception, and Nicholai had come to put an end to it.

Once and for all. It was time for his brother to come back into the fold. Now. Before it was too late.

The dark quiet of the hallway contrasted sharply with the bright light and noise where the real show occurred. Uncomfortable with the cameras overhead, he moved faster than they could record. Anonymity was key. Invisibility had kept their race alive throughout the ages; honor and duty had kept their House strong. Why couldn't Alexi understand that?

"You could have knocked," Alexi said.

Nicholai shrugged. He'd thought he'd slipped into his brother's room unnoticed. "Such respect is earned."

Alexi leaned back in his chair, his pose nonchalant. "I take it, then, that this is not a social visit."

"No it is not." Nicholai surveyed his surroundings with disdain. "I cannot believe that you risk so much for this." He made a sweeping gesture with his hand to encompass the room.

"Risk is relative, brother. You, of all people, should know that."

Always pressing the edge, Nicholai thought, intense weariness threatening to overwhelm him. How many times had he wished he could trade places with his twin so that Alexi would understand the weight of the mantle he carried. And yet he loved his brother. More than Alexi would ever know. "You will cease this madness immediately. You will stand by my side at the ceremony, a member of our House, with pride in who and what you are."

"And if I decline?"

"You have no option."

Alexi smiled. So innocent. So confident. So untouched by the burden of leadership. "Get a life, Nico."

"Funny, but I thought I was trying to save

yours."

"Well, well. A sense of humor from a man who has none. I'm impressed."

Did Alexi think this was some kind of joke? Did he think the continuation of their race was funny? How could he believe that the years of tradition, the honor, and the pride could be dismissed with a wave of the hand? "As Head of this House..." Nicholai began.

"By sixty-three seconds."

"I order you to—"

"To what? Disappear? That would solve all your problems, wouldn't it?" Alexi sneered. "Stick around for the show and you'll see how it's done."

Deep in his heart, Nicholai ached for his brother. He had no idea why Alexi thought he wished him gone, or why Alexi thought he had to go to such extremes to be noticed. But Nicholai had a family, no, a race to protect, and Alexi was endangering them all.

All right, he told himself. Be honest. You also have a position to protect. "Challenge me."

Alexi looked amazed at his words, then gave a snort of disbelief. "Do I look like a complete fool, Nico?"

"You make a spectacle of yourself every night, Alexi." He watched his brother's eyes widen as his barb hit home.

"So what? Haven't you ever heard of hiding in plain sight?"

"Not when you flaunt your powers for all to see. But this is not about the game you play. This is about the absolute disdain you show for who and what you are. The other Houses are making noise."

"That pack of flea-bitten hyenas?"

"That so-called pack of flea-bitten hyenas—"

"Won't let you become Head of the High Council," Alexi interrupted, "if your no-account brother keeps causing you a problem."

"Yo, Prince," a voice called from the other side of the door. "You're on in ten."

"Yo, Prince?" Nicholai mocked.

At least Alexi had the grace to look a bit abashed. "Show business."

"Alexi, when will you learn to take things seriously? Those so-called hyenas have the power to destroy us. Back them into a corner and they will lash out. As it is now, I may not be able to protect you."

"Protect *me*?" his brother's asked, Alexi's shoulders shrugging with disdain. "Then don't."

Aghast, Nicholai could only stare. "You do not mean that."

"No," Alexi replied, his smile saccharine sweet. "Of course I don't."

"Alexi, I love you. You are my brother."

Alexi snorted. "You love the Nobility. You love being a prince. You love being a prince of the Nobility." He turned away. "I can't do this right now. There's a place where I'm actually needed. We'll talk after the show."

Nicholai wanted to say more, but Alexi was already leaving the room. "I'll be waiting."

As Nicholai followed, he asked himself some tough questions. Was that what was driving Alexi? A need to be recognized? Nicholai loved his work; being named to the Council was an incredible honor. But was Alexi right? Did it mean more to Nicholai than his own family? How could Alexi think such a thing? Didn't he realize that all the work he poured into the Nobility was for him, their family, their House?

Nicholai was tempted to wait outside in the car with young Andre, his driver. He preferred to be away from the irritating confusion of the casino, but he was also curious to see what his brother did on stage. As a performer, Alexi became the center of attention. Once Nicholai realized that, he realized Alexi had often been pushed aside in his favor as they were growing up. In answer, his brother did many things to get attention.

But Nicholai had been groomed to become Head of the House since birth. He'd been groomed to become a member of the High Council since his early twenties. He had accepted his role and now Alexi had to accept his. There was no choice in the matter. The time had come for Alexi to take his rightful place within the Nobility. End of discussion.

An usher greeted Nicholai, taking him to a table in the back of the room where he could remain unnoticed yet watch the show from a decent vantage point. A glass of Courvoisier, properly warmed, awaited. At least in this his brother performed as he should. The rest? The rest was not nearly as harmless as Alexi deemed.

The lights dimmed. Pyrotechnics shot out from the edge of the stage creating a wall of yellow light. After a moment the entire room went black except for a single spotlight illuminating his twin, music playing softly in the background. Alexi never spoke as an announcer welcomed the spectators to the show. The music became a bit louder as Alexi began with slight of hand. Amused, Nicholai smiled. The same tricks Zandor had shown them as boys. Nothing overt. Nothing to make the other Houses react as they had. When Alexi used his powers, he made every effort to camouflage his actions. As would any magician.

But Alexi was not a magician. Nor was he human. He was of Noble Blood.

Nicholai could not understand. To him, this behavior, this blatant exhibitionism, was demeaning. Why would Alexi, a True Noble, his flesh and blood, lower himself to a human level?

Nicholai found his answer at the beginning of

each deception as he held his breath with the audience, only to let it go once the trick was complete. Adrenaline surged through his body at the sound of their applause. And the applause only grew louder and louder. They loved him. They loved Alexi. Humans loved his charisma, his verve and his showmanship. He could feel their adoration for his brother ripple over his skin in a shower of reverence; hear their praise as they spoke with one another. How intoxicating for one who'd spent his whole life in the shadows.

The room went black again. This time Alexi spoke, his voice clear and strong. "In a moment I will be placed in handcuffs, a straitjacket, and hung upside down in this." The stage illuminated slowly to reveal a huge square of steel fashioned in the shape of a bank vault. "I ask for three volunteers to come up on stage and verify that all the locks and fastenings are secure."

An usher touched his shoulder. "If you will follow me, sir?"

Having no choice, Nicholai rose. He caught the smirk in Alexi's gaze. His brother would have much to answer for later.

"Once inside," Alexi continued. "The door will seal and the air will be sucked out. I will have three minutes to reach the door and open the lock." A large digital timer illuminated over his head.

Nicholai knew that their lung capacity would enable Alexi to remain conscious for much longer than that. When Alexi stopped in front of him to have his bonds checked, he winked. "Later," Nicholai growled, before moving back into the shadows on the side of the stage.

A collective gasp rose from the crowd as the strap lifted his brother by his feet and hung him upside down. Nicholai shuddered. To be locked in, totally enclosed, deprived of Sun or moonlight—

unthinkable. "Prince of Darkness," the announcer called out. "Are you ready?"

Alexi nodded. Nicholai watched his brother intently until the door shut. He was certain he'd already released the handcuffs under the straitjacket. The clock began to count down immediately.

A knot formed in his stomach. Sweat dotted his brow. He could not even contemplate what was going on inside that vault. Total darkness. No air. Nicholai had never told anyone about his secret fear.

"Thirty seconds."

The knot grew. Nicholai comforted himself by calculating Alexi's progress. He should be just about free of the straitjacket by now and working on the strap holding his feet.

"One minute."

Something was wrong. He was certain. Then he chided himself. What was wrong was his fear. Nothing more.

"One minute and thirty seconds."

Alexi should be out by now. He frowned. His fists clenched. Panic struck. *Andre. Come to me. Alexi's in danger.*

"Two minutes."

The murmur of the crowd grew. Even *they* were expecting him by now. Was Alexi playing with him? Making him suffer for…what? Loving him? A white-hot needle of searing pain sliced through his brain. He collapsed to one knee, his hands clutching his head.

"Two minutes and thirty seconds."

"My Lord? Are you all right?" Andre stood by his side.

By sheer effort of will, Nicholai rose. No time to explain.

"Three minutes."

The crowd noise grew louder. The pain in his

head blurred his vision. "The curtains," he choked out. "Close the curtains."

Nico. Help me.

****

Nicholai paced in the center of the penthouse suite in the heart of New York City, his rage a living thing. He stopped, swerved, and came to a stop in front of the huge picture window facing the city. A city his brother could not see. Pain knifed through his heart. "My brother lies in a coma. Do you really expect me not to react?"

His mentor, Stefano Benedetti let out a deep breath before taking a sip of the drink in his hand. "I expect you to do what I've trained you to do. Watch, wait, listen, gather your facts, then decide."

"Easier said than done." Disappointment threatened to overwhelm as he asked the question he'd dreaded asking. "Are you going to postpone the ceremony?"

Stefano gave no hint of his thoughts away. "You really need to learn to curb your emotions, Nicholai."

Emotions be damned, he thought. "I have worked most of my adult life to become Steward to the High Council."

"Yes. And you have worked very hard. However the Council deems it appropriate at the moment."

"Appropriate," he repeated, bitterness riding his tone.

Stefano's countenance softened. "I know, my young protégé. But you still have lessons to learn."

"You can stand there and speak to me about lessons at a time like this? Do you expect me to simply sit back, watch, wait, and listen while Rhys-Jones tries to obliterate my family?"

"You do not know that he is behind this."

"I do not know that he is not."

Stefano nodded. "All the more reason to gather your facts. I have advised the rest of the Council that you are to perform the investigation. They agreed, with a bit of arm twisting."

At least he'd been given the some mastery over his own fate. He nodded his thanks as the elder man took another sip of his drink. "Now to practical matters. We believe it will be best to advise the rest of the Houses without a full gathering."

Nicholai agreed. "A full Council meeting could get out of hand."

His mentor stared at him, seeming to debate what his next words would be. "As you know, a true Noble was made last night." The thought still floored him. He couldn't comprehend the audacity of someone breaking their most ancient of laws. "We believe the making caused your brother's illness. She—"

"She?" he cried. "A woman?" Stunned, Nicholai could barely breathe. Rhys-Jones used a woman to destroy his brother? Destroy him?

"I can still read your thoughts, Nicholai. You have no proof and until you have proof, you cannot accuse. Do you understand me?"

Nicholai calmed down. He heard the veiled threat behind the words. Behave, toe the line, or the Stewardship would no longer exist. "Yes," he bit out.

"As I was saying, there are certain problems you are going to encounter in your investigation. The first being that we do not even know who this woman is, what House she is from, nothing. Not to mention that her very existence will cause incredible turmoil between the Houses."

Not know? "Have you been able to find out anything? I am more inclined to believe she was bought and paid for by my enemies, one House in particular."

Stefano rose without replying. The interview was over. Once again, he was floored by the power the man wielded. Not many could dismiss Nicholai

Valentin with a wave of the hand. "You must find the answers we need without emotion, Nicholai."

The words between the lines sounded loud and clear. This was going to be his final exam. If he failed, he could kiss all he'd worked for good-bye. Even worse, if he failed, his brother might die.

Chapter Two

Nicholai's only thought was to get home as he left the hotel. During the plane ride back to Nevada, he wondered if he could have changed the course of fate. He couldn't stop the thread of anger simmering in his veins any more than he could stop the acid churning in his stomach. So how could he have changed fate?

Damn, he railed against himself. Twice as helpless as a newborn babe. No idea how to bring his brother back, no idea who the woman was that had caused his brother's illness, only the cold knowledge that Rhys-Jones was behind the events that had taken place. Nicholai ended up sitting in the solarium simply cradling his brother's head. All I ever wanted, he tried to explain to Alexi, was to protect you. I thought—I thought that becoming a member of the High Council would give me, *us*, enough power to survive. Put us above the possibility of a threat. No one would have the nerve to destroy the family of a member of the High Council, definitely not the senior member. What have I done?

He ran his hand over the silken threads of his brother's hair. So alike, yet so un-alike, he thought.

Jet-black hair, flawless skin. The slight notch in the top of their ears that marked them as True Nobles. How he wished he could see his own clear gray eyes stare back at him. How he wished his fingers felt warmth as he dragged them lightly over his brother's face. Or that his eyes could glean some kind of color in Alexi's skin. Something. Anything.

"My Lord. The plane is ready."

He lifted his head to stare at his Steward. His face portrayed a mask of ice. Only his gaze showed the emotions roiling beneath the surface. Beneath his hand, Alexis' heart beat strong and steady. That was his one saving grace, the one fact that kept him in his anger and pain from destroying everything in his path.

"My Lord?" Sergei repeated.

Nicholai rose, placing Alexi's head on the pillow with a brother's gentleness. *Why didn't you listen to me, brother? Why did you keep flirting with danger? Damn you, your foolishness opened you up to attack, made you vulnerable—hell, made us all vulnerable.*

I should have tried to bring you under my wing, Nicholai thought. I should have worked with you. Maybe then you could have seen what it took to be the Head of the House, perhaps even the Head of the Nobility. "Will he awaken, Sergei?" he asked, giving voice to his greatest fear.

"I do not know. There is no telling what the making will do." Sergei's voice broke. He could not continue. Neither of them dared say anything more. The death of his brother was not something Nicholai would contemplate.In the past lesser Nobles, those with less than enough Noble blood flowing through their veins, had tried to use the Water of Change to become True Nobles. So many had died from the attempts that the Water was now forbidden.

"He will gather strength from the Sun and that will heal his body." Sergei tried to give him what comfort he could.

"But what of his mind, Sergei? What of his mind?" he asked, frustration pouring from his tone.

"I cannot answer, My Lord. You and Alexi are True Nobles. Born that way, the strongest of us all. If you had less Noble blood, if you were not True, I do not believe Alexi would be alive right now."

"Do you think he could stay like this forever?" His stomach fell to his feet as this terrible thought pounded in his brain.

"Again, My Lord, I cannot answer. Nothing like this has ever happened before."

Nicholai forced his mind from the possibility that Alexi might not survive. He sighed. A thousand questions and so few answers. "Alexi is her link? They are connected. They have to be, otherwise he would be with us now."

"As are you."

Nicholai dismissed the possibility with a wave of his hand. He was not the one lying unconscious. "I have been directed by the High Council to investigate how she was able to steal the Water of Change."

"Are you so sure she is the cause, my Lord?"

He refused to answer. He reached over and brushed the hair off of Alexi's brow. "Watch over him, Sergei."

"Already done, my Lord."

He looked up at his long time friend and confidant, his gaze turning to steel. "I swear to you, I will find the truth."

He looked down once more at his brother. *You will come back to me, Alexi.* "I will find out who put her up to this, and when I find that they were trying to destroy me and my family, I will obliterate them." He paused, bent down, and kissed his brother on the forehead. "Then I will destroy *her*. Personally."

****

The room reeked of disinfectant and that distinctive odor found only in hospitals. Moving her head she remembered waking to excruciating pain and falling back into blessed oblivion several times during the night. Try as Tara might now, however, oblivion would not come.

"So you won't die after all."

Die? Where was she? She opened her eyes. At first, all she saw were the steel railings guarding the bed. Then she saw a water pitcher sitting on the side table. *Property of Jersey Shore Medical* the label read.

Moving slightly, she focused on a pair of hands gripping the steel bed rail. Strong. Deeply tanned. Well-shaped and finely manicured. A man's hands. She'd seen these hands before. In her dreams? In reality? She wasn't sure.

Lifting her gaze, her breath caught in her throat. Midnight black hair and chiseled features. Incredibly clear gray eyes staring at her with intense anger. Why? Thick dark brows drawn together into a double crease over an aristocratic nose. Her gaze shifted slightly. There were slight notches in his ears that gave them a rounded but definitely pointed tip. "Elrond," she breathed.

"I beg your pardon?"

"Elrond Halvelven. From the novel. You know—" All of a sudden she couldn't remember the name. It was on the tip of her tongue then floated away just out of reach.

He scowled. "I am afraid not."

He seemed to be unable to mask the anger or the intensity of his gaze. What had she done to him to make him want her dead? She was in a hospital. Had there been an accident? Her fault? "What happened? Dear God in Heaven, don't tell me. Have I killed someone?"

"Not yet," he hissed.

"Wait a minute," she began, clutching her head with her hands, her stomach a sea of acid. "If I did something, if something happened, you have to understand I didn't mean to hurt anyone."

"Of course not."

He didn't believe her. Why? In fact, he seemed to think that whatever had happened wasn't an accident. "Look, I don't know you. At least I don't think I do. And that has to mean you don't know me. Whatever happened has to be an accident."

He didn't answer right away which increased her confusion, then her ire. "Why won't you answer?"

He opened his mouth to tell her then froze. No, that was wrong. He retreated behind a thick wall of ice. Why was he being so cold? And who the hell was he?

"I don't know what you want from me. I don't even know where I am. So back off."

Just as he took in a breath to answer, the door to the room opened and another dark-haired, deeply tanned young man appeared. "Get the doctor. She is awake."

A minute later an elderly gentleman in a white coat with a stethoscope appeared. "I see you've decided to rejoin the living." The doctor smiled. In comparison, his attitude was like the equator to the stranger's Arctic. "Good. I'm Doctor Bowers."

"Nice to meet you. I'm—" All of a sudden she realized she didn't know. She glanced first at the doctor who shrugged, then at the man standing nearby. The doctor gave her hand a reassuring squeeze. "I don't know. My mind. I just don't know."

Like lava bubbling up from the depths fear coursed through her body. But unlike that heated rock, this emotion did nothing to warm her. She wondered if this man, so beautiful yet so cold, would cool the magna and encase her—trapping her in a cave of nothingness.

"I was afraid of this." The doctor seemed to be speaking to both of them. Why? It was obvious that the man standing next to her bed didn't care about her. More like he wanted to finish the job and drive the jackhammer in her head all the way down her spine.

Dr. Bowers turned his attention just to her. "You were found at the bottom of a stairwell in an old house not far from here. You must have fallen. You seem to be suffering from temporary amnesia, Tamara."

"Amnesia? Tamara?" Why didn't the name feel right? The doctor handed her a New Jersey driver's license. "Tamara Duncan," she read out loud. Yet she found no familiarity in the words.

"We were trying to locate your next of kin," the doctor continued.

"I don't have any." Now how could she be so sure of that?

"When your fiancé arrived."

She burst out laughing. She was a Hatfield. He was a McCoy. Not her fiancé. "I have no ring," she said, looking down at her left hand.

He smiled. Too bad the smile didn't quite reach his eyes. "You haven't told me you accepted yet."

Thank the Lord, she thought to herself. Better to shack up with Jack the Ripper. "Oh."

"A pocketbook was found in a car at the front of the house. We assumed it was yours."

"I'm not sure."

He nodded as if expecting this. "Doctor?" Mr. Hatfield asked. "If I may have a word?"

"Of course. We'll be right back."

Tamara Duncan. She read the words over and over again. *She could hear a gruff deep voice telling her a story. "You were found right here on the steps with a note on your blanket. Take care of my Tamara, it read. Well, we've done that, now haven't we?"*

Father Duncan. The Sisters. The retreat by the sea. She could hear the gulls crying. The sound comforted her. The ocean soothed her. Sunlight streaming through many windows. Crystal figurines making rainbow colors. "Ahh," she cried as she thought her head would explode.

"That is enough." Such raw abrasiveness made his words harsh. "You cannot fight yourself this way. You are not strong and you need to rest."

"Why would you care? And how could you possibly be my fiancé when you seem to hate me so?"

His gaze made the words a lie as soon as they left his lips. "I do not hate you."

"Bull. You can't hide your feelings. I know them. You're so mad right now you could spit."

He frowned as the thought that she could read his mind, reached him. "Yes," he replied. "I am. But that does not mean we do not need each other right now. You hold answers I need."

At least he was honest with her. "You seem to do the same for me."

"I have gotten the doctor to release you but only into my care. Your choice. Either you stay here or you come with me."

"Not much of a choice," she muttered. She wanted to go home. But she had no home. Only an address on a piece of paper. She felt so empty inside. So confused. Statements that had to be true meant nothing to her yet he felt right. As crazy as that was right now, he felt right. Besides, whatever she'd done, he would tell her. He was her only link to her past and he might be able to help her remember her life. If he didn't end up killing her first. "I'll come with you."

He seemed to relax and withdraw all at the same time. "Good. Shall I help you dress? Or would you prefer I wait outside?"

Dress? She wasn't even sure she could stand. "Outside." The light in the window beckoned and she walked over careful not to make any sudden moves. She lifted a slat on the blinds. A buzz ran through her. All of a sudden she needed to get away, away from the smell of decay and death.

As long as she didn't make any sudden turns with her head, she was fine. She even felt human when she put a bit of toothpaste on a toothbrush she found on the stand next to the bed and scrubbed her teeth.

Opening the door, she saw both men standing in the hallway. She squared her shoulders and stepped into the hallway. "Tamara, this is Andre."

"Hello." She held out her hand, which he did not take.

He gave her a slight bow instead. "My Lady."

She frowned. "Lady?"

No help from Neanderthal man. No help from his young lapdog. About to reconsider her choice, he gave her a slight smile. "I will explain later."

He had a lot to explain. But at least he didn't touch her. She wasn't sure what she'd have done if he'd touched her. They stepped out into the bright sunlight and Tara became blinded. She watched them put on very dark sunglasses, then Andre handed a pair to her. What blessed relief to see again when her skin began to tingle.

Her supposed fiancé watched her closely while Andre simply looked bewildered. Tiny bolts of lightning. Surging draughts of power. The air cleared. Her vision sharpened. She could smell the odor of potatoes frying from the hospital kitchen. Tiny details. She could even read the license plate on a car hundreds of yards away.

She felt as if she could fly. It was like being on the most incredible speed trip. She felt as if she could jump right out of her skin.

She caught his gaze. He had known this would happen, regarded her warily as if trying to gauge her reaction to...to what? "What is happening to me?" she gasped.

He reached out and touched her. Images, sights, sounds, exploded in her head, a running collage of a past, present, and perhaps a future, she could not comprehend. A battlefield, banners fluttering in the wind, the acrid stench of blood hanging heavy in the air. A huge stone fireplace inside a castle great-room, the scent of fresh reeds upon the floor. A feeling of warmth and security. A brick house, an austere room, a plain table and three chairs. Nighttime, dark and cold. A lake. Cries of agony accompanying the throes of death. "Oh My God." Then the world went black for a second time.

****

Would God be able to help? An interesting question. Nicholai had not liked rendering Tara immobile, but he feared a scene even more than he feared the scenario unfolding before him.

Every House had been summoned to the place where they had met for centuries. It sat on the cliffs high above the Hudson River, in close proximity to the greatest city in the world—New York. Here, where the Nations of the World of men had united themselves.

The Hall reminded Nicholai of a fortress, albeit a rich one. The stone castle, with two towers flanking the Hall and huge arched windows faced the river. Great blocks of slate-colored stone rimmed each window, and a massive set of wooden doors with gleaming gold trim formed the entrance.

The interior was rich with treasure accumulated over the centuries. He stared at relics of ancient days such as swords and shields, with tapestries lining the walls to show their heritage. Paintings from the Renaissance Period, a supposedly more cultured era, hung next to each other belying the jealousy that raged between the artists. Gold and silver coins, jade statues, pieces chosen not only for their worth but their exquisite beauty. All this made up only a portion of their wealth. There was no such thing as a poor Noble.

Each House aligned themselves according to rank, their crests hanging proudly upon the walls with the Ruling Houses closest to the dais. But their numbers were dwindling. Of the original families, less than a hundred remained. Of those, only a handful had more true blood than not. Upon the dais sat three ancient, high-backed wooden chairs and a plain wooden table. No other adornments were necessary.

All sound ceased as the High Council took their seats. Stefano Benedetti, the senior member of the Council spoke first. "You have been summoned to this meeting upon the threat of death. Let each of you stand true and take account of your House."

A roll call ensued. The leaders of each House answered. For this meeting only the leaders and their second-in-commands had been summoned. Nicholai noted belligerence on as many faces as he saw bewilderment. His best friend, Dmitri Borodkin, was one of the few who returned his gaze with concern. And a bit of curiosity.

When the last House had finished silence reigned once more. Han-Sing, the second member of the High Council, spoke next. "The High Council has summoned you all here under the gravest of circumstances. A True Noble was made last night."

Even the discipline of a Council meeting could not stem the murmur that ran through the crowd.

"Silence!" Stefano thundered. "We ask that Nicholai Valentin take the floor."

Nicholai explained exactly what happened including the nightmare of retrieving Alexi from his steel coffin. He felt the displeasure of the crowd at his brother's antics but continued without interruption. At first he had not been sure whether or not his suspicions were true. His final confirmation was in meeting Tamara Duncan and her behavior as they left the hospital.

"The making has given her temporary amnesia. At least, what we believe is temporary amnesia. She has no idea who she is, she does not know the extent of her powers and cannot remember how she was made. She remains with me until the High Council rules."

"How do we know she's not lying? How do you know this whole setup was not planned?"

"We do not," Stefano answered for the Council.

"Why Valentin? Why can she not remain with my House?" Charles Rhys-Jones asked, stepping forward to claim the floor.

Nicholai waited patiently for permission to speak. Stefano granted his request by nodding and raising a hand for silence. "With all that I have told you, who among you would dispute my claim? She is connected to the House of Valentin."

"Silence." This time Ariel Gold spoke, the third member of the High Council and the first woman to ever hold that coveted seat. She stared at Rhys-Jones until he moved off the floor and back to his House. "One of our most sacred laws has been broken and you quibble about trivialities? Do not press this Council too far. Any of you. Great harm has been done this past night. We have been told the woman does not even know she is of Noble Blood."

A collective gasp rose from the crowd. "The Water of Change has been forbidden for centuries," Stefano continued. "Let it be known now that any House found to be connected with this crime will be obliterated. Down to the last infant. And your name will be stricken from every record ever made."

"Impossible," Rhys-Jones cried as he stepped forward again. "You would wipe out an entire House for that which is ours by right?"

"The laws were made to protect us, not for debate," Stefano replied. "The risk of the Change is too great. Too many have perished in the attempt."

"We perish anyway," Charles Rhys-Jones interrupted. Yet Nicholai read the cold calculation in his gaze. If the Water of Change were again made available and he forbade his House to use it, he might grow strong enough to become *The* Ruling House. "There are no infants. We have not had a True Noble born in what, a decade?"

"Twelve years," Ariel answered, her tone level. "Do you believe that this Council would allow—?"

"It is not the Council's right to decree," Rhys-Jones countered. "Each Noble must make his or her own decision." Nicholai watched as others nodded in response to Rhys-Jones' statement.

"Then less than half of you would be standing here," Han-Sing retorted.

"Hold." Stefano's voice rang through the hall daring dispute. "This Council was not called to debate. A heinous crime has been committed. The perpetrator or perpetrators of this crime must be found. This Council now charges every one of you with the task of finding them. Do you all understand?"

The room rang out with a chorus of "Aye."

Stefano caught Nicholai's gaze for a moment. That was when he realized what his mentor was trying to do. He was testing him again. As angry as Nicholai was, he was now going to have to prove that he could put his personal feelings aside for the good of the Nobility. "For now, and until we can prove otherwise, the woman is to be protected by the House of Valentin. She must be taught our ways. Once she stands as a member of the Nobility, she may decide her own fate."

"And if she rejects her heritage?"

"Then she will be destroyed."

The ramifications of this statement stunned the entire assembly. Destroy a True Noble female? When she could possibly bear one or many True Noble offspring? Nicholai didn't care. If Alexi died, she would die. End of discussion.

All of a sudden, Nicholai realized what he had to do. "In the name of Tamara Duncan." He caught his mentor's gaze as the man realized what he was about to say. At first, the elder man seemed stunned, as if he had not thought of this possibility. Then he nodded imperceptibly. "In the name of Tamara Duncan," he repeated, his voice clear and strong. "I invoke the Rite of Sanctuary."

Nicholai waited for the outburst that never came. The Rite of Sanctuary had kept their race alive during the many human wars, decreeing that a Noble, any Noble, could not take the life of another Noble no matter what side they took. In these modern times there was no need for the Rite, no one would willingly take another Noble life now. There were too few of them left.

"Does anyone challenge the Rite of Sanctuary? If so, let them speak now."

He caught Stefano's gaze once more. Nicholai made sure his mentor knew exactly why he'd done what he'd done. Then he let the man know what was in his heart. Alexi might never wake up. Alexi might live out his days wandering in an existence of nothingness. If that happened no Right on this earth would keep the woman safe. Or the enemy who was trying to destroy his family.

Nicholai had no proof but now he had the means to keep searching for the truth. Rhys-Jones was out to destroy his House and his family. Nicholai was certain of it. And the key was a woman with no memory.

"So be it," Stefano's voice rang out again. "The Rite of Sanctuary is decreed. Let the woman remain in the House of Valentin until the coming of the New Moon. Then she will stand before this Council and we will test her Nobility. Teach her well, Nicholai. Your life, and hers, depend upon it."

He nodded. "I understand."

"Until we find out who she is and who perpetrated this crime, the Stewardship Ceremony will be postponed."

Nicholai looked over to see Rhys-Jones smirk at him. He did as he was taught and remained impassive. "This meeting is over."

The High Council rose as one. "True Blood to True Blood."

The assembly chanted in return. His voice joined them. "True Blood to True Blood."

****

Tara awoke to a starlit sky. She marveled at the beauty of the night then realized she was staring through the ceiling of the room. As she looked around in stunned surprise, she saw that all the walls were made of glass. Fascination kept the nightmares and the pain at bay until his voice brought them back.

"How do you feel?"

Used. Abused. Alone. Frightened. "What do you care?"

"I had no choice."

Not that she expected more. "Thanks a lot. Where am I?"

"In my home in the desert."

"Desert?" she asked.

"Outside Las Vegas."

"Oh."

"You sound bitter."

"Bitter?" she repeated, not believing he could

ever be nice to her. "You don't know the half of it."

He sighed. Why did he bother? He didn't care. "I am afraid I do," he replied from a chair near her bed.

"Then tell me, Oh Kreskin the Great," she sneered. "What am I feeling right now?"

"Used. Abused. Alone. Frightened."

She blanched. Could he read her mind? "How in hell—?" She stopped. She dared not give him any more of an edge than he already had.

"An interesting choice of words. Some have used "hell" in context to our existence."

What was he talking about? "Our existence?" she asked, hating her need of him. She wanted answers and all he was giving her were more riddles.

"Life. Death." He rose and walked over to the bed. A simmering anger shimmered just below the surface of his gaze. "The limbo some of us sleep in."

She frowned. Now he really made no sense. "I don't understand."

His hand swept back his rumpled suit jacket to rest on his hip. "My brother lies in a coma in the next room," he accused.

He blamed her. "I caused an accident, didn't I?"

"In a manner of speaking."

"Damn you!" she exploded. "You spew out accusations in half sentences and hints I don't understand. Don't you get it? I don't remember. If you would just tell me what happened, I would be more than grateful." *Not.*

"That would take quite some time."

The tiny softening she'd been feeling at the bewilderment in his face died as he intended. He was playing games with her. "I don't know what you're talking about and now I don't care. I hope you get exactly what you deserve."

"You would say that to me after the havoc you have wrought?"

"Me? What about you? Do you have any idea what it's like to walk around with a gaping hole in your mind?"

"No."

"Then you tell me I put your brother in a coma. But you won't explain how. You're crazy."

His gaze told her otherwise. "I cannot explain thousands of years in a mere sentence."

"Try me."

"All right. You are not human."

She laughed. "Now that's the first thing you've said to me that makes any kind of sense at all. I'm not human. I have no memory and my body feels like a Mack Truck ran over it about ten times just for the hell of it."

He refused to soften. "You will have to forgive me if I don't feel sorry for you."

Bastard. "I wasn't asking for pity. Just answers."

"You will have them soon enough. And then you *will* ask for pity."

"I doubt that. I won't be around here very much longer."

Tara tried to lift her arm. She couldn't. As if she was totally exhausted and any movement would require the last of her strength, the appendage simply refused the commands of her brain. "What the—?" Looking down, she saw she wore no clothes except a small bikini-type bottom covering the "v" between her legs.

"A thousand pardons," he bowed with a mocking smile. "To explain now would be redundant. The Sun rises."

He ripped off his suit jacket and threw the garment across the room. His tie and shirt followed. He caught her gaze as he undid the belt to his pants and shucked them off. Was that enjoyment she read? He was having the time of his life. "You have no right to play games with me."

"Games?" She didn't like the manic undertone in his voice.

He'd drugged her. "Touch me and you'll regret the day you were born."

To her utter surprise, he threw back his head and roared with laughter. "You are absolutely right, I will. So you have nothing to fear in that respect."

He swept the bedcovers aside. She shrank from his touch. He frowned but slid his arms underneath her to lift her out of the bed. Tiny sparks rippled through her at his touch. Why? "Hold onto me," he commanded.

That was the last thing she wanted to do but her legs simply wouldn't support her. "What is happening to me?"

The sky had turned different shades of gray and now the horizon appeared nearly light. From the next room she heard a low murmur. Many people. Chanting something. He stood behind her chanting the same words. *Words?* They were like no language she'd ever encountered.

He held her upright with his hands but touched no other part of her body. As the Sun burst over the horizon, her skin began to sizzle with the same energy boost as before. This time she welcomed the feeling with delirious ecstasy. She wanted, no, had to have the Sun. Like food. Like air. Necessary to her basic survival. She had to have more. More.

The chanting grew louder. The desire grew greater. Where before the shock of the full exposure to the Sun had overwhelmed, now the gradual rising fueled the fire in her veins. Her skin danced in pleasure, heat pumped through her veins. She drank and drank as if the well of energy would never run dry. The more she craved, the more she fed. And when the room finally exploded in golden light, she screamed her passion out loud.

Her rational mind couldn't accept what her heart already knew. She wasn't human. She wasn't quite sure what she was, but she wasn't human. And neither was he.

Help me.

She could sense the fight within him. He hated her. She needed him. He needed her more. She swayed as her body and mind went into total overload. "You see," he whispered with intense sadness. "There was no way to explain."

Chapter Three

Did he dare feel sorry for her? She sat on the bed she'd been lying in, dressed now that the feed was over. Her luminous brown eyes tugged at him, so tough yet so vulnerable.

"Who am I?"

Why did her hair have to be such an exquisite shade of chestnut? "An interesting question, one my people have not been able to ascertain yet."

She hunched over, trying to almost crawl inside herself while her body tried to expand and drink in every ray of Sun the solar let in. "What am I?" she asked, her voice barely above a whisper. Her strong chin worked as if she were trying not cry.

"That will take longer to explain. Perhaps we could focus on you first."

Her shoulders straightened. Her jaw tightened, making the questions in her gaze tear at him even more. He decided to start with the mundane. "The clothes fit you?"

"Perfectly."

"The food?"

"I wasn't hungry." She threw him a look.

"You may not feel the need to eat for a few days

until your body adjusts."

"Adjusts to what?"

He held up his hand. "In time. Tell me, were you really found on the steps of a church?"

Her brow scrunched as she tried to remember. "I think so."

So many questions, he sighed to himself, and no way to verify the answers. Did he know what it was like to have a gaping hole in his mind? No, but he knew the frustration her amnesia caused. "My people have not been able to find out much."

"To be a person means you're human. We're not, are we?"

"No. Not exactly."

"Great. Now I'm like a Hertz commercial." She rose and began to pace, her movements necessary due to the amount of energy she'd consumed. "I think you'd better explain."

He ignored her. He had to. He needed answers, any answers, to his questions first. "The name Duncan. Was it yours?"

She moved with a graceful fluidity. Already her body was changing, growing stronger and more solid. In less than a week she would burn away all her excess fat. "No. I remember being told that Father Tim gave me his name."

She moved to the center of the floor and turned her face to the ceiling, drawn by her need for the Sun. That, too, would lessen in a short time although the need never went away not even after a glorious feed like this morning. "By whom?"

"Sister Mary Edward." She looked startled as if she didn't know how she knew that.

"You grew up on Long Beach Island in New Jersey." That was what Sergei was able to ascertain.

"I remember a Retreat. Seagulls. Nuns. I guess they raised me."

"But you did not become one," he replied, stating

the obvious.

She looked down at the floor as if she were ashamed. "I didn't fit in."

"Now at least you know why."

"Do I?" she asked, her tone bewildered. "Right now I don't know anything."

What could he say to that? "Can you remember anything else?"

She closed her eyes. "I'm sitting on Sister's lap. She's rocking back and forth. I'm crying."

He could picture the scene in his mind. "Go on."

"The other children had been making fun of me because I had no parents."

How could she remember something so vivid but not her own name? "And?" he prodded.

"Whatever she said must have made me feel better because I got off her lap and told them all off."

"That is all you can remember?" he asked, his impatience growing.

"Damn you, don't you understand? I keep hitting this black hole."

"I am sorry. We will begin with this nun, Sister Mary Edward. Do you know where she might be?"

She gave him a helpless shrug. "I don't know."

"My people will find her."

His words seemed to upset her. "That's the second time you've used the word "people." We're not human, remember?"

"I am well aware of that fact. I believe you are the one having identity problems right now."

"Then for the love of God, would you please tell me who I am?"

"A protected member of my House, the House of Valentin."

"And that makes me what?"

"A True Noble, of highest rank within our society."

"What society?"

"The Nobility." He gestured to the edge of the bed for her to sit down and pulled up a chair next to her. "I'm going to tell you a story."

****

The sickness came upon her again and Mur fell to her knees. Bending over, she retched until she thought her stomach was going to end up all over the ground. Despite her misery, she knew a deep contentment. She was with child.

A foot in her ribs brought her back to reality with a jolt. Og was not one to worry about anyone but himself. But he was the best hunter in the clan and she never lacked for meat.

Scrambling to her feet, Mur saw the problem immediately. They were out of water. Og shoved the skin at her with a grunt of disgust and Mur hurried to the small pool she'd found not far from their cave. Perhaps some berries would sooth Og's ire. They would be ripe now. Sweet. Og liked sweet berries.

Mur stopped in total surprise. The glowing rock was a color too beautiful to describe, not the color of the sky, not the color of the great water she had seen as a child. It seemed to live, pulsing bright and dark in a mesmerizing pattern. She reached out but only to remove the skin from the water, careful not to touch. A sharp warning ran through her mind and ended in a pit of fear in her belly. Yet the need to possess the rock grew stronger with every second she stared. Surely Og would be pleased. The rock would give him great stature within the clan.

Her hand trembled as she reached out. Her fingers broke the surface of the water but this time they tingled. She moved very slowly until they rested just above the rock. As she was about to touch the stone her mind called to her to draw back. The ground trembled. The bad omens were everywhere and she tried to obey. Too late. She lost her balance and the world exploded.

A foot in her ribs brought her to reality with a jolt. Shards of light danced inside her head finally becoming one. In an instant, Mur knew she carried two babies made of the same being. One was the light and the other—oh, the other frightened her badly—just as the deep darkness of the cave at night frightened her. Og grunted in disgust, snatching the water skin from the ground before whirling away.

Mur rose, her head pounding in pain. She staggered, as much from the weakness of her body as the certainty of what had to be done. One of her babies would live. One would not.

****

"The entire clan drank from the pool."

Horrified, she didn't know what to say. "So you're telling me I'm a mutant?"

He shook his head, his innate pride making a mockery of her choice of words. "You are a member of another race. Physically and mentally superior. We are the Nobility."

"So what you're telling me is that I'm a member of the X-Men."

He gave her an affronted look. "You have a great deal to learn."

"So do you. Especially people skills. Oops, I'm sorry, I'm not a people, am I?"

He didn't meet her gaze. "I suppose I could have been a bit gentler in my handling of this situation."

"Why? Do me a favor. Don't change now. I'm getting used to your attitude. It's refreshingly consistent."

"When you were made—"

"Made?" she asked, cutting him off. This was getting better and better. Now he was telling her…ah, hell. How did she know about Play-Doh and X-Men? Why couldn't she remember her home? What she did for a living? Her friends? If she had any.

"Tamara?"

"You sound so concerned."

"I am. My brother is lying in the next room."

"Your brother," she cried, tears threatening. "Damn you to hell and back again. You treat me little better than a criminal and you want my pity? Don't you realize how I feel about this whole mess?"

"I have thought of little else."

"What about the holes in my mind? Not only do I not know who I am, I don't know what I am."

"You are the most valuable member of our race right now, a True Noble female of child bearing age."

"Excuse me?" She couldn't believe what he'd just said.

"If you were not under my protection and the Rite of Sanctuary—" He held up his hand already knowing she was about to interrupt. "The Rite of Sanctuary means exactly that. No Noble may deliberately take the life of another Noble."

A shiver ran up her spine. He was serious. "Go on."

"If you were not protected, one of the Ruling Houses would have abducted you by now, chained you to a bed, raped and impregnated you."

She stared at him. "You're scaring me."

"Good," he snarled, rising from his chair. "Because I would have done the same."

"Why?"

"Because family is everything to us."

"Then women in your race count for nothing except their ability to procreate."

"*Your* race," he reminded her with stiletto-like intensity. "And no, this is not the Dark Ages." He sighed, running a hand through his hair. "Our race is dying. The Water of Change is forbidden because the odds are not good that the Noble taking the Water would survive."

She finally put two and two together. "You mean

someone gave me this water you're talking about?"

"Because you have no memory, I do not know. I have no idea how the change occurred."

"But I didn't even know it, or you, existed."

"That we existed?" he repeated. "I cannot be sure of that either. Because of your amnesia."

"I see."

"Do you? I do not think so."

"What do you mean?"

"We are a race of order and hierarchy. There are True Nobles of undiluted blood, Nobles born to the mating of two True Nobles. These are the strongest."

Order and hierarchy. That was comforting. "Undiluted blood?" she asked.

"Unmixed with humans," he replied with disdain.

"Racist," she muttered.

"No, proud. Proud of who and what I am."

"Oh." He didn't seem to appreciate her sarcasm.

"And lesser Nobles, those who have portions of human blood inside them," he continued, ignoring her. "All take their place in society according to rank. As do the Houses. There are Ruling Houses and secondary Houses, tertiary and so on."

"Is yours a Ruling House?"

"Yes."

No wonder he was the way he was. The head of a Ruling House. "Are you a prince or something like that?"

"Something like that." Now the lord and lady routine made sense.

"So even though you profess to care, you'd force me to bear children against my will without an ounce of remorse. You really are something, you know that?"

"At least I would make the experience pleasurable."

Tara laughed. "Oh joy, oh bliss."

He was beside her in less than an instant. "There are those who would tie you to a bed and not let you up again. They would force you to bear one child after another until you could not have any more or you were dead. They would not let you raise any of those children. Not one of their people would lift a finger to help you unless they were ordered to. Can you at least understand that?"

She shivered again. "Yes," she replied, still scared but also appalled. "You have to understand how barbaric that sounds."

"I do." He seemed about to say more then stopped. "The more True Nobles within a House," he continued, and not with his first thought, she was certain. "The greater the stature of the House. My House, the House of Valentin, is blessed. One of our gifts, as a race, is the ability to bear twins. One of our bane's is that one twin usually dies at birth. Alexi is not only my brother, he is my twin."

"I see," she said. No wonder the man was so upset.

He reached out to place his hands on her upper arms. Again, her flesh tingled as it met his. "You feel that?" She nodded. "There is a connection between us. I am not sure what that is yet but you may be a member of my House. However, your true connection lies with Alexi." He paused then decided to continue. "Your making is what caused his coma."

"Is that why you're so concerned with my past?"

"Yes." He let go and placed a gentle finger under her chin, the first softening she'd seen within him. "I would hate to tell my brother his lifemate is his sister."

"Lifemate?"

"Humans call them soulmates. We know better. The connection is not necessarily as ephemeral as humans would believe."

"Then I guess we need to find out who I am.

Especially since you already have me wedded, bedded, and having children to increase the status of your House."

He frowned. "Are you always this cooperative?"

"You get what you give," she replied with a falsely sweet smile.

"All right. Then perhaps we make a pact."

"A pact?"

"Yes. A truce. We help each other find the truth."

She wanted that badly. "What if you find that I had something to do with this mess?"

His gaze narrowed. "Meaning?"

She swallowed. "That I drank the water knowing the consequences."

"Then Rite or no Rite, you will regret the day you were born."

At least he was honest. "You're not going to believe me, but deep down I know I would never deliberately harm another being. Ever. So just remember something."

He raised a brow as if nothing she said would change his mind. "And that is?"

"Paybacks are a bitch."

****

Nicholai found Sergei hovering faithfully. "How is he?"

"Resting easier, my Lord. And he continues to feed. From a physical standpoint he seems fine."

Nicholai allowed his gaze to roam over his brother's face. His first instinct was to try to reach Alexi. Then he stopped. What if he caused more damage? Biting his lip with indecision, he whirled away to stare out into the desert. The small solar was fashioned in the same manner as the larger one with only glass for walls. "I believe the girl is his lifemate."

He turned to find Sergei staring. "His lifemate?"

"I told you before. Mine is not the connection."

"We shall see," came Sergei's enigmatic reply.

The door to the solar opened, startling them both. "What are you doing here?" Nicholai asked in a harsh tone as Tara walked in.

"I don't know. I felt a need to come here."

"To gloat?"

She stiffened. "I beg your pardon?"

"Or merely to enjoy your payback. Oh. Excuse me. Allow me to make introductions. Alexi? This is Tamara Duncan. Tamara? My brother Alexi."

"Nicholai," Sergei gasped.

"Leave us," Nicholai ordered. Why was he pushing? Pressing? Even *he* didn't understand.

Sergei bowed. To *her*, not to him. "My Lady."

She smiled as the door closed. "At least someone around here wants to treat me with respect."

"My deepest apologies," he mocked, giving her a sweeping bow, "that I have not shown you your proper due. But you see my brother is the one who should be greeting you, not I."

"You know, you're beginning to get on my last nerve. My very last nerve."

"Too bad."

"Are you drunk? Or are you normally this obnoxious?" She threw up her hands. "Why am I even talking to you? I came here because Alexi needs me."

Nicholai stopped dead. "Are you sure?"

"Yes."

Terror clawed inside his belly only to be overpowered by a sweet surge of hope. His hesitation was clear now. He was not the one meant to bring Alexi back, she was. "Place your fingers here and here." He pointed to Alexi's temples.

"And do what?"

"Call to him. With your mind."

"Whoa. Wait a minute. I'm not sure I can, let

alone have a clue as to how."

"You must." He grabbed her arm. "You were meant to do it."

She broke free of his hold with ease. "Let go of me. I don't have to do anything."

He sighed. "You are right. Forgive me." He stepped away to stare at the night sky one more time. "I have been debating whether or not to try. But I do not believe I am the one who should."

"And you believe I am?"

"You are his lifemate."

"Let's get one thing straight. Right here, right now. I'm nobody's lifemate. Got it?"

He nodded. He had to. "All right."

"And I'll tell you another thing. I came here, not because I'm a member of The Nobility, but because I'm human and I believe in humanity and all it stands for. Goodness. Caring. The teachings I was brought up with."

Nicholai didn't care what her motivation was as long as she could help him reach his twin. "Fine."

"Last and certainly not least, you need an attitude adjustment. You've been acting like a spoiled little prince. Your race is dying because no one can live on pride and conceit alone."

"Are you finished?" he asked in a very quiet tone.

"For now."

"Good. Can we get down to business then?"

She wanted to answer but clamped her jaw shut instead. "Yes," she finally bit out.

"Thank you. Now. If you would place your fingers here." He pointed to Alexi's temple. "And here."

She reached down next to him. "Like this?"

He turned to answer and watched her entire body freeze. Her face turned gray as ash, her eyes blank and glassy as marbles. Horror seared his soul.

What had he done? What the devil had happened to Alexi? "Tamara?" He never finished his thought. As his fingers touched hers his skin crawled as if a thousand snakes slithered over him.

I am a Prince of The Nobility. Fighting his terror, he realized whatever was happening was based in deceit. Like magic. Smoke and mirrors.

Of course. Mirrors. Crack the mirror; reveal the deception.

The world exploded. He ripped Tara's hands away from Alexi and they both staggered back. "Tamara? Listen to me. Listen to the sound of my voice. Follow the path. Come to me."

Her eyelids fluttered. She took in a huge gulp of air and started flailing in his arms. "It is all right," he soothed. "You are all right."

She screamed and her eyes rolled back into her head. She began to convulse. She couldn't breathe. Then her body went into overload and she went limp in his arms. As she came to all she kept saying was "Oh my God, Oh my God."

"It is all right," he repeated. "You are safe now."

Mighty tremors racked her body and he wrapped his arms tight around her. Her breath hitched again and again. "I can't—"

"I know," he whispered. "Do not worry. You are with me." As he said them, he wondered why the words felt so right.

"And what about me?"

Nicholai whirled and found Alexi staring at both of them.

Chapter Four

"Alexi!"

She heard the cry, but the sound came from a terrible distance. Shudders wracked Tara's body. Terrifying images threatened to overwhelm. Yet through all the horror, his arms felt right around her. They comforted, soothed, gave solace where there was none. "Shhh."

She couldn't answer, her throat locked by the unspeakable. "It's over now." A hand reached out, touching her forehead to brush aside a lock of her hair, but it reminded her of one of the demon claws that had tried to tear her limb from limb. With a cry she tore free of his grasp, and threw herself into a corner where she tried to huddle inside herself. "It's over now," Nicholai repeated over and over.

"Alexi?" Tara remembered nothing but a barren plain, a wasteland stretching into gray then the blackest of black. But the name. That name. She knew that name. Spoken in a voice that set her teeth on edge, made her skin crawl. "I'm all right."

Strong arms pulled her onto the bed and cradled her as if she were a child. A familiar scent reached her. Clean but from the earth. Like the desert. "Barely."

Tremors that began in her body ended in the cocoon that protected her. Tara tried to stop shaking. She wanted to stop shaking. She really did. "But she is not. Not yet."

"Oh my God." The words took on a life of their own as she whispered them over and over again.

The solar. Glass walls. A table. Chairs. Two men. Exactly alike. Twins. Her heartbeat began to slow down. "Tara? Can you talk to me? Can you tell us what happened?"

Nicholai. He was a Hatfield. She was a McCoy. The thought seemed so mundane after so much fear.

"Don't," Alexi cried. "She's not ready to answer. Neither am I."

Silence stretched between them all. Shock kept her from speaking. "You saved my life," a gentle voice finally told her.

Yes, she had. Pride stiffened her backbone. She wrenched away from the man who hated her and focused on the one who didn't. His grateful gaze said all that needed to be said.

"I have been half-crazed, out of my mind since you collapsed, brother. Can you not tell me anything? What happened to you?"

You wanted answers, she said to herself. *You're going to get them.* Tara reached out. As she touched Nicholai's temple with her outstretched fingers, she knew he was seeing a small portion of what they'd both been through. Nicholai jumped back as if burned. "Dear Lord in Heaven."

Tara watched Nicholai leave the small solar then return a moment later with two snifters of liquor in his hands. She didn't really like to drink but welcomed the smoky bite of the whiskey and the burn that turned to glow in her belly. She nodded her thanks.

"You know," Alexi said after she watched him down the drink in one swallow. "I'd given up on that type of faith a long time ago. Perhaps I was a bit hasty."

Nicholai nodded. "Perhaps we all were."

With a gentleness she'd never received from his brother, Alexi urged her to finish the whiskey. "Drink, sweetheart. It will help."

As she tipped her glass, she happened to glance up and catch Nicholai's gaze darken. She wondered why. "Tamara?" he questioned.

"I'll survive."

She watched as Alexi looked first to her then to his brother, bewilderment etching his features. The man shrugged as he said, "You saved my life. I am in your debt."

Tara rose. She felt uncomfortable. "I'm not interested in your gratitude."

"You have it anyway." Tara felt some of the horror of the dreams return as she watched Alexi's face turn grave. "Nico, we are in danger."

"Yes," Nicholai sighed, and his shoulders slumped slightly. All of a sudden Tara caught a glimpse of the mantle Nicholai carried. "The paths you walked along—"

"Are best left unsaid," Alexi finished.

"Yes." Nicholai raked a hand through his hair. She felt his gaze follow her as she sat down in a chair and cradled the brandy glass in her hands.

"The legends are just myths."

"Are they?" She watched Alexi raise a brow then purposely turn to stare at his brother. "Even you cannot be that naive."

"Why now?" Nico asked.

"Who knows?" His shrug ended in a shudder. "I cannot explain the type of being that can do this, only that it can and will destroy us all."

"I can." Both men turned to stare at Tara. "Only one being is powerful and evil enough for this and you both know who he is."

Both men turned to her, pity in both their gazes. They knew she really didn't understand. "What you can conceive of through your human existence cannot compare to the evil we are talking about," Nicholai answered

"How can you be so certain?" Tara asked.

"Because you see only through the eyes of good and evil. There are legends handed down through our people that make the Devil look like a cartoon character."

Tara winced inside as he threw her words back at her. "It all makes sense," Alexi added. "We are being systematically destroyed. Driven out of existence. Piece by piece. No new births. Unexplained deaths. Sometimes of child bearing females, sometimes the design pits House against House which ultimately causes us to aid the plan of our own imminent extinction."

"The High Council."

"Is blind," Alexi cried, interrupting his brother.

"Perhaps. Perhaps not."

"Mark my words, Nico. We are facing the horror of our beginning. Now. In the present. As it was foretold."

"I do not know this. Neither do you. We must advise the Council. Explain what has happened."

Alexi slammed his hand down on the bed. Fascinating, she thought. I'm not the only one who finds the man irritating to the nth degree. "Think outside the box for once, will you please? They know and they're terrified because they don't know what to do. Don't you get it?"

A staring match ensued and Tara was tired of feeling like an outsider in the game. "Would someone mind explaining what you're both talking about?"

****

Mur felt the heaviness move lower inside her belly. Fear slithered through her at the thought that

her time was near. She knew what she had to do yet wondered if she would have the strength of will to carry out her plan. The dark one had to die so they could all live. Even now she sensed him questioning her purpose.

Of them all, she had the greatest power. She knew the exact moment Og drank the water. He would become leader of the clan and they would not only survive under his leadership, they would thrive. But they would pay a dear price for that growth. For she now knew that when the change occurred, it magnified the traits one carried. Og was a tyrant. His would be an omnipotent reign.

How she wished she had not touched the stone. Then she realized that the water would have done the same to her. She'd followed her destiny, a path she could not comprehend. Perhaps, in order to have great good, great evil had to be the balance. But evil such as the dark one had to be destroyed.

Og sensed the dark one, was drawn to it as a moth to flame. He hovered, cared for her with false tenderness, all the while seeking its power. Already she feared they could communicate, but until born, the dark one was too weak to hurt anyone. So she hid her thoughts in a swirling mass of fear and turmoil, all too real and spurred by the one she carried in her womb.

The light one had to be protected. Tana would help her in this. She'd lost her little one in the making and Mur sensed her profound grief. When her pains began she chose Tana to aid her, taking her outside the cave to show her where to draw more of the water that had changed them all forever. She let her see both babies and begged her to take the light one back and care for it.

The birthing nearly killed her. Tana took the light one back to the clan while Mur took the dark one. And she walked. The dark one fought her, but he was not strong enough to match her yet. He called upon creatures in the night but she hid until she was safe. To go on. To walk. And walk.

Now was the time. Death was upon her. Without sustenance and exposed to the frozen reality of winter, they were both dying. She thought of the light and knew she'd done what she must to protect her people.

The snow no longer felt cold. A tiny trap of remorse bit at her for her actions. Such was the pain of choice. Her part was done. For better or for worse. Only time would tell the final outcome.

****

Long Beach Island, New Jersey. Nicholai was unimpressed. The island reminded him of many similar communities along the Atlantic coast. He preferred the crisp clean magnificence of the desert to the damp crowded salt air of the sea. Yet Tara's body language fascinated him. As soon as the distinctive odor of the bay became apparent, she relaxed. She belonged here.

"Sergei."

"Yes, my Lord?"

"We will go to the rental first."

"No," she countered. He watched her chin set in defiance.

"It has been a long flight," Nicholai answered.

"Neither one of us is tired and you know it," Tara told him.

"Yes," he agreed. "But the doctor was quite clear. He said your memory would return gradually. Considering all that has happened, I did not see the sense of trying to use a sledge-hammer to smash something loose."

"Too bad. This is my home."

"But we came here for a purpose," he said, trying to dissuade her.

"To find Sister. I know."

"Do you?" he asked with brutal honesty. "Or is it because you have been told?"

Her gaze caught his. *Bastard.* He laughed. "Yes, I am."

"I don't like mind games."

"You play them quite well."

"Is her amnesia real?" she asked, mirroring the thoughts that haunted him night and day. "Or does she have an ulterior plan?" She laughed. "Yes, I suppose I do."

He swallowed to try to remove the sour taste in his mouth. The whole fiasco had him on edge, off balance. He needed her and hated his need. He wanted the truth. He wanted to know who was trying to destroy his family. His only solace was that Alexi was alive. And well. "As you wish then. Sergei? Take us to Tamara's townhouse."

"Very good, my Lord."

He watched her closely as they pulled into the parking lot. Would she remember more? Her expression never changed. "You should have listened to me."

Her jaw worked. Her eyes filled with tears. And more. He told himself he didn't care about her hatred. "Someday, man, I am going to enjoy those paybacks," she promised.

He shrugged. "Shall we go in?"

She drew in a long breath letting the air out slowly. "All right."

He produced the key that had been in her pocketbook the day they found her. "Here."

"How dare you," she hissed. "How dare you go through my things."

"I will dare anything to protect my family and my people. You had best remember that."

Her fingers twitched. He could see her savoring every moment of the vision where her hand would imprint his cheek. Yet she did not strike. He admired her self-control. "Don't forget what I said before either."

She moved past him and up the walk. They climbed a set of stairs and stopped in front of a door. He waited as her gaze roamed the small foyer and moved to travel the living room. "Anything?" he asked again.

The house was immaculate, modern with collectibles everywhere. "If I had a choice, you'd never know. What a pity I don't have that luxury."

Statues, prints, artifacts, shells, crystal. "This continual taunting serves no purpose." She stopped and walked over to her dining room table. "What is it?"

"A Circle of Friends." The unique candleholder was indeed a circle of figures holding hands. Unbroken. United. Strong. "Jeri gave it to me. To tell me what mattered most."

"Jeri?" he asked gently.

"My best friend."

He raised a brow. This was interesting. "Jeri who?" he probed.

She gave him a bewildered look. "I—I don't know."

"Thought so," he replied. "Let us go."

"No." She spread her feet as if bracing for a fight.

"I do not think you understand. I rented a house."

"I really don't care. This is my home. I'm staying here."

"The doctor said you must take your time."

"The doctor isn't God and neither are you."

"I could make you go with me," he warned.

She laughed. "That's so typically male of you. No, make that omnipotent. Yes, Lord. No, Lord. And if that doesn't work, might over right. What makes you think you can get away with it?"

"You go girl."

Nicholai whipped his head around. A statuesque African-American woman stood in the doorway, her huge earrings dangling in a mesmerizing fashion. "Damn you, Tara. Where the hell have you been?"

****

Her hug was like coming home, being right with the world, and so comforting Tara wanted to drown in the feeling. "Jeri?"

"I was worried sick, child."

The scent. So different, so totally Jeri. Pictures flashed through her mind. A fireplace. A bottle of wine. Popcorn. Movies. Laughter. So much laughter. "I'm sorry. I seem to have lost my way."

They broke apart. Jeri turned to Nicholai as Tara wiped her eyes. "Child. You crying?"

"No," she tried to lie. "Nicholai, this is Jeri."

Jeri held out her hand. A brow went up when he refused to shake. Tara didn't understand why. He answered that question when he said, "You are one of the gifted ones."

Jeri's jaw dropped along with her hand. "I never thought I'd see the day."

"You use that word quite freely," Nicholai answered.

"Yes," she chuckled. "My Mama told me I would have a different kind of sight."

"Did she also tell you the rest?"

Tara watched Jeri shrug. She sensed anguish in the woman, a pain she hid quite well. Tara wondered if she'd known about this before. "Only that my gift would allow me to see far more than a pair of eyes ever could."

"She was right." Nicholai turned towards the doorway. "Let the poor animal in, Sergei."

"But My Lord, he might hurt you."

"He is not going to do anything," Nicholai replied in exasperation.

A black Labrador with a harness trotted into the room and sat down by Jeri's side waiting for his master's bidding. Tara watched Jeri reach down and stroke the dog as he sat down next to her. "Jeri?"

"You'd better explain, Tara."

She hadn't known her best friend. She hadn't remembered Jeri was blind. A sick feeling welled in the pit of her stomach. "There's this hole in my mind, Jer. This big gaping hole. "

"Give me your hand." The initial comfort gave way to a tingle then that same electrical sensation she felt when she touched Nicholai. "Oh my God. You're one of *them.*"

Tara yanked her hand back as if burned. She tried to steel herself to the hurt. "Them?" She looked up to find Nicholai's gaze on her. She expected satisfaction but found concern instead. *Why?* Why would he behave now as if he cared?

Nicholai's gaze left hers to travel to Jeri. "You always knew that though, did you not?" he asked.

Jeri ignored him and turned towards her. "You've been the daughter I never had, child. That will never change." She held out her arms. "Yes, I knew you held the promise. But I never dreamed in a million years that you'd ever become a Noble."

Tara let her soul decide. Jeri was the mother she never had. "I lost my memory with the change. But there are some things I'll never forget." With a cry, she ran into Jeri's arms.

"It'll come back to you. Already is, I'm guessing."

"We need your help," Nicholai told Jeri as they let go of each other.

She guided Jeri to the couch and sat down with her. "The change was forced on me. At least, I believe it was. Nicholai isn't as sure because of the amnesia—"

"I get the picture."

"We need to know what I was doing three days

ago. Did I mention anything to you? Say anything that might give us a clue?"

"Let me see. You said something about an estate sale. I wasn't paying attention because you're always going off with that Morgan. Not that I don't like him, I just don't trust him."

"Estate sale?" Nicholai interrupted.

"Buying," Jeri replied. "For the store."

"Store?" Tara asked. "What store?"

"Oh Tara, you have lost your memory. The Treasure Trove. Your store that's across from mine on the Boulevard."

That same picture of sunlight streaming through crystal flashed before her eyes again. "The Treasure Trove," she repeated. Another picture. "Serengeti."

Jeri squeezed her hand. "You'll be all right. If you can remember that, the rest will come."

Tara looked up to find Nicholai watching her. He seemed to vibrate, like a coiled spring ready to explode. "Since you seem to know more now and you are closer to this woman than I, I suggest you perform the connection."

"Connection? I don't understand."

"Just as you did with Alexi."

"I thought that was only with other Nobles."

"The gift of this woman's sight is the gift of her Noble blood. And you have the ability to give her far more. You can give her the gift of your sight as well."

"Jeri? Is that true?"

"So I've been told."

"Have you ever done it before?" she asked her friend.

"No. I never had the opportunity."

She didn't need to say more. Tara would have given Jeri her heart if she wanted. She reached out and touched the elder woman's temples in the same way as she had with Alexi. Then she heard Jeri gasp. A flower. A sunset. Memories she didn't even remember. "Oh Tara," the woman breathed.

"Go slow," came Nicholai's warning.

Tara gave Jeri a montage of pictures of a life Jeri had never really seen before. Memories of a sunset over the ocean, children playing on the beach, seagulls swirling overhead. The Sisters at prayer. Her first images of the hustle and bustle of New York City. Then she took back. Since Jeri was blind, Tara received senses instead of pictures. The cool, crisp texture of the leaf of a tree. The soft, silky threads of animal fur. The peaks and valleys of a person's face. Her face. She'd had no idea so much could be learned from them.

As she let go, she found they were both crying. "Thank you," the woman said.

"Don't thank me, Jer. We both gained. I remember even more now." She turned to Nicholai. "We'll find Sister here on the island. At the Retreat."

"Excellent."

"Sister Mary Edward?"

"Yes."

"You'd better hurry," Jeri advised. "I don't think she's been well. They've been saying prayers for her at mass."

"We will," Nicholai answered.

"Jer?"

"You felt it too, didn't you?"

"Felt what?" Nicholai questioned.

"I'm not sure." She turned to Jeri. "I felt something like a shadow. A dark shadow that hovered in the background. It was hard to pinpoint but definitely there, almost watching, as if it were waiting for something. Did you feel it too, Jeri?"

She nodded. "Not something I wanted to investigate."

"We may have to." she sighed. "Whose voice did I hear? The one with the slow incomplete kind of speech?"

"That would be your assistant." Tara recognized disdain in the woman's tone and wondered why. "Morgan. Morgan Pennington."

Morgan let the icy water of the ocean roll over his body. Only here could he truly be free. No laughter. No jeers. No taunts. No cruelty. Only the constant roll of the waves, rocking him, as his mother had so long ago.

Morgan.

No, his mind rebelled. Let me have this moment of peace.

Morgan, there is work to do.

He rolled over and began to swim to shore. "Yes, Master. I hear and obey."

Chapter Five

Sister Mary Edward was sitting in her favorite chair watching her favorite television program, *Jeopardy*. She couldn't abide all that nonsense shown on other programs, and the news seemed more like a soap opera than reality these days. The other Sisters didn't mind the small television as long as she kept it low. And since she felt pretty good this evening, maybe she'd even stay awake long enough to see *Wheel of Fortune*.

So much for growing old. The little pleasures in life truly became little. The sights and sounds of the sea, a nicely prepared meal, a favorite television program. Perhaps she was being spared her discretion's after all.

So much to atone for. Was love a better excuse than cowardice? Was He jealous that she'd loved a child more than Him in spite of her vows? Hadn't He given Tara to her for that very purpose? To love and nurture?

A light tap on her door startled her out of her thoughts. She shifted and settled deeper under the throw covering her shoulders. "Come in."

Sister Mary Edward waited. Her brows pulled down in what Tara used to call her "stern-mother" look. "Come in."

Her mistake, she supposed. Old age no longer creeping up on her but hammering away at her body. And mind. She re-focused on the television in order to catch the last question. "Edward IV," she murmured. "Sorry, the answer is." A quiet chuckle ended the sentence. More self-deprecating than anything else because the answer was really Edward V. Thank goodness she wasn't teaching anymore.

Another light tap on the door caused her to whip her head around. How very strange. "Come in," she told the potential visitor, her ire increasing. When no one opened the door she wondered why anyone would wish to play such a game with her. Reaching over, she picked up the cane lying against the chair, set the piece in front of her, and struggled to rise. Weakness tried to suck the very strength of will from her but God always provided a way. Her movements slow, what used to take a moment now seemed to take hours. She opened the door more startled than anything else to find a young man standing there. "I called. Didn't you hear me?"

He cocked his head. Non-descript looking. Sandy brownish hair beginning to thin. A long face and nose supporting huge horn-rimmed glasses. Pale blue eyes. He blinked. Once. Twice. "No."

Turning, Sister Mary Edward started back towards her chair. "May I help you?"

No answer again. What a strange fellow. Then she realized. She would have to proceed at his speed. "Help…me?"

She chuckled. That usually happened with the special ones as she used to call them. God had his reasons but it pained her to watch them struggle so. "No," she shook her head as she pointed to the chair. "Help me. To sit back down if you please."

He nodded and came to her side with a look of eager willingness. *You poor thing, you.* "Ah, that's it." Her bones creaked as she fell into the chair. "Yes, thank you." Once she was settled under her throw, she smiled up at him in gratitude. "Now. Who are you? What is your name?"

"Morgan."

"Do you have a last name, Morgan?"

"Pen—"

"Just Pen? Like this?" Sister Mary Edward made a motion as if she were writing in the air.

He shook his head. Poor soul, he seemed to be struggling deep within himself. Perhaps this visit was meant by God to be her last task as a teacher. To help this young man. Give him the tools he needed to survive. "Take your time, child. One word at a time."

"No." He blinked again.

How sweetly frustrating. No, not just Pen? Or no, he doesn't want to take his time? "Not just Pen?"

He nodded, eagerly, his face seeming to light up with success. "Must…find…"

"Must find what, Morgan?"

A look of shadow and fear crossed his face. "He…said."

"Who said?" She shook her head. This was all getting so confusing. "Morgan? Morgan," she used her stern-mother voice. "Focus."

As their gazes met a chill ran down her spine. The eagerness was gone, replaced by nothing. In all her life, she'd never really understood the words blank stare before. "Pen…Dragon."

Horror clawed its way up her throat. "Impossible."

He smiled. No innocence here only malevolent purpose. "Get out," she cried. "Get out. Now!"

He flicked the door closed with his heel, reaching out at the last minute to stop the door from slamming. The quiet click of it shutting frightened her more than anything had before. "I don't know what you're talking about. I don't know why you're here." To her everlasting shame, though, she did.

"The...ring."

"Why? Why now after all these years?" Her heart hammered in her chest. She couldn't catch her breath.

He didn't reply. He didn't have to. "I don't have it. I gave it to her."

He shrugged. For a split second she thought she saw pity in his gaze. "This won't help you," the woman cried. "She'll find out and then she'll hate you."

She caught the longing from the depths of his soul. In that last brief instant, she realized he was just as much a pawn as she was. Then his eyes became mirrors, mirrors to her soul.

"Hail Mary, full of Grace." Tasks would now remain undone. "The Lord is with Thee." Pain ripped through her chest.

"Blessed Art Thou Among Women." Her heart exploded as a hand closed over her mouth and pinched her nostrils shut.

A curtain of black descended and then at last there was peace. Her final thoughts were of the past, rocking in her chair, holding the baby who had stolen her heart.

****

Nicholai watched Tara pace the tiny vestibule with a mixture of concern and amusement. Her long straight chestnut hair, usually left loose, had been pulled back into a tight bun. The austerity of the style seemed to accentuate those huge, expressive brown eyes, making her look vulnerable not strong. Yet he knew better. She moved with the lithe grace of a caged tigress. One that refused to acknowledge captivity. Her head snapped up as a door opened. "Tara, I never thought to see you again."

The nun's demeanor changed instantly when

she saw him. "Visitors are discouraged from entering the Retreat."

"I apologize for taking the liberty of bringing my fiancé," she bit the word out to his infinite delight. "Sister Margaret. May I introduce Nicholai Valentin? Sister Margaret Theresa."

"We wish to speak with Sister Mary Edward for a moment. With your permission of course," he added with a slight bow.

He watched the elderly nun consider his request. "I'm not sure. She's not been well. Perhaps, Tara, you should come back later."

"Are you trying to tell me the shock of seeing me might hurt her, Sister?" He could tell the thought did not go over well with Tara.

"Yes, no. You left with some very ugly words hanging between you."

Nicholai was stunned by Tara's reaction. Tears flooded her eyes and she clenched her jaw to stem their tide. "Mostly my words, Sister. Words I now regret very much. I would make my peace with her if you will allow it."

"That is a difficult request. My heart lies with your search for forgiveness, however, my head tells me she might be too frail."

Tara walked over to Nicholai and gazed up at him with intense adoration. "I would like her to know that in finding love I have found the way to release the bitterness in my heart."

Consummate actress, he thought. He grazed his lips against her forehead in a gesture of love. "We would like her blessing before the marriage."

That seemed to turn the tide in their favor. "Sister," Tara added. "You know how hurtful words said in anger can be. Let me take them back before it's too late."

Sister Margaret nodded. "All right. But it is late and many of the Sisters have retired. Your discretion would be appreciated."

He gave her a solid dose of the Valentin charm. "They will never know I was here."

Sister Margaret accompanied them down a long hallway then turned down another. The Retreat spread out much like a Spanish hacienda with only one level, for many of the nuns could no longer climb stairs.

They stopped in front of a room. The door was closed but a light shone from underneath. With his sensitive hearing Nicholai could hear a commercial coming from a television set inside. He glanced at Tara to find she heard the same. She took a deep breath and knocked.

No answer. "Perhaps she's sleeping," Sister Margaret said in a low tone of voice.

"I'm sure she won't mind the inconvenience once we speak," Tara replied. She knocked softly again, and before the elder nun could stop her, opened the door.

"Oh no!" she cried, running to kneel by the woman in the chair. Her head lay slumped on her chest, her arm hung over the side, limp and lifeless.

Wait. Listen. They both did. And soon sensed a tiny thread of her life force remaining. Holding on. "Tara, your hand."

She reached out and cradled her surrogate mother. "Please," she begged. "Don't go."

"Sister. Quickly. I think she is still with us. Call an ambulance."

The nun nodded once, turned on her heel, and left the room. He heard her prayers as she half-walked, half-ran down the hallway. "How bad?"

"I may not be able to reach her."

"Try," he urged.

She placed her fingers on the Sister's temples in the same way she had with Alexi and Jeri. Then he added his power to hers by connecting with her. She tried to shrug him off, but he wouldn't let her. *Do not fight me. She will not last long.*

Nicholai focused first on the heart. To give the body life. Then he delved into the mind. Impressed, he found Tara trying to shield her thoughts from him. Without training. *You must say your farewells. Now.*

Tara balked. "Not like this," she whispered. He felt like an intruder. *You must. No choice.*

The love between the two staggered him. Pure. Unsullied now that no words could interfere. *Her heart. Hurry.*

All of a sudden he sensed something. They both did. Terrible fear. Confusion. Before he could respond, heartbreak rendered him helpless. So many words would never be spoken. *Tell her, Tara. You can.* And he broke his connection with them.

Moments passed and he knew the elder woman's life force was slipping away. He opened his eyes to find Tara's head cradled in Sister Mary Edward's lap. She looked up at him and he would never know which got to him more. The quiet heart-wrenching agony on her face or the profound gratitude for the privacy he'd given her. He nodded and turned away just as Sister Margaret came rushing back. With a sad shake of his head, he ushered the nun out of the room. Tara's one keening cry would stay with him forever.

"We must let her grieve in her own way."

He found Sister Margaret eyeing him with a newfound respect. "Come to my office, please. The ambulance is on its way anyway. We'll take care of the arrangements from here."

She led him to an austere but very busy looking office. With a gesture, she urged him to sit down. He didn't realize how much he needed the drink until he found her offering a glass of brandy. "Thank you." He took a sip, enjoying the bite and the warm glow it left behind. "Very good."

"The monsignor likes an after dinner drink when he visits."

She studied him for a time. He wondered with droll humor if he passed muster. "Do I pass inspection?"

"You do." He smiled. "My heart tells me you will be very good for Tara. I can only hope so. She's going to need you now more than ever."

"I know." He took a sip and curiosity got the better of him. "Tara is, how shall I put this? Very closed-up inside herself. She doesn't give information easily. I try not to pry too hard."

Sister Margaret nodded. "She's always been so, so alone. No real friends. Living here in a retreat. Not that we didn't try to make life as normal as possible for her."

He frowned as he tried to imagine not belonging to a family. His heritage, his House, they were ingrained in his bones; they made up the very fabric of his being. To not belong? "Was she, was she unhappy as a child?"

The nun considered his question carefully. "No, I don't think so. In fact, she seemed happiest when she *was* alone. Playing on the beach, swimming in the ocean. Yet, somehow, it just didn't seem right. She was…"

"Different?"

"Yes."

"She is extremely…gifted."

"Yes. I just wasn't sure what her talents were. No one was."

"I see. This fight they had. What caused the rift between them? They seemed to love each other so much."

She took a sip of her drink. "I suppose I'm as much to blame as anyone else. Sister Mary Edward and I always assumed she'd follow in our footsteps and join our Order. She certainly seemed to have a propensity for the Calling. I'm afraid neither one of us wanted to let her grow up. We both pushed at her. Until we realized we'd pushed too hard. She reacted in exactly the same way she always had. You could never tell that child no without a reason."

Nicholai smiled. He'd been the same way. "I understand."

She smiled back, so very sad and so very bittersweet. "No matter what. Tara would listen then go off and make up her own mind. But this time we didn't give her a chance, I guess, to use reason. As I said, we pushed."

"And she reacted. How?"

"I'd told her she was too young to make a decision and that we knew what was best for her. She said she needed to figure out what life was all about first. She was right, but at the time I was so angry with her for being obstinate that I didn't see her side of things." The elder nun sighed. "The police caught her in the back of a car with a young man."

"I get the picture."

"I don't think you do. Once I stopped being so angry with her I prayed. God lectured me for being a hardheaded fool. I apologized but I think it was already too late. But Mary? Mary is, was, older than I. She came from the "old" school. She took the Calling very seriously. She felt betrayed. She wanted Tara to follow in her footsteps. Tara didn't truly understand what that meant. She went along with the idea to please Mary. And Mary didn't understand that Tara could never be what she wanted. The one who'd really been betrayed in all of this, was Tara. In the child's defense, I think she was only gathering information."

Nicholai nearly choked on the brandy he was about to swallow.

"Tara was always curious. We couldn't stifle the

child. She'd go to whatever lengths she had to in order to find the information she needed. In a way, I believe she was simply conducting an experiment."

"An interesting way of putting it."

"Mary was horrified," the nun responded.

"Come now, Sister. Certainly you do not expect me to believe this was the end of the world, do you?"

"Of course not. But sometimes, when people grow apart, they can't seem to find their way back to each other again."

How true was that? he wondered. Then he sensed her presence. "Tara?" he asked, rising from his chair.

She fell into his arms and had no need to act. "I must take her home now, Sister."

Tara pushed away from him. Sister Margaret went to her and held her without words. None were needed. "I'll make the arrangements, child." Tara nodded.

"My cell phone number." He handed her a card.

Once outside the Retreat, Sergei got out of the car and bowed to Tara with great respect. "My sympathies."

"Thank you." Tears welled up and yet again she refused to cry. Why would she not yield? Did she think that showing her emotions would make her seem weak? He had yet to meet anyone stronger.

When neither he nor Sergei moved to get into the car, Tara looked back and forth between them. Nicholai began the chant with Sergei giving the correct responses. When they were done, Tara asked, "What was that?"

"The death chant of our people."

****

She didn't want to argue but she didn't need a keeper. She wanted to be alone. To remember all the things she hadn't said. She certainly didn't need help. Especially not his. Nor that incredible stare that saw right through her, that made her feel all the guilt she could bear.

"You don't have to stay with me. I'll be fine. And if I need someone, Jeri will come over."

"You are a stubborn woman. But this time I will not yield. I am spending the night and that is final."

"Why?"

"Must there be a reason? All right then, I'll give you a reason. Protection. Or did you not see the marks on her face."

"Marks? What marks?"

"Bruises. By her mouth."

"From what?"

"A hand, perhaps? To keep her from shouting out."

Tara paced enough to put tread marks into the carpet of her living room rug. "Someone was in the room before us."

As she looked up at him she saw him nod. "I believe so. Someone who wished to frighten her so that she would not say anything to us. Instead, with her frail body, she died."

"But I don't understand." Anguish flooded her as she thought she might be the cause for hastening her foster mother's death.

"I think I am beginning to."

"What do you mean?"

He sighed. "Someone does not want you to find out who you really are."

She frowned, speaking her thoughts out loud. "That doesn't make any sense. Why not just leave me in the hospital where I could vegetate and not remember who I was?"

"Because I stepped in and ruined the plan."

"Now you're really not making any sense. How could anyone possibly know that the change would cause amnesia in the first place?"

"Perhaps amnesia was not what was intended."

Her jaw dropped. "You mean someone wanted to kill me?"

"I do not know!" he admitted. "But add up the facts. Why you? Why not someone from one of the lesser Houses? Why not try with one of their own House? Or else one of the gifted ones, such as Jeri?"

"Because if they changed someone in their own House, they'd bring about their ruin. No one would risk it. But an outsider, an unknown. That makes sense."

"Especially to someone who already knew who you were. Correction. What you are. Of Noble Blood."

"But I could have died."

"Then no harm done. No one would really know."

That was cold. "Gee, thanks."

He came around to stand in front of her so fast she had to pull herself up short or bump right into him. He grasped her upper arms in a vise-like grip. "I am not the villain here, can you not understand that?"

"A little hard under the circumstances. You haven't exactly been warm and cuddly."

All the anger seemed to drain right out of him. "You are right."

Tara did a double take. "Say again?"

"I said, you are right. I have not exactly been my most charming."

"Oh my God, an apology. Will wonders never cease?"

"Tara, that is enough."

"You think that's enough? I've been through hell and back and you think that's enough?"

"Yes. I gave you the time to say good-bye."

"And I'm supposed to be forever grateful. Well, you can just forget that because—"

She never got the rest of the words out because

the next thing she knew, his mouth had closed over hers.

Chapter Six

He kissed her to shut her up. Perhaps in the back of his mind, he even thought he could pare some of the barbs off that tongue of hers. Except in the instant their lips met, everything changed. Her mouth opened in surprise and ended with a sweet catch of her breath. The tension in her body, that innate vibrant energy so totally hers, mellowed. Softened. A word he would never have used to describe her before.

Intrigued, Nicholai decided to explore. He ran his tongue around the outside of her lips to gauge her reaction. She shivered. Fascinated he delved even further, tasting the inside rim of her mouth. She moaned. He turned his head for better access and she slanted against him, an invitation he couldn't refuse.

What madness was this? he wondered, exploring the inner recesses of her mouth? How could he possibly allow himself to lose control this way? Their actions served no purpose; indeed, they represented great peril. Yet she was so tempting, so sweet, he couldn't tear himself away. Even the lower half of his body responded, almost with a will of its own. Madness, yes. Sweet madness, he thought as his hips flexed into hers.

Her hands, hands that had begun pushing at his chest, now twined their way behind his neck. She had no idea of the box she was about to open, the potential storm she could unleash. His blood raged, begging to be let free. She was the vessel and his seed craved release.

"No!" he cried, pushing her away. They'd crossed a line that should never have been approached. She smiled, her eyes heavy-lidded and her breath as uneven as his. What a fool he was to think he could teach her a lesson.

"Why did you do that?" she asked softly.

A hundred reasons. A thousand reasons. None of them good. He scowled. "To shut you up."

Her brow arched. "Telling me to shut up would have done the trick."

"I did not think so at the time. Besides, I thought you might like some comfort."

"Comfort?" She cupped her chin with one hand, her arms crossed over her chest, mocking him with her serious consideration. "Hmm. Comfort is chocolate. Comfort is a good book, a glass of wine and a fire. Comfort is a hug to make the pain go away. But the funny part is that I understand. I really do. I looked easy, available, nothing fancy, just out and out sex. A diversion for me, a freebie for you."

"Nothing is for free," he answered, thinking again of the consequences he'd just ignored.

"Boy, don't I know that," she spat at him. "What was the plan? Catch me at a weak moment?"

"There was no plan."

"Oh, come on. You expect me to believe that? You've calculated every move you've made so far, so don't bullshit me. I know what you were thinking. You were going to screw my brains out, get me pregnant, and achieve the ultimate objective. Damn the consequences, full speed ahead."

Her words tore at him like little daggers. "You know nothing."

"Don't I?" She came up and got right in his face, her gaze blazing. "All you ever do is use, use, use. *Your* life, *your* House, *your* race. You consummate bastard. The end does not justify the means."

He lashed out at her. Not physically because he didn't need to. They had the connection. Without touching her, he gave her pictures of the two of them together, suckling her breast, lapping at her core, their hips straining together to reach the ultimate release; pictures she'd never be free of. When he finally realized what he was doing, shame seared his gut. He broke the connection instantly. "I…am," he let out a shaky sigh. Remorse tore through him at the sight of her pale face and unshed tears. "I am sorry. I have never done anything like that before."

"No? You sure about that? Because if this was the first time you've tried to wound someone, you're really good at it. I mean, not just talented, I'm talking expert here."

"I said I was sorry, did I not?" He raked his hands through his hair. He was not very good at apologizing.

"Sorry's not going to cut it this time."

He wanted to reach out. Cup her cheek with his palm. "All right, what I did was unforgivable."

"Damn straight," she replied, presenting him with her back.

"Besides, you belong to Alexi."

"Alexi!" she exploded, turning back to face him. "What about rape? Or don't you consider the mind an organ of the body?"

"You were willing," he replied, his tone sullen. He was not used to being reprimanded.

"So this is my fault now?"

"No," he answered, weariness flooding him. "I

had no idea, that is, well, I have never lost control before."

"Oh my goodness," she taunted. "The great Nicholai Valentin toppling off his moral pedestal. And all because of a mere woman."

"You mock me one more time..." he threatened.

"And you'll what?" She smiled and he realized he'd fallen right into her trap. "Watch out, darling. Your Neanderthal is showing."

"Bitch," he growled.

"For every action there's a reaction."

She was right. She was only answering him on the level he'd stooped to. "Yes."

"And now if you don't mind, your Highness, I'd like to be alone."

"I am not leaving. But I will see Sergei housed before I return."

"The door will be locked." Was she speaking literally, figuratively, or both?

He answered in kind. "Do you really think that will keep me out?"

The weariness in her tone answered both. "No. The spare bedroom's in there." She pointed to a door.

As he turned to leave she asked another question. "Is there anyone you care about besides yourself?"

He refused to answer. She wouldn't like the truth. Neither did he.

****

Tara felt dread as she listened to the door open and close. She'd opened a bottle of wine hoping to soothe the hurt he'd inflicted. She wanted to dull the guilt and pain she couldn't assuage. Nicholai hung up his coat. Funny, she hadn't thought he knew where the closet was. "I have brought some food."

"I'm not hungry."

"You must eat. We will not see much of the Sun tomorrow."

"I can't."

He ignored her and began setting out aluminum tins on her dining room table. "Just an FYI. You will not like what the wine does to you if you drink too much."

"That'll fit. I don't like myself very much right now. Almost as much as I don't like you."

He nodded. "You have to understand, as a prince, I do not apologize often. On the other hand, you might want to be thankful you got an apology at all. None of my people would expect one." He pointed to the bottle next to her elbow. "Why not bring that over to the table."

She rose, not sure why. She could smell the food. He'd gone to *The Owl Tree*, one of her favorite restaurants on the island. "I'm not one of your people."

"I know. Nice wine, by the way. You have good taste."

"Very true. That's why I don't like you."

He ignored her. Again. Which rankled about as much as his attitude that he owned the place. She was going to say something when he came out of the kitchen with plates and cutlery. When she glanced down and saw her favorite meal, a rack of baby lamb chops with garlic mashed potatoes, sitting in front of her she couldn't believe it. "That's my favorite meal."

"I know." He smiled like a little boy with a secret. "Compliments of a short stocky blonde waitress."

"That would be Emma. But how did you find that out?"

"I peeked into her memories."

Horrified Tara asked, "You invaded her mind? For a meal?"

"No, no, no," he insisted. "Never. I just let her see you in her mind and then I saw you eating dinner and what was on the table."

"You can really do things like that?"

"You can too, if you wish."

She shook her head. She wasn't sure if there was a word for his level of arrogance. "You treat them as playthings, inconsequential playthings. The same way you've treated me. We're not inconsequential. We're human beings."

He frowned. "One of the first steps you are going to have to take is to realize you are not human anymore. For your sake I hope you get this through that thick skull of yours soon. We do not have much time by order of the High Council."

"What do you mean?"

"That I was charged with making you into a Noble, teaching you your powers, our ways, our laws."

"Your rules. Not mine."

He threw up his hands, exasperation showing clearly on his stern features. "You do not have a choice. The High Council will order your death if they feel you pose a threat to our race. They have before." Tara gasped. "Since the beginning of time we have tried to coexist with the human race. We could easily have become dictators and taken over the world. We chose not to. We guide, we prod. Lord knows there have been times when not taking a human life nearly killed us."

Puzzled Tara said, "I don't understand."

"We follow a code. Much like that non-interference directive on that television show, *Star Trek*. We try to stay out of human affairs. In the past there have been times when that was incredibly difficult. Hitler would be an excellent example."

His words hit her like a sledgehammer. "You'd have saved the world from a great deal of ruin if you'd killed that bastard."

He shook his head. From his gaze she read the horror of that time. "For every action there is a reaction. By the time we realized what a maniac he was, he was already in power. If we had simply killed the man, we would have plunged the world into an economic tailspin it would still be recovering from. Why do you think he finally lost the war?"

"He made some really bad military moves." She stopped as understanding dawned on her.

"It took years to get one of our people into his inner circle."

"But the lives he took."

"Are but a fraction of those who would have starved if we had killed him."

He shook his head, his shoulders seeming to bear the weight of the world for a moment. "We follow fate, Tara. We do not direct it. Now come. Sit. Eat."

Trying to absorb the ramifications of his words, Tara picked at her food. As she did, she found she was rather hungry. "You hold that much power?"

He took a sip of the wine and saluted her with the glass in appreciation. "Yes, I suppose. In a sense." He took a few bites of his fish and smiled. "Very good." He took another sip of wine then continued. "You made a reference to the cartoon *X-Men* before. I am not dense. I knew what you were referring to. Now think a moment. What would happen if all those mutants rose up and declared dominion over the human race the way the humans fear they will?"

"They'd win, wouldn't they?"

"Of course. And become no better than any other dictatorship in the course of history. Do not forget, we still have personalities. Many of my people are not kind just like many humans. We are not that different."

"Yes, you are."

"We wish only to coexist. We use economic power to gain access to the highest councils and try to advise the best course of action."

"For the Nobility?"

"I would be lying if I said no. But why can't there be a middle of the road? Why can't decisions be made in the best interests of both races? We would not last long if the human race decided to annihilate itself, now would we?"

"I guess not."

His meal finished, he sat back and toyed with his wineglass. "You know, one of the most frightening moments in history was the Cuban Missile crisis. We were terribly concerned when the Manhattan Project was completed. There was no way to stop Hiroshima and Nagasaki. We had no idea how you would maintain the balance of power. In the end, I suppose, the fear of death won out for all of us."

"Radiation poisoning can kill you?"

"Us," he bit out. "And yes, probably, although none of us have ever really been exposed."

"And you've been orchestrating the peace talks, getting the Berlin Wall torn down, etc. etc.?"

"Not alone. Many in the human race want peace as much as we do. And the Middle East will continue to flare up no matter what we do. We try to live. We try to survive. We do the best we can under the circumstances given. No crystal ball, no Kreskin hat."

"You mean there's something you can't do?"

Her sarcasm obviously got to him. "I am not a god."

"Gee, you could've fooled me."

Strangely enough, he laughed. Just when she thought she'd gotten to him, too. Darn. "Rather than worry about wounding me, I would advise you to worry about yourself. We still need to find out who you are. I am going to return to the Retreat and see if I can find out any more information."

"Breaking and entering is illegal."

"Not if you do not get caught."

"I'll come with you."

"No. Tonight you need to grieve."

As much as she hated him being right, he was right. "OK. I'll stay home. Just don't call me for bail money."

He laughed. "Perish the thought."

****

Sergei stood in the living room of the rented house, scowling as if he were a true Cossack. "I do not like this, my Lord. You should not go."

Nicholai, not feeling any possible danger from a group of retired nuns, simply laughed. "You worry too much."

Sergei shook his head. "What you propose is illegal. What would happen—?" Aghast, he choked out the words. "What would happen if you were caught?"

"I will not put myself in that position."

"You cannot be certain. Even with your powers." Sergei growled, obviously not getting anywhere with the conversation. "You are as stubborn as your sire."

"No," Nicholai replied, a smile playing about his lips. "I am worse."

There were times when Sergei was inventive with his cursing. Then there were times when he was flat out straightforward. This was one of those times. "What do you hope to gain with this absolute nonsense?"

"Answers."

"Are they worth the risk?"

"Sergei, please." Nicholai hoped his tone would warn his old friend.

"You test my promise to the limits," Sergei bit out.

"But your loyalty always remains true. Why is that?"

Sergei growled again. "You arrogant young pup."

"Enough," Nicholai cried, trying very hard not to laugh. He really did enjoy baiting the elder man. "No more arguments. Please."

Sergei scowled at him even harder. "At least let me drive you."

Nicholai raised a hand to cut his friend and mentor off. "And risk the sound of a car awakening someone? This island is like a morgue." He cocked his head to listen. "I hear very little but the sea. Besides," he cajoled. "The locals already gossip about the limousine. We should have rented a car."

"I'll exchange the vehicle tomorrow."

"No, that might draw even more attention. Let me go and do what I need to do with none the wiser."

Sergei still looked unhappy. "You will be careful?"

He reached out to give Sergei's shoulder a quick squeeze. "Of course."

As Nicholai stepped out of the house, a swirling mist enveloped him. The damp air chilled him and he shivered, wishing for the dry wind of home. He felt smothered but knew the fog, floating like a cotton cloud would cover his movements. And the brisk walk would help him clear his mind so he could think.

So many questions. Who was Tamara Duncan? What made her worth the risk? More and more, as Nicholai went over the events of the past few days, he was becoming convinced that she had not instigated the change herself or had any prior knowledge to her true heritage. If this was true, then what purpose did she serve? Who had the most to gain from wreaking this havoc? Was the end result of creating a True Noble female of childbearing age worth the risk? Could the creator of this game have foreseen she would lose her memory? Were they aware of the connection she shared with

Alexi, and somewhat, himself? Nicholai shook his head. Although his first inclination was to believe these events had been planned, too many details had been left to chance. Unless the planner felt they were insignificant. But if that were true, was he then focusing in the wrong place?

Nicholai reached the Retreat without being seen. He'd marked the window of the sister's room as they'd left and now opened the portal to her room with ease. As he climbed inside he left the curtains open. A large spotlight on the grounds gave him just enough light to see.

Talk to me, old woman. What secrets did you hide? He stood in the middle of the room and cleared his mind of his own thoughts. He drank her in, her scent, and her essence. He tasted a trail of age and pain and fear. What was that? Disbelief?

Why? Had the Sister not been able to believe someone wished to end her life? Or was it that she couldn't believe the someone who had come to take her life would actually do so? Perhaps both.

Turning, Nicholai exhaled and opened his eyes. He inspected the room thoroughly, leaving nothing untouched. A frugal woman, he thought, even by what he assumed would be a nun's standard. Some clothes. A picture album he would leave as he hoped the nuns would give it to Tara as a keepsake. A porcelain angel standing on the dresser. He touched the piece and Tara flashed through his mind. This piece he would take, he decided, unsure if anyone would understand the significance to both women.

However, he found nothing else. No papers, no safe deposit box key, no help of any kind. Disappointed, he left the Retreat. He'd hoped for answers. Instead he only had more questions. As he walked, he found his hand curling around the angel in his jacket pocket. Had he done the right thing or would she hate him even more now?

Walking faster, Nicholai tried to clear his thoughts. Tara was a jumble inside his head and he couldn't afford the distraction. Yet he couldn't get her out of his mind. Why? Then he felt the whisper, like the fog swirling around his feet.

He shivered, not from the cold. Disregarding the possibility of being seen, he stopped to examine the porcelain figurine under a street lamp. At first he felt nothing out of the ordinary, then he noticed that the base of the statue, the underside, had a different texture. He chipped at a piece with his fingernail. A small flake of white came off.

Another dilemma, he sighed to himself. He didn't want to hurt the angel, but he was curious. Was something hidden inside? Taking a key out of his pocket, he used the point to dig. What came off in his hands was like plaster-of-Paris, as if the inside had been sealed after the figure had been formed.

What treasure do you keep inside you? he mentally asked the statue.

All of a sudden, the key went through empty space. He used his finger to pull at the remains and something fell to the pavement at his feet. As Nicholai stared at the ground, horror filled his soul.

Chapter Seven

Tara awoke to the sense that something was wrong. As her eyes snapped open she found Nicholai bending over her, a look of horror and disbelief etched into his stern features. She shrank back. He was a monster. He hated her. He'd done nothing but make her life miserable since the moment they'd met.

"Who are you?" he growled.

The words came out in a grating rasp. A terrible knowledge surrounded by anger filled his gaze. Bewildered she asked, "What are you talking about?"

He seemed out of breath. Why? What new torture was he planning to put her through now? "This." He shoved his palm under her nose, so close to her face she couldn't even see what was in his hand.

She slapped the offending appendage away. "Hello, Tara," she mocked. "I'm very sorry for your pain. Yes, I know. There are no words. Not really. Not even when you just lost the only person who ever really loved you." She swung her legs over the edge of the couch and rubbed her face with her hands. *Not when so many things you said in anger can't be taken back now.* Misery, guilt, confusion all made her continue to lash out at him. "Gee, Tara. I wish there was something I could do. Something I could say."

"Enough," he cried. He grabbed her shoulders and hauled her up to stand before him.. His pupils seemed twice their normal size. He was breathing in short, sharp gasps; nostrils flaring. She'd never understood the word fey before. She did now. "Do you know what this is?"

She stared at the black oval disk sitting in the center of his hand. "A dragon by the looks of it. Made out of a red stone. A ruby I'm going to assume. But I'm no gemologist. Nice work. And your point is?"

His jaw worked. His eyes widened. His disbelief matched hers. "You have no idea what this is?"

God, how she wanted to hate him in that moment. But she was too tired to muster the effort. "No I don't. Since you never believe anything I say, I'm not sure what good it would do anyway. I am, as Jeri likes to say, a collector of stuff. As a collector of stuff, my guess is some sort of signet. From the shape and design, another guess would be a herald. From a ring?"

Some of the wildness left his gaze. "You really do not know," he breathed.

"Damn you to hell and back, I told you that, didn't I? What the hell is your problem anyway? When are you ever going to listen to me? Why do I have to constantly repeat myself before you either believe me or the words reach inside that goddamn thick skull of your?"

"It is hard to hear one of the dead."

"Come again?"

Only when he let go did she realize how tight his grip had been. She rubbed her arms to get the circulation going again. "It is hard to hear the dead." His gaze kept returning to the piece and he stared at it transfixed.

"Look, I've had just about all I can handle tonight. I think you'd better leave. Why don't you go wherever it is you need to go and sleep it off, OK?"

"I am not drunk."

"You sure about that?" He simply stared. "Well if you aren't drunk, you can join me while I try to get as drunk as possible. Because being sober right now, right here with you, is more than I can stand." She walked over and uncorked the wine she'd opened before. It was still sitting on the portable bar. She held up a glass.

He shook his head. "I wish I could."

"You are the most obstinate, infuriating—," she exploded. More words failed her. She took a healthy swallow to drown some of her anger. The liquor plunged into her belly making her stomach roil. She shuddered waiting for the wine to settle. "I could go on and on, but I won't. Explain or get out. Better yet, just get the hell out. I'm not in the mood for any more of your bullshit tonight."

His hand opened and she saw the imprint of the stone on his skin. All right, so he wasn't exactly unaffected. "This is the seal of the House of Pendragon." He shuddered as he spoke the name. "I found it hidden inside this." He drew a porcelain angel out of his pocket.

"How dare you! How dare you go through her things." Tara snatched the piece out of his grasp. She stared at the statue remembering the day she'd first seen it. She'd been seven years old. She'd spent all summer and fall saving any money she could earn doing favors for the nuns to buy the piece as a Christmas present. How Sister had loved and treasured the statue.

"She knew."

"Knew what, thief?"

Her barb had no affect on him. "She had to know."

At the very last inch of her rope Tara asked, "Had to know what?"

"That you were a Pendragon and that you were marked for death."

"Who and what is a Pendragon?" When he didn't answer, she continued. "Sister Mary Edward was a nun, not a Noble. She had no idea what a True Noble really is, how could she? How could she possibly become embroiled in your world?"

"So much makes sense now."

So much for listening. "What makes sense?"

"You. The change."

Steaming she bit out, "Would you care to explain that?"

He still didn't seem to hear her. He seemed to be speaking to himself. "It would not matter if you died during the change or not. You were already dead."

"Wonderful." She went to take a swallow from the glass in her hand but thought better of the idea. Her stomach was already in trouble. "I really have to hand it to you. You know exactly how to make a person feel totally worthless. There's just one thing you and everyone else have missed. I'm alive. Very much alive. And I intend to stay that way."

He looked at her. Really looked at her. As if seeing her for the first time since he'd barged into her home. "Not when the High Council finds out who you are."

Crazy. Totally insane. She'd have turned her back on him except for the incredible sadness mixed with pity in his gaze. "You know, I am damned tired of being a puppet in a game I have no control over. So before I ask why, let's start with how. As in, how do you know I'm a Pendragon?"

"I do not."

She pinned him with her gaze. "Bingo. You don't have any proof. All you have is a theory and some circumstantial evidence."

"But—"

"No," she cried before he could continue. "No more buts. I'm tired of being a but."

"It stands to reason."

"What reason? Whose reason? What about a little help, a little loyalty? If nothing else, how about the benefit of the doubt? If for no other reason than I saved your brother's life."

"After you nearly killed him."

"That wasn't my fault."

He nodded. "In that, at least, you may be right. Someone may be pulling both our strings. If so, the only reason I can think of is to create havoc within the Nobility."

"Why?"

"That I cannot answer. Revenge against a House, perhaps. Total dominion over the Nobility, the desire for absolute power, the annihilation of the human race. I do not know."

Silence passed between them in slow seconds. "I don't understand. Something tells me I never will. So maybe I need to backtrack for a moment. What happened to cause the problem with the Pendragons?"

"The Head of the House of Pendragon was found guilty of being a traitor. He was killed and every member of his immediate family ordered put to death. His House was named outcast. Those who were found innocent were assimilated into other Houses. Those who were not were banished, maybe a fate worse than death."

"On circumstantial evidence?"

"My grandfather argued that very point."

"Your grandfather?"

"He and Christian Pendragon were best friends.

****

Not a sound. That was what frightened Christian Pendragon to the core. Not one word, no greetings, no change in their expressions, only stone cold silence. Except for Gregori. The fear in Gregori's gaze matched his own.

"Once before we came together," Kenjo Tenaka began. "In secrecy. Only a select few. For reasons of security."

How well he understood that now. Hitler was everywhere. Dangerous and poised on the brink of world domination. "Two years ago we asked a grave service of you, Christian Pendragon. To give up your wife, your House, your life, and keep the humans from annihilating themselves."

They thought he was Nazi. Two miserable years of watching in disbelief, standing by while atrocities were committed that he would never be able to forget. Two years of working to become part of Hitler's inner sanctum. Now he was able to suggest strategies, make decisions, all leading down a path of ultimate destruction. "The less who knew what you were about to do, the better."

Christian agreed. "So I also believed. And still do. Which makes this meeting ill-advised."

Kenjo stiffened. The rebuke, though lightly given, remained between them. "The Council does nothing that is ill-advised."

Point taken. "Then why have you brought me here? You risk the work that I have performed. Some of the seeds I have planted are just ready to take hold."

"Are those seeds for your own end?" Tenaka asked.

Christian blanched. "What are you talking about?"

"You stand accused of treason."

"Treason?" Bewildered, his gaze flew to Gregori's. A cold dread settled in the pit of his stomach as he realized his best friend did not wholly believe in his innocence.

"Christian Pendragon," came another voice, solemn and strong. Antonio DeMarco was the second member of the High Council that was part of this scheme. "You are hereby charged with attempting to steal the Water of Change and create a True Master Race for Adolf Hitler."

"That's insane!" he exploded. "He's a madman. To create even one would jeopardize the entire Nobility!"

"Exactly."

Righteous anger boiled inside him. "I have just spent the last two years of my life trying to destroy this monster and all he stands for without changing the course of whatever human history is about to unfold. Without getting myself killed in the process. I have given up everything I hold sacred. And you dare to accuse me of this nonsense?"

"Hold." Antonio DeMarco held up his hand for silence. "We do not do this lightly or without proof."

"What about motive? Or have you forgotten that Edward Rhys-Jones has sworn to avenge his House against mine?"

Their silence told him they had not forgotten. Yet something wasn't quite right. Had he missed something? Something vital? "Bring the prisoner in."

Prisoner? Christian recognized the man immediately. One of Hitler's "golden boys." Horror filled his soul as he realized the import of what had been done to this man. He was a True Noble now and he was pure Nazi. "I swear to you, I had nothing to do with this."

"We have proof. Your signature on papers outlining the creation of the True Master Race."

"I had no choice. He wanted me to devise a plan. They were naught but papers. To refuse would have probably gotten me killed."

"You were seen near the Swiss border two weeks ago."

"I was sent to inspect troops. To make sure they were ready for an upcoming battle." Christian now knew he was being framed. "Don't you see? This is all circumstantial evidence. Someone is setting me up."

"Albert Manneheim," Kenjo called to the prisoner. "Do you know this man?"

"I do."

"What did he say to you?"

"That he would make me strong. Very strong. A true Aryan god."

"Members of the Council." Gregori gave Christian an imperceptible nod before taking the floor. "We have only this man's word against one of our own who has proven his loyalty to the Nobility countless times. We cannot simply condemn on the face of such little evidence."

"You call this man's very existence a little evidence?"

"No, I do not. What I do believe is that our first problem is not how he was created, that cannot be undone. No, I believe our first problem is what to do with him now he has been created."

"The Council is not stupid, Gregori Valentin."

Christian watched Gregori pull himself up to his full height. He knew the true depth of their friendship. "Neither am I."

As if he were the best defense attorney ever created, Gregori stood before them all. "What are we? A pack of humans? At the least provocation, we immediately turn on our own? In this time of human war when we need to believe in each other more than ever, all we can think of is trying to condemn ourselves? At least give Christian Pendragon the chance to defend himself. Gather proof of his innocence."

"We have all the proof we need."

Christian heard the voice and had his answers. Edward Rhys-Jones. He'd been set up. He looked at

Gregori then at his enemy. "They'll let anyone into a secret meeting these days."

Realization followed realization. Rhys-Jones had suggested he infiltrate the Nazi Regime. With the High Council terrified at the thought of Hitler winning, with Tenaka and DeMarco unable to return home because of their countries' involvement in this war, he'd played upon every fear they had. How could he have been so blind? "Including a traitor."

Rhys-Jones knew nothing of Christian's psychic abilities. He saw the plan as soon as he probed. If Christian suggested he go back to finish his work he'd fall into the trap, if he tried to defend himself, all the Houses would find out their small group, Tenaka, DeMarco, Gregory, had called these secret meetings. The Council wouldn't allow that. But there was one avenue Rhys-Jones had forgotten. He prayed he wouldn't have to use it. "I'm touched you consider me worth such effort." Turning to the Council members he continued. "You all find yourselves in a very awkward position. The other Houses will not appreciate being left out of these decisions. On the other hand, if you let me go back, you run the risk of my trying to continue to create this Master Race. At the very least, allowing Hitler to win. And then there's him. Nice creation, Edward."

"Th—" The man stopped himself just in the nick of time. "This is ridiculous. Pendragon is merely trying to extricate himself any way that he can."

Christian remained calm as he addressed the Council. "My word against his. What will you do now?"

He saw indecision in DeMarco's gaze; Tenaka was as hard to read as ever. Of them all, he was the best at blocking his thoughts. He also knew they'd recognized the play might go this way.

"Throughout our history," Tenaka began and Christian's heart sank. He'd hoped— "We have

resolved issues with ancient rituals. I invoke the Rite of Trial by Combat."

Not even a choice. He looked over at Rhys-Jones first. The man actually had the gall to smirk. Then he looked at Gregori. He nodded. In spite of the concern written all over his face, Gregori nodded in agreement. "I choose Gregori Valentin as my second."

"Edward Rhys-Jones?"

"I choose Albert Manneheim as my champion. I will second."

"Coward," Christian taunted, but he recognized the logic behind the move. Christian was in top physical form and at least twenty years younger.

Walking over to Gregori he chose not to speak. 'He is newly made and not used to his powers. That is to our advantage.'

Gregori answered, also without words. 'He is young and very strong. He shows no fear.'

'Should this go awry, you must protect my family. I will not allow them to die because of my stupidity. I did not see this coming.'

'Neither did I. You have my word. Christian—'

'I know old friend. Now is not the time for words. Remember your promise and believe in the truth. No matter what happens, you know the truth.'

****

"My father told me about the fight once," Nicholai continued. "As his father, Gregori had told him. As a lesson in courage."

"You call this courage? I call it stupidity. Super men on a super testosterone trip. Setting each other up, House against House."

"It has always been this way."

"Then you all need a good slap upside your damn fool heads."

Nicholai wasn't sure if he was insulted or not. Truth be told, he agreed that this feudal fighting was terribly unproductive. And terribly dangerous to all of them as a race. When they fought among themselves they were vulnerable to attack from anyone, even humans. "You are right. But we are a race steeped in tradition."

"Traditions can change."

"Yes, they can." Nicholai eyed Tara from a new perspective. When she wasn't being belligerent, she was quick and able to reason with intelligence.

"So what happened?"

He smiled. She was curious in spite of herself. "Both Pendragon and the Aryan were near death when the Aryan lost his footing. Christian, seeing an opening, tried to end the fight with a final blow. It was a trap. He died with a knife through his heart."

He watched her shudder. Funny how she could be so hard and yet so vulnerable at the same time. "Oh my God." She took a deep breath. "And the Aryan? This Albert Manneheim?"

"As Christian Pendragon's second, my grandfather destroyed him. They all knew he could not be allowed to live."

"Just like that? Oops we've made a mistake, let's fix it?"

He frowned. She really had a way of distilling things down to black and white, which didn't sit well with him at all. "No. Not exactly. He was nearly dead anyway."

"And that made everything OK?"

"As his second, my grandfather had the right to kill him."

"Damn you and your rights! You allowed how many people to be destroyed because of your rules, your traditions." She spat the words out at him. "And you call yourselves Noble."

For the first time, Nicholai was able to set aside his immediate anger. From her perspective, she was right. "Humans make mistakes too, you know."

His words seemed to reach her. "How many died

because of this?"

"You would rather not know. Even one, from your point of view, would be too many."

"You're right." She sighed as the weight of the story along with her grief threatened. "Did anyone try to find the truth? Prove that this Rhys-Jones character was behind the whole plot?"

"My grandfather tried. But with the end of the war and trying to help the humans rebuild their world he was unable to do so."

"Don't tell me you care after all."

"One for you," he said, inclining his head. "As I was saying, my grandfather tried, but Edward Rhys-Jones was killed in an automobile accident shortly after the war."

"How convenient."

"My father thought so also."

"That still doesn't mean I'm a Pendragon."

"I cannot prove otherwise. Therefore I am obligated to bring you to the High Council for judgment."

"Just like that? Sorry. It's been fun, but—"

Nicholai searched his heart. She was a pawn. They were both being used. His House was in danger. "I think we should return to my home first. My father's notes are there. He did try to continue the search. Perhaps we can find something that will lead us to some answers."

"So you're not going to turn me in?"

"Not just yet. Although if I'm forced to choose, my people come first."

She nodded. "No sense sacrificing the many for the few or even the one."

Chapter Eight

The Sun. Always the Sun. How could her eyes, as tired as they were, open of their own accord? How could her feet carry her, of their own volition, to the tiny deck outside her living room? How could her mind, normally sane and logical, accept his presence as he stepped behind her? What was this need that not only consented to the hands on her shoulders but actually welcomed them?

The Sun. Golden glorious rays. A soft warm caress. A lover's touch. That spark of anticipation deep inside her belly as the sky lightened. She'd never known so many shades of gray could blend into pale yellow then burst upon the horizon with bright white light.

Nor had she known that the white light would burst inside of her, ripple under her skin, tantalize and tease her every sense. Such power. From her muscles to her bones to her individual cells, they all cried out with anticipation. But none more than her core, that deepest part of her, the place that made her—her.

She wanted. Not just the energy she absorbed and drank in like a greedy infant. She wanted more. Not just the molten heat deep inside her belly. She wanted *him*.

The pressure of his fingers increased. If she turned, he'd know. Deep inside, she was certain he knew already. Her body betrayed her, circling to meet his gaze. She'd never realized there were rings of fire around his irises. She'd never realized his eyes were almost silver, brilliant like a flash of light against polished chrome.

She'd called him Elrond that first time they met, likening him to the Master of Imladris. A leader who was hard from battling the forces of evil but just. A leader who was weary from shouldering the responsibility of saving a world he would eventually leave. Yet he never wavered from his purpose, never said no.

Tara whispered an ancient tongue without thought. How did she know the language? He answered in kind making the question superfluous. His fingers lifted from her shoulders to skim the skin of her neck. She shivered. His hands caressed her cheeks, moving to mold each side. He urged her closer.

What madness was this? When her mind cried out to resist, when her pride begged redemption, all she could do was lean towards him. What insanity caused his head to angle ever so slightly? What lunacy caused hers to turn in kind?

Their breath became one. So close. The Sun, now a glorious orb behind them, bathed their bodies in resplendent light. Their lips parted; ready to drink in the taste of one another. His hands tightened drawing her closer...closer...

Tara reared back and broke away. Shaking with the war inside her, she could not meet his gaze. He hated her. He would give her up to the High Council in a heartbeat.

A gentle finger lifted her chin. He was breathing hard, his confusion as great as her own. Doubt warred with desire. She could read the questions in his gaze. Was she truly the enemy? No matter who she was, was she still guilty until proven innocent? Was this incredible attraction between them merely Sun and hormones or something more?

Neither of them spoke more than a few necessary words as they showered, dressed, and prepared to return to his home in Las Vegas. The flight became a test of her willpower. She wanted all her thoughts, all his thoughts out in the open. She wanted to battle, rail and exorcise the demons tearing at her. Did he believe in her? Could he believe in her? If she were this terrible entity would he try to destroy her?

His hand reached out. She was certain he was fighting with himself as much as she was with herself. He would begin to speak only to clamp his jaw shut, then repeat the actions moments later. Yet his hand never moved from hers for the entire flight.

After they landed, Alexi stood on the tarmac to greet them. She watched the easy-going camaraderie between the brothers with envy. They were lucky to have one another. They'd never known the ache of a lonely childhood.

"Hello, sweeting," Alexi said, reaching out to hug her.

Unfamiliar with such natural warmth, Tara wasn't sure how to react. She'd never known a man to be simply friendly. "Alexi."

He grinned. A quick glance between Nicholai and herself made their situation quite obvious. "My brother can be a real ass, don't you think?"

Unable to help herself, she laughed. "I didn't know it was a historical trait."

Alexi laughed out loud, causing Nicholai who was talking to Sergei, to flick them a quick glance. "Indeed, there are times when the blinders he wears are nearly impenetrable."

What a relief, she thought, to talk to someone who understood. Well, not everything of course. But then, she didn't have a handle on their relationship—relationship? "Why don't you hate me, too?"

"Hate you?" Alexi's gaze flew back at his brother then to her. One of his brows rose. "Did he say that?"

"He didn't have to."

"I see," Alexi murmured. With a shake of his head, he grinned again. "What a maroon."

It figured that Alexi would know Bugs Bunny. She smiled but could only mask the hurt inside. "What's going to happen to me, Alexi?" The smile fell from her face as reality set in.

"I don't know. But my grandfather swore he would save your family."

"That's if I am a Pendragon," she interrupted.

He nodded. "I believe he did save your family and that you are a Pendragon."

"Then I'm doomed."

He frowned. "No. We won't let that happen. *You* didn't do anything to anyone. The sins of the father or anyone else shouldn't be visited on his heirs. Anyone with two eyes in their head can see that."

"Tell that to the High Council."

"Not me. Nicholai. I don't count. He does. He's next in line for a seat on the High Council."

Why didn't he tell her that? She turned to berate him as he approached and gasped. His face, etched in stone, was the color of old plaster. "Sergei just informed me that the High Council has called an emergency meeting." He took a deep breath and exhaled in a rush. "Tomorrow night."

"Damn," Alexi cried.

Her heart plummeted. "So little time," she whispered.

"How could they have found out?" Alexi asked.

"My thoughts exactly," Nicholai replied.

"A traitor?" she asked, putting word to what neither of them would.

Nicholai sighed. "Possibly, but from now on, no one and I mean no one, except the four of us, is to know what we're doing."

"Four?" she asked.

"I trust Sergei with my life," Nicholai replied.

"I do too," Alexi seconded.

"Well I don't," she argued. "This is my life we're talking about here."

"I know," Nicholai burst out.

"Easy, Nico," Alexi tried to soothe.

Nicholai looked straight at her. He seemed to be trying to swallow the fight inside him, push it to a safe place, and not let it cloud his judgment. "We all go into this trusting only ourselves, all right? However we need Sergei. He has answers we need."

Tara knew she had no choice. "Very well."

"You and Alexi go back to the house. I have an errand to attend to, then I will meet you there."

She wanted to ask what was more important than her life at the moment but he seemed, again, to be asking for time. Maybe even faith, she wasn't sure.

"Don't worry, sweeting," Alexi said, putting a comforting arm around her shoulders and urging her towards the limousine. "He may be a maroon, but he's a bulldog when his back is up."

She nodded. As she stepped into the car, she caught Sergei's gaze. He remained completely impassive. And, impervious to the probe she tried. *What else do you know, old man? Even more important,* she wondered, *would you use that knowledge to save me?*

****

So many years, Sergei thought, walking down the hallway to the huge library next to Nicholai's study. The young one believes I am a traitor, even that pup Alexi could not quite meet my gaze. So many years, he repeated, feeling his age.

Lies, deceit, deception. Move after move. Feint to parry. One House gaining here, another losing there. Chess game after chess game with no end in sight. God, he was tired. So very tired of all the nonsense.

The humans could not know the havoc they wrought. The Nobility was a whisper, a phantom, and a part of their deep unconscious. Yet they had the power of such destruction. How many times had their race been forced to save them, stop them from their insane stupidity?

All for a promise. Made to the one man he loved above all others. Gregori. How he missed his mentor. How he wished he could confer with the man, discuss and not be the one to make so many important decisions. The plots would never end; they would ebb and flow as with the tide of the ocean. Only now, the surf was up and the waves were building. What if he was wrong?

Sergei opened the door to the library, closing the portal behind him before facing his charges. "You sent for me?" he asked them.

"My father kept a journal, Sergei," Alexi answered.

"A journal, Alexi?" The young woman's gaze tried to burn a hole through his brain. He would have smiled, but she looked so vulnerable in her wrath that he didn't have the heart. She would never know that he'd been tortured by the best, the Gestapo, in the disappearance of her grandfather. Only his Noble blood had kept him alive.

"Yes," she told him. "A journal."

"A private journal," Alexi added, daring him to dispute its existence. "I saw it once. As a child."

"A private journal should remain private, shouldn't it?"

"In any other case, I would say yes," Alexi replied.

"Maybe you want to see me get fried for something I didn't do," Tara accused.

"Every paper your father had was in his study. I assume Nicholai went through them."

"He's stalling. I believe you already know. Am I a Pendragon or not?"

Should he tell them? But he had no proof. "If you know, you do not need me."

"No games, Sergei," Alexi told him. "We do not have time."

"Your loyalty lies with the House of Valentin." Was this an outright challenge from her? How interesting. "I'm expendable."

She was very direct, perhaps too direct. "You are absolutely correct."

"Sergei!" Alexi growled.

"The order has already been given, young one. Your brother was most specific. I am to aid you in any way."

"And?" Alexi asked.

Tara cried, "Am I a Pendragon?"

"Yes."

Sergei whirled as they all did. Nicholai stood beside an ancient looking woman, with snow-white hair and a tanned well lined face. She was wearing a gypsy peasant blouse and skirt. "You have grown to be a beautiful woman, *dochinka*."

"Witch!" Sergei spat at her, his disgust knowing no bounds.

"That is not what you said long ago, Sergei Ivanovitch."

She cackled and a chill ran up his spine. "Will you now right the wrong that was done?"

"I do what my lord commands."

"As always," she replied with disdain.

"Tara," Nicholai began. "This is a friend."

"I am Irina Petrovna, Tamara Pendragon. I saved your life once, long ago."

"You should not have brought her here, my Lord," Sergei protested. "She is outcast."

"For saving a child's life?" Irina's voice dripped acid. "As far as you are concerned, perhaps. But I am a member of a House again." The woman drew herself up to her full height. "You men. You cannot see around your own noses. Swords and axes, beating your chests to be the best, to be the one and only. So many lives wasted."

"And you know better, old crone?" Sergei asked, his tone no less destructive.

"Sergei, please," Nicholai requested. "Both of you. We cannot fight among ourselves right now."

"There is evil at work here. Can you not feel it?" Another chill ran up Sergei's spine. "My Lord, she is crazy. You cannot possibly believe a word she says."

"Do they know?" The old woman seemed to be talking to herself, her gaze sly. "Do they know what awaits them? Can they see the shadow hiding in the wings?"

"My Lord, look at her. Her mind is gone," Sergei cried.

"I don't think so," Nicholai replied.

"Neither do I," Tara joined in.

"You must understand the plan. Do you know his plan? Do you?"

"Enough, Irina Petrovna. You must tell us what you know." Nicholai's temper had been tried long enough. "Can you tell us, old one? What plan? Who is this dark one you keep talking about?"

"The ends of the circle meet. The past repeats."

"She is crazy, my Lord."

About to berate Sergei, Nicholai stopped. Tara had a hold on his arm. "Let me try." She looked to him for approval.

He nodded. "Go ahead."

"Irina?" Tara asked with a gentle tone.

"You are such a beautiful woman. I always hoped—"

"What do you remember, Irina? Can you tell us what happened?"

"He knows. He knows." She was pointing to Sergei.

"Sergei?" she asked.

For a moment Sergei seemed to shrink, and look his age. "Your grandfather believed Christian Pendragon was innocent. He believed he'd been used by the High Council to save their precious Houses, and then eliminated because he knew he'd been used. In his innocence, Lady, your grandfather never saw the danger he was in until it was too late. He only saw the human threat. When he finally realized the game they'd played with him, he had no choice. He called for a Trial by Combat to clear his name."

"Trial by Combat," Tara spat out. "Good Lord, what is this, Camelot for crying out loud?"

"Tara, please," Nicholai replied. "I understand your disbelief. Our traditions do seem quite Medieval at times. However, they've kept our race from annihilating themselves since the very beginning. Without them—" He shook his head. "I don't know."

"He's right," Alexi agreed. "We're an awful aggressive race."

"Swords and shields, knives and axes," Irina told them, her voice dripping disdain. "Nothing changes."

"Your turn will come, old one. But first I need to piece the past together. Sergei, if memory serves, Christian Pendragon had two children, a boy and a girl."

"Nelson was able to save both of them. Having been able to get away from Reich headquarters for a few days, Christian sent his wife, Sarah, and the children to a safe house where he could join them."

"My grandmother survived?" Tara asked, bewildered.

Nicholai watched a pained, sorrowful expression fill Sergei's countenance. "No, Lady. When she found out what happened, she went after Edward Rhys-Jones. Your grandmother knew who was behind the whole plot even though Gregori killed Albert Manneheim. She went after Rhys-Jones."

Sergei took a deep breath and exhaled. "I tried to stop her, but there are times when a mate dies the other mate dies too, even though the body lives. They were meant to stay together. The attempt was futile and—"

"Aye," Irina agreed. "A true love match. I remember."

"Not yet, ancient one," Nicholai interrupted. "Continue Sergei."

"Nelson took the children to a hiding place. With all the chaos of post-war Europe, they were able to get lost for a while. Eventually they landed with a band of gypsies."

"My band," Irina Petrovna declared. "We were some of the blessed...gypsies that escaped the Nazi net." A flash of pain worked across her face at the memory. "We kept them safe, but the dark one is relentless."

"There is no dark one," Sergei cried. "The darkness lies in the House with no honor. Rhys-Jones had no honor. He made an attempt on the children. The boy died. They thought the girl did too. Nelson saved her."

"Who is this Nelson you keep talking about?"

"We are Stewards, Lady. Sworn to serve. I serve the House of Valentin. Nelson served the House of Pendragon."

"And the child, Sergei? The daughter?"

"Elizabeth, My Lord."

"Elizabeth?" Nicholai whirled to see tears fill

Tara's eyes. "My mother's name was Elizabeth?"

In that instant Nicholai realized the torment of abandonment. He was a prince, born to rule, pampered, well loved, so much so that even his twin was jealous. But this woman had never even known the name of the woman who gave her life. "Tara—" He stopped knowing he had no right to offer comfort.

"Yes, child," came the oh-so-soft reply. Nicholai watched the old woman's face light up with love. She held out a hand to Tara, a hand that he could not offer. "I am gypsy, but I also know of the Nobility. Some of my kin are members of your great Houses. We cannot resist the blood. True blood to True blood."

Nicholai murmured the chant with her. "How did you save her?"

"She was placed with a family on an estate near our encampment. We told them she'd been orphaned and we could not keep her. The lady of the house wanted a baby girl very much. We kept a close eye on her as she grew until she was ready to know the truth. But Michael Rhys-Jones found her first. Devil that he is, he planted one of his own in the house and she fell in love with him. We could not stop the marriage. My mother begged me to serve her, stay close. I helped her—" The woman cut herself off in mid-sentence.

The ensuing silence ran deep inside Nicholai. "Go ahead, Irina Petrovna. Tara needs to know the truth. We all do."

"He did not care for her. It was all an act. I do not know why. But he broke her heart. She asked me to take care of the infants and she killed herself."

"You let her? You just let her kill herself?" Tara cried.

"Tara, listen," Nicholai replied. "No one has control over another's life. Irina might have saved her for a month or a year, but when the heart is broken, there is no life, just existence."

"I don't agree, Nicholai." She turned to the old woman. "Wasn't there something you could do?"

"I am sorry, little one. I have asked myself that question a thousand times over the years and I still have no answer."

"Irina?" This time Alexi asked the question. "Correct me if I'm wrong, all right?" The woman nodded. "Did you say infants?"

The woman cackled a broad grin spitting her face. "Yes. Yes I did. Tara, *dochinka*, you have a twin. A twin brother."

Chapter Nine

Tara's knees buckled. The next thing she knew, a strong pair of arms encircled her and she was urged to sit in a nearby chair.

"Are you all right?"

Concern? Did she really believe he cared? "I think so." So many nights, crying in the dark, wishing for a family. She beckoned the old woman to her. "Are you certain?"

"I do not lie."

Nicholai stepped back but not before his finger traced her cheekbone. The movement was not lost on either woman. "I wasn't implying that you do."

The woman held up her hand. Shiny bracelets clicked together telling her to hold her tongue. "I watched you come into the world, little one. You and your brother."

Stunned, she wasn't sure how to feel. *A brother.* The whole story seemed just that—a story, a fairy tale, unreal. "You said my mother killed herself. What about my father?" Fear threaded the ancient woman's gaze and Tara reached out to reassure her. "I won't harm you."

She read an old agony in the woman's gaze. "But you will hate me."

"I can't," she replied with a wry shake of her head. "You can't take away something a person's never had. Tell me. Please."

"My lady," Irina Petrovna began, drifting back into the past. "She was quiet. Unassuming, but very pretty. When she smiled, the world smiled with her."

Tara drank in the words. "Elizabeth." *Elizabeth.* "My father?"

The woman's gaze darkened. "Harold," she bit out. "I tried to tell her I tasted evil within him. She wouldn't listen. Charmed, she was. Enamored by a serpent's tongue. But oh how she smiled. The only time, I believe, she was truly happy."

Tara tried to absorb the woman's words. How would she have felt? Years of mistrust and loneliness. Could she blame her mother? "Did he love her?"

"I don't know. Perhaps a small part of him tried. I don't think my lady would have responded if he hadn't. But evil holds no capacity to love."

"I see."

"Do you, child?" She gave Tara a strange stare. "They were married for about a year when she got pregnant. Everything changed as soon as he found out."

"I wonder why," Nicholai said, joining the conversation.

"I did also, my Lord. But Elizabeth was so happy. She'd been so alone, now she would never be alone again."

Tara knew that feeling all too well. "Can you think of a reason why he would want me," Tara paused. "Us. Why he would have wanted both of us dead?"

"No, little one. Nothing except the darkness. And the sight."

"The sight?" Nicholai queried. "You bear the gift?"

"No, not me, my mother. She was the one that knew. She warned me what I would do would change my life, but that my fate was already written. So is yours. Both of you."

Tara shivered. "Why do you say that?"

Nicholai looked pensive as well. "What did your mother see, old one?"

"That the past holds the key to the future."

"Explain," Nicholai commanded.

"I followed him to the lake. He was going to drown you both while the household slept. Make it look as if you'd been kidnapped. When I caught him, I told him he'd never get away with murder. He laughed and said he'd kill me too. Then he picked up your brother and started to put him under the water. I picked up a heavy stick and began beating him with it. Beating him. Beating him."

Tara pictured the events as if they were happening right before her very eyes. "He let go finally. Didn't he?"

"Only to see my lady." Irina Petrovna shuddered. "I never want to see that kind of a look on anyone's face again."

The silence grew to a roar in her ears. Just listening to the story filled Tara with horror. What her poor mother must have felt—

"Finish your story," Nicholai coaxed.

"I breathed life into the boy and set him down. My lady was already struggling with her husband," she spat the word out as she would a curse. "I jumped on him too. He fell into the water. We held him down until he stopped breathing."

"Oh my God—," Tara cried.

"We had to, Tara. He would have killed us all." She sighed with terrible sadness. "I looked at my lady afterwards and knew she was already dead. She told me to take care of both of you, guard you with my life if necessary, and then she walked out into the lake. I picked you both up and ran back to my mother. She was already waiting, packed and ready to go. We fled our homeland and all that we knew."

"Grayson," Nicholai exclaimed. "Now I know who you are talking about."

"Yes." She nodded. "We were blamed. Our people had to scatter for a long time afterwards. My mother and I came here, to the United States. Not many wanted to help us. But my mother had the gift, so she was feared. We settled in New York but there were too many eyes. Too many tongues. We knew we would be caught soon. There is always one who will betray."

"But how did you come to find the Retreat?"

"Luck, I suppose. Or perhaps my mother just knew you would be safe there. We kept your brother for a while, but only a short while. Then we gave him to the Church too. They had an adoption agency."

"Do you know what happened to him?"

"No, I am sorry. My mother and I worked as housekeepers. There are many rich people on the island. I watched you from afar. Then my mother passed away. By then I had learned of my Noble blood and joined the House of Deveraux. But I will always be a Pendragon at heart."

"You had no further contact with my brother?" Tara asked.

She shook her head. "I came back to see if you were all right when you were about thirteen. I found you still living with the nuns. I tried to find out about your brother, but the adoption agency would not give me any information. I had no proof of any ties to you. Besides," she continued. "You were both still in mortal danger. You still are. The evil one wants you dead."

"There is no evil one!" Sergei exploded.

"Wait a minute!" Tara didn't want tangents or

arguments; she wanted family. She wanted answers. She wanted to find her brother. "My brother. What is his name?"

"Morgan, my lady. You brother was named Morgan."

****

"Tara, listen to me," Nicholai answered. "If he is still alive, we will find him. I promise."

"Me, too," Alexi added.

"I can't believe this, I can't believe any of this," Tara kept muttering over and over again.

"I know, Tara," Nicholai told her. "But before we try to find anyone, we must reason this out. Someone decided they were going to destroy the House of Pendragon. First we need to find out whom, and then we need to figure out why. And if we're next."

"Rhys-Jones would stop at nothing to gain control of the Nobility," Alexi answered. "But I don't think he's smart enough."

"I do not either," Nicholai agreed. "Sergei?"

"Your father felt the same way."

"My father?"

"Aye, my Lord. At first he believed the High Council was protecting itself. Then he realized they might have been manipulated as well."

"How?" Nicholai asked, disturbed that he could not find any logical reason behind that statement.

"Germany, Italy, Japan," Sergei began. "Germany ripe for a dictatorship after the hardships following the First World War. Italy and Japan with members on the High Council. Look at the catalyst for the First World War. Assassinations are planned, not random acts. Your father wondered if there wasn't just too much coincidence. Throughout too much of our history, the history of the Nobility, we have seen tensions brought to bear so that one House wars with another. Divide and conquer. Is that not the easiest way to win a war?"

"But that doesn't make sense," Alexi argued.

"Yes, it does," Nicholai murmured, deep in thought. "What better way to keep our attention focused within. Just have each House mistrust the other. Feed on that suspicion, stoke it into a fire, and watch the blaze burn them all down. Then go after the High Council."

"Nicholai?" Tara asked, bringing him out of his thoughts. "If everyone is dead, who is there left to rule? There would be no Houses."

A shudder ran through him. That would mean the end of his race, his people, and his reason for being. But she was right. "The evil one wants to destroy, not rule," Irina Petrovna whispered.

Did that make sense? Some kind of master puppeteer pulling all their strings? No, but Nicholai couldn't rule out the possibility either. "Sergei," he finally said, his decision made. "Take Irina Petrovna upstairs. See that she is settled and comfortable. She will stay with us until we are sure she will be safe if she goes home. Then call a meeting of the Stewards."

"*All* the Houses, my Lord?"

"Yes. In times of trouble, the Stewards have saved us before. They may just have to do it again. Let them know that their Houses may be in danger and that I do not call the meeting lightly. If they protest, tell them that they must know what is going on before the meeting tomorrow night. At least we will have been honest with them. Then try to find Connor, Nelson's son."

Sergei frowned. "Why, my Lord?"

"Because I remember Nelson and he would never give up until he found the answers he sought. He may have charged his son to continue. If he did, Connor may have information we need. He may also be in great danger."

"Yes, my Lord." He watched as both of the older people left the room.

"This is pretty far fetched, brother," Alexi told him. "And if it is true, you just told the entire Nobility you know the plan."

"Something like that."

"Why?" Tara asked. "No one would betray their House."

He watched Alexi nod in agreement. "Not necessarily. Think for a second. What if the threat really is against all of us? Forewarned is forearmed."

"Point taken, brother." He saluted them both but didn't seem to be able to contain the grin on his face. "Then I leave you to your next battle."

Nicholai couldn't believe his ears. Alexi was her lifemate, wasn't he? "Are you sure?"

His brother laughed. "There are times when I am a putz, but I'm not crazy. Of course I'm sure. Although I'm not sure I envy you. Or the conversation you're about to have. Enjoy, brother."

"Coward," Nicholai growled. Wasn't he one also? How was he ever going his plan to her?

"Too true, too true." And then Alexi quit the room also.

He turned to Tara without a clue as to how to broach the next subject. "What was that all about?"

"I will explain in a moment. First I need to know if you understand that this has nothing to do with the charges against you by the High Council."

"Yes. I'm still going to go on trial." Her voice lowered almost to the point he could not hear. "I'm dead, aren't I?"

With her almost chameleon-like moods he wasn't sure how to answer. "Not exactly."

Her lips tightened in anger. "Are we playing Hertz again? Because if we are, I have to tell you, I'm not in the mood to play games."

"No games, no joke. Just a solution to an

immediate problem."

That got her attention. "Such as?"

"The High Council will not destroy you if you are pregnant."

Her jaw dropped, the look on her face comical in its disbelief. "I beg your pardon?"

"I said the High Council will not kill you if you are pregnant."

"I heard you." Then he watched the light bulb go on in her head. "That's what Alexi was talking about. You thought he— Oh, my God. How could you? How dare you?"

Nicholai wondered if he could have blundered through this any better. "I had to make sure he would not challenge me."

"Challenge you? Of all the Medieval, Arthurian nonsense. What do I look like to you, a piece of meat? A thing to be used?"

"No, of course not," he cried. "I wanted to explain."

"Explain what?" she goaded. "A roll in the hay? A few quick ejaculations?"

"Damn you!" he exploded. Nicholai walked up to her and shoved his face right into hers. But his anger drained as he saw the incredible hurt in her gaze. "So that I would not have to fight him. Perhaps to the death. To make you mine."

"I belong to no one!" she roared back.

"I know," he whispered, retreating into himself. "But I would rather have you alive than dead. So you either," his mouth curled in disgust around the word, "submit to a few ejaculations or you do not live to see your next sunrise."

He turned away and walked over to stand by the window. The Sun warmed and soothed him. But not as much as the hand that touched his shoulder.

"I'm sorry," she said.

"I am no stud horse, you know."

"Yes, I know." She sighed. "This isn't your fault."

"Some of it is, I suppose. My family swore to protect yours. We failed."

"So that's all I am to you. A debt of honor."

"No. At first I thought you were an enemy sent to destroy my family. Now I know you're just as much a victim as I."

"Then I don't understand. Why do this?"

She would never know the true price he would pay. This would end a dream that began when he was just a boy. But a seat on the High Council was not worth a life. Any life. "Because I want to."

"What?" she cried. "Screw my brains out?"

His stomach churned with distaste at her words. "Crude does not suit you." She seemed torn by that. Then he realized she didn't understand the full import of what he was talking about. But before he explained, he owed her another apology.

"What if I said yes? How would you feel?"

"That you were being honest."

He winced. "I have not given you much faith, have I?"

"No. You've been rude, crude, and any number of other things I don't want to go into right now."

"I am sorry for that," he answered with a sigh. "You will never understand how I feel about Alexi. I am not sure you will even understand how I feel about my people, my responsibility towards them. I was ready to destroy you first and ask questions later."

"I'm glad you didn't," she replied with a small laugh.

No humor there. "Instead I seem to have destroyed something far more precious."

"My trust," she finished for him.

"Yes. And that makes what we are about to do that much harder."

She threw him a look. "Strangers have sex all

the time."

All right, he really botched this now. How the hell was he going to explain? "This is not just about a function between two bodies."

She burst out laughing. "That was one helluva way to put it."

"You do not understand," he continued. Her laughter faded at the urgency in his tone. "A male Noble can have sex anytime he wants. Constantly for that matter. Complete with orgasm." Nicholai took a deep breath then took the plunge. "But he can withhold his seed. Not ejaculate, to use your terminology."

"So?"

"Our race mates for life for the purpose of procreation. Once I spill my seed inside you, we will be mated for life. You will become my lifemate."

"I've heard the word before."

"Yes, but you never really understood its true meaning. We will be bound together."

"Let me get this straight. You mean this is irreversible?"

He nodded. "Should we survive the next twenty-four or so hours, then we will be bound for our natural lifetimes."

"You're not joking, are you?"

"No. I will try to be as careful as possible, but there will be times when I will not be able to resist my need of you. Then, I am afraid, you will not have a choice."

She shivered and he felt her fear. "Is that what you meant about the rapes and tied to the bedpost?"

He'd forgotten his words. "I wished only to make you understand that we can be a primitive race as well as an enlightened one. But that is what I meant." He reached out wanting to reassure her. "I would not wish it to be that way between us. Ever. I will try to make the experience as pleasant as possible."

"Oh joy, oh bliss."

His hand fell away before he touched her. "Do you wish to die?" he demanded. She shook her head and he swallowed the anger that threatened. "Then use your brains instead of your mouth. I am trying to save your life. Is that not worth some sacrifice?"

"Yes." She turned away, unable to meet his gaze. "But what about love?"

"Dreams are broken all the time." He certainly knew the meaning of that now. But there was always hope. "That does not mean they cannot be repaired. Or changed. Is it so hard for you to believe that we can carve a future out of this adversity?"

"And if I meet my soulmate later? Or you meet yours?"

He didn't want to look in that direction. "It has happened before."

"And?"

"I have no answer for you, all right?" he cried. "We will deal with what we have to deal with now and when the time comes. I did not make the rules. I did not create your fate. Right now you have a choice. Live or die. The future after that will have to take care of itself."

So many emotions, he said to himself as he watched her. He would have to teach her how to hide them. At the moment though he was glad for them. He needed to know how she really felt. "My life seems like it will never be my own. Never has been. My grandparents, my parents, and now me. All faced with the lesser of two evils. I wish I knew why."

"Fate has never been kind to you," he commiserated. "That is how destiny works. So if I have no control over events that are happening to me, I do have control over how I will react to them. Defeat is not a word in my vocabulary, do not let it be part of yours."

"It's so unfair," she whispered.

"So?" He picked up her hand and squeezed. "So what if we have not had time for courtship, at least we are attracted to each other. So what if I have not been kind. At least you have seen me at my worst. If you agree, you might see someone you even like."

"Now that would be interesting."

Lifting her arm up, he pressed a light kiss on the back of her hand. "I take hope where I can find it, Tara. Can you?"

"I don't know."

"You do know the worst case scenario."

"Yes." He ached for her as her tears threatened to fall. Still, she was so strong because not one drop slid down her cheek. "I just don't think dying is preferable to rape."

He shook his head. "Do you really believe I would rape you?"

"Yes. No. I don't know."

He let go of her hand to cup the side of her face. "I swear on the House of Valentin that I will not hurt you. Can you believe that?"

"If you insist."

"I do. Making love is preferable to both rape and death."

She tore her head away. "Don't be too sure."

Confused, Nicholai could only stare. "What are you talking about?"

Chapter Ten

Tara could feel the fire of Hades creeping up her cheeks. How the hell was she going to explain? "I'm not—" Good grief, this was beyond embarrassing. His keen glance made her feel naked. A state she'd never really, well except once…

"Experienced?" he finished for her.

Someone find me a shovel quick because all I want to do is dig a hole and crawl way down into it. "Yes."

Randy Meyers. She found out later that she was part of a bet that he couldn't get into her pants. Trouble was, he couldn't. He was not a generous loser, either. "You are not supposed to be."

"I'm not?" she asked, looking up at him.

He stepped nearer to her and she could feel the heat and sizzle of his body. "No."

She lowered her gaze again. "Yeah, well, you'd want me to say that, wouldn't you?"

"If that was your wish. And I know it was." Both hands cupped her cheeks now. "So hard and yet so vulnerable."

"Don't you dare pity me."

"Pity? Never." His vehement reply almost made her believe. Almost. "You are too strong to pity. But there is no law that says I cannot hurt for you. Especially when there are so many things about yourself you do not know."

"Such as?" His thumbs grazed both her cheeks in a gentle rhythm.

"Your Noble blood. You did not have many friends because you already knew you were different. The same with any amorous contacts you may have had."

"I thought there was something wrong with me," she confessed. "If they'd had Viagra back then I would have taken some."

"None needed." He kept up the steady caresses against her skin and sparks ran up and down her spine. "You see?"

"Then why couldn't I feel before?"

"Because True blood runs to True blood. A human would have to have had at least a small amount of Noble blood in them for you to respond."

Light bulbs popped all over inside her head. "It wasn't me?"

"No. And I am sorry that you had no one to teach you. Noble girls are taught these things as they reach puberty."

That earned him a hearty laugh. "I grew up in a convent full of nuns. Get the picture?"

He smiled with her. "Yes." Then his smile faded. "Was the experience terrible for you?"

"Disastrous."

"The boy?"

"Randy. Took his name a bit too seriously. Of course, when he couldn't complete the act, the name-calling got more pointed. And a whole lot uglier."

"He would never have been able to, just so you know."

Stunned she said, "What?"

"Your body knew what your mind did not. That he was not a Noble."

A sense of utter relief ran through her. "That's not just a saying, is it?"

"No," he replied, his tone gentle. "We mean it. Literally. I guess you could say we just know, if someone is one of us or not, even how much Noble blood they have. The boy had some Noble blood but not as much as you, therefore, not enough for mating which, in turn, caused your ambivalence." He shrugged. "I've always thought the ability was a survival mechanism, survival of the fittest. Alpha to alpha, Beta to beta and so on."

"I was afraid I was frigid."

"Oh no, Tara. You are far from cold." His head inched closer.

Her heart raced as panic set in. Standing in the Sunrise and feeding off the power was one thing. This was different. This was real. "I'm not sure."

He stopped. He was so close she could feel his breath on her lips. "I know. But before you make your decision, I want you to know there can be joy in this for both of us."

"Joy?"

His lips captured hers. Kissing had always been a little disturbing to her, something that she knew she was supposed to enjoy but never quite could. Nicholai changed that for her in the span of a heartbeat. Tiny electric bursts ran from her lips to her arms, all the way down to her toes, and back up to pool in her belly. Better than the Sunrise, she decided. Much better.

He pulled back. "Yes," he whispered.

Whoa! Wait a minute. This experiment was far from over. Tara wound her arms around his neck and pulled his mouth down to hers, kissing him for all she was worth. He forced her mouth open with his tongue and went on to explore. Thoroughly. All of a sudden, she couldn't get enough. She wanted more, like a morning feed. No matter how surfeit she felt, she wanted more.

Again he pulled back. This time, as she opened her eyes, she read desire in his darkened gaze. His hips had somehow managed to find their way against hers. His erection pressed hard against her core. "You see what I mean?" he gasped.

Tara nodded then let her forehead rest against his. A thrill of excitement ran through her followed by a shot of pure unadulterated fear. She had no idea what she was doing, what the outcome would be. "Do it now," she commanded.

He rolled his head from side to side. "That would be unfair and I have been unfair enough." He lifted his head and she noted that the harsh granite-like intensity in his countenance had softened. "You must make your own decision and not one made in the heat of the moment. Besides, I will need time to make arrangements."

"Arrangements?"

"I would like to make our wedding night as close to a wedding night as possible. For you."

"Wedding night?" Tara swallowed hard.

"If we mate, we mate for life," he reminded her.

She had forgotten. Smack square in the heat of the moment. A slow smile curved her lips as she repeated the words to herself. *The heat of the moment.* "My answer. In one hour."

His smile matched hers. "Done."

****

One small kiss. Nicholai wondered at the weight that lifted from his shoulders. "Sergei."

"Yes, my Lord?" the elder man stopped in the middle of pouring a glass of brandy.

"Can you have everything ready in time?"

"All will be as you wish." Sergei walked towards him, handing him the libation.

Nicholai accepted the glass with a nod of appreciation. "Will you join me?"

Sergei shook his head. "I am getting old and there is much to do. The liquor will put me to sleep."

Old. Sergei? He'd taken forgotten that Sergei had always been a part of his life. Then he remembered he'd been part of his father's life also. "The Stewards?"

"Being notified as we speak."

"Good. Now tell me. We have no audience. Why—?"

"Did I not tell you?" Sergei finished for him.

A shaft of annoyance ran through him, for the omission as well as the interruption. "Yes."

"There was no need."

"No need?" he exploded. "I am Head of this House."

"Until this House decides you are not," the elder man answered softly.

"Are you challenging me?"

Sergei chuckled. "You still let your emotions rule, young one."

Nicholai grimaced. He'd fallen right into that trap. "And you are still a sly old fox, my teacher. But the responsibility of the people still rests on my shoulders, not yours. I should have been told."

"Perhaps."

The door to Nicholai's study opened and Alexi entered. Nicholai gestured for him to pour himself a brandy then turned back to his mentor. "Explain."

"I promised your father to protect the House of Pendragon. We agreed to keep the secret."

"We?" Alexi queried, walking over to the bar.

"Your father, Nelson, myself."

"Before or after the murders?"

"Before, but especially after. In the interest of keeping attention away from the survivors, we kept a low profile. I suppose we monitored the situation, as you would say now."

"Did you know the children survived?"

"Yes, but we couldn't find them. Then we decided that if we couldn't find them, no one else could, and that was their best protection."

"And that is why you did not tell me?"

"Yes, my Lord."

Satisfied by the logic, Nicholai took a sip of his drink. "You have not commented on my decision. Either of you."

Alexi laughed. He gave Nicholai a salute with his glass. "You have no choice. Never did."

"I agree, my Lord."

"Easy for you to say."

Both men nodded but only Alexi had the audacity to grin. "Come on, Nico. You know this was meant to be."

"Again, that is easy for you to say. Do not forget what I forfeit by this act."

Alexi really poured it on as he added, "You act as if this is a fate worse than death. She's worth your stupid Stewardship and you know it. Have you kissed her? Wasn't her kiss worth a thousand Council seats?"

"Alexi!"

Sergei coughed to cover a snicker. "Children, please."

Nicholai threw the older man a look. "Point taken. Just remember my life is my own and this was my decision. Now as far as you are concerned, old man." Their gazes met. He could dish out more than he received when he wanted to. "I will need you to act in my stead with the Stewards. Along with needing to be appraised of the situation, tell them I ask for a Council meeting. Round table. This may spark some ideas as to what is going on. Make sure you mention every detail including this evil force business. Understood?"

He watched Sergei sigh but knew he was right to insist. "Very well."

Sergei made to leave the room. "And Sergei?" The man stopped and turned. "Thank you."

Alexi raised a brow as soon as the door closed. "Why did you do that?"

"Do what?"

"Antagonize him," Alexi accused.

"He needed to know who was boss."

"I see."

"I am not so sure, but someday maybe you will. Someday you will take your responsibilities seriously."

"Maybe. I just don't think you're giving up the entire world," Alexi continued, swallowing a mouthful of his drink. "Do you think you will enjoy your bondage?"

"I believe I will."

"She's been through an awful lot."

"I do not pity her if that is what you are asking."

"No, it's just that she deserves the best you can offer. More than anything, she could probably use a friend right now."

"A friend?" Nicholai snorted then stared into the glass wishing the amber liquid inside could give him the answers he sought. "That is humorous. I am not exactly her most favorite person on the planet."

"You can change that."

"Can I? Sometimes I feel she will only accept what she chooses to accept."

"So you're both stubborn mules. Work things out."

Nicholai nodded. "I owe her the effort, at least."

"We've been very unfair to her." Nicholai heard regret in his brother's voice.

"I am glad you made that plural. But I will take most of the blame for being an ass."

Alexi laughed. "Now, if I'd said that—"

"Yes, and I would have too."

"Seriously, though. Did you tell her you're an—"

Nicholai glared at him even as he tried to hold back his laughter. "I tried. But how do you make a person understand your entire life in one sentence. She could never understand this." He swept his arm around to encompass the room. "She could never understand the responsibility I carry for our people."

"What about the Stewardship?"

Nicholai smiled. "All right, so you know me too well. No, I did not tell her that. I could not. She'd think I was an arrogant, ambitious ass. Which I am, of course. Up to a point."

"Here, here."

Nicholai took a sip of his drink then swallowed. "We are stagnating, Alexi, and I am scared. You think I am ambitious. So would she. But you are wrong. I am scared—scared we are dying of dormancy. Maybe Rhys-Jones was right. Maybe we need to make the Water of Change available."

"I don't know, Nico. Think of the risk."

"Think of the risk if we do not. Not one true Noble born in what, twelve years? How long can our race survive without pure blood?"

Alexi shrugged. "Would being human be so bad?"

Nicholai hated the thought. "You ask that question from a secure position."

"True. I have, however, tried to reach out in understanding."

"By demonstrating simple magic tricks?" Nicholai scoffed. "Do you not see, Alexi? Our line must continue."

"Or what?"

Nicholai threw his brother the same look he threw his mentor moments ago. "Now I wonder which you play, devil's advocate or simply buffoon."

"Neither. I just want you to put things into their proper perspective. Nothing is worth your life. Or hers."

His heart warmed as he read the concern in his brother's gaze. "Thank you. But as you said before, I do not have a choice. Therefore, I plan accordingly. Should something happen to me, you will take over the House."

Alexi blanched. "Me?"

Nicholai clapped his brother on the back with affection. "What made you think you would get out of this unscathed? Hmm? Everyone must sacrifice and now you will know what you have always wanted to know, what it feels like to rule."

An overwhelming feeling of love engulfed him as he watched Alexi swallow then square his shoulders. "I'll do my best, Nico. But as far as I'm concerned, there won't be any need. You'll be here."

Nicholai didn't really believe in God. Then again, he'd never had a reason. But he found himself quoting a human phrase without hesitation. "From your lips to His ears."

Tara looked out of the huge picture window marveling at the green oasis surrounding the house in contrast to the broad band of desert on the horizon.

"I never asked before. Do you like my home?"

Amazing what the promise of sex would do to a man. Then she sighed, angry with herself for being petty. Their predicament wasn't his fault.

"I love my home. I miss the ocean. But it is very beautiful here."

"And you feel out of place?"

"Out of everything," she cried, turning towards him. "God, this is so awkward. I don't even know if I like you."

He smiled. "I know. And putting the cart before the horse does not help." He moved to stand beside her. "Speaking of horses, I raise purebred Arabians here. Do you like horses?"

"I—I guess so. I've never been, wait a minute.

Yes, I was. A pony ride. At a carnival."

He laughed. "Perhaps you would like to take a walk and see some of them?"

Was this an offer of peace? It would also give her a moment to dig below the hard exterior and get to know the man underneath? Tara hesitated. He was so much easier to hate. And if things went wrong, so much easier to blame him. "All right."

He led her out of the house down a small driveway, towards some fenced in areas of grass. They passed a large barn off to her right. A light breeze caressed her skin. The air was dry but smelled sweet from the scent of the grass. In the distance she could see some peaks. And beyond the pastures only brown scrub. "This was all wasteland before my great-grandfather came here. Amazing what patience and hard work can accomplish."

Was he being figurative, literal, or both? "It's very beautiful."

"Look over there on the top of that rise. Do you see him? Is he not magnificent?"

The stallion stood tall and proud in the distance, surveying his domain. All of a sudden Tara realized they were made from the same mold. The arrogance that grated on her so was as necessary as the air both man and animal breathed. Neither could falter one step or question one action. Decisions weren't thoughts or even instincts because leadership was ingrained in their cells. This was the mantle they both carried. "Yes."

He turned towards her to look directly into her eyes. "Your decision?"

She wanted to tear her gaze away but couldn't. "It never really was a decision."

"I know. I do not want to hurt you."

"That won't be possible either."

"True. But a small amount of trust will go a long way."

"I can try. I just wish—"

"That we had started off differently with each other?" he finished for her. She nodded. "So do I. But I do care. I know you don't believe that right now, but it is true. Tonight I will try to prove to you that I do."

"What, no slam, bam, thank you, ma'am?"

His face closed and his gaze narrowed. "One of these days I am going to tame that tongue of yours."

She nearly told him to try it. "You don't exactly look like a whipping boy, but I've been using you as one."

"You have every right to be angry but not with me."

"I'm not angry with you."

"Scared?" he probed.

"Yeah."

"Do I frighten you?"

"Personally?" He nodded. "Why, no."

"Then it is the unknown that bothers you." She nodded her head yes. "I am glad." He reached out and took hold of her hand. "Come. The ladies of my House await you."

"Excuse me?"

He took a deep breath, letting the air out slowly. "My people do not know you are being forced into this. They believe we have fallen madly in love with each other. I did not correct them because, well, there are going to be hard times ahead. I thought this could be a night of celebration."

"I don't have much to celebrate."

"Ah, but you do. You have your life and another Sunrise to look forward to."

He was right. "Will there be a ceremony?"

"A small one. Symbolic mostly. Will you miss your human traditions?"

"I guess. I'd always dreamed of a church wedding."

“Then again, I must disappoint. Our traditions are very different. But I suppose the purpose is the same. Our hands will be tied together and there will be the branding.”

“Branding?” she shivered, totally freaked out.

“To mark each other for all eternity.”

Chapter Eleven

Nicholai watched from afar as was his right. He'd never known that bathing a woman could be such an erotic experience. At first Tara was stiff as a board, shy beyond belief. She didn't want to undress in front of a room full of women. But the whirlpool and the heated water did wonders to relax her. A long thorough massage followed by which time she was putty in their hands. Of course, the ribald comments the women made didn't help. In the end, she was manicured, waxed, styled, and dressed in the traditional wedding garment. There would be no undergarments and the dress bore a high neck line with no sleeves and a diamond-shaped cut out in the front showing most of her cleavage. The back dipped almost to her waist and the collar was held together in the front by a pin bearing the crest of the House of Valentin. Remove the crest and the top of the dress would fall away to his view.

For himself, Nicholai dressed in a tunic of scarlet satin like that of the Cossacks. Trimmed in gold thread, the pants were of the same material. Again, no undergarments, only two well placed buttons in order to shed his clothing at a mere touch. His job would be the harder for he would be forced to hold himself in check until the ceremony was finished.

Sergei stood under the moonlight in the garden next to the pool where she was bathed. The House gathered around as close as possible. Next to Sergei Alexi stood beside a heated ornate brazier, the fire one of many that lit and warmed the area. Nicholai entered first then he turned to watch Tara approach.

Was this the Amazon who fought his every move? Whose tongue pierced worse than a thousand daggers? Head held high, eyes clear and her gaze locked on his, only he felt her fear. He tried to tell her with his gaze that he would try his best to be the prince she dreamed of. Her tiny nod told him she understood.

"I, Nicholai Alexander, Head of the House of Valentin, come before the people with a question. Will you accept this woman, Tamara Elizabeth?" She gave him a look of pure gratitude as he added her mother's name to hers. "As my lifemate? For all eternity?"

Sergei's voice rang through the air. "Tamara Elizabeth. Are you of Noble Blood?"

"I am."

"Do you swear fealty to the House of Valentin for all time?"

"I do."

"Will you bond with Nicholai Alexander for all eternity?"

She swallowed at that question, but Nicholai could not blame her. "I will."

Nicholai held out his right arm and pulled back his sleeve. Sergei directed Tara to do the same with hers. He used a golden rope to tie their wrists together. Chanting in the ancient tongue, he told them they were bound, now and forever. Then the rope was removed. Using tongs, he held out a fiery circle of gold, fashioned in the crest of the House on both sides. Nicholai nodded to her. *Be strong, it will not hurt but for a moment.* He positioned his wrist on one side, she on the other, and they pressed their wrists together.

Capturing her gaze, Nicholai bent his head. Indeed, he felt no pain as his lips touched hers. There was only the warmth of their kiss and the love of the people surrounding them. Breaking the kiss, Nicholai lifted her wrist to his lips. He kissed the wound knowing as he did so, the fire melted away. Her gaze, full of pain, changed to confusion. She'd never seen him gentle before.

He held out his wrist for her to do the same. As she did, the wariness that was always part of her seemed to vanish. He smiled. She smiled back.

A great roar rose from the crowd. Alexi was the first to congratulate both of them, then Sergei. As they passed through the throng of people, comments flew. Yet what struck him the most was their acceptance of her. She seemed a bit baffled by their show of loyalty but walked beside him with regal acceptance.

The crowd moved to an open area on the other side of the house. Tonight they would celebrate. Already Nicholai could hear hands clapping in time to the music. He smiled.

With her hand clasped in his, Nicholai guided Tara back to the pool. At some point during the ceremony a platform had been brought out, not quite a bed, but more like a dais with a soft covering and pillows strewn about. A white, gauze-like linen made up a canopy and draped around the sides like a tent.

Knowing she was nervous, Nicholai walked over to a bucket and pulled out a bottle of champagne. Adding a fresh strawberry to each glass, he poured in the liquid. "You were wonderful. I am sorry for the pain."

"Thank you."

"To us," he toasted, touching his glass to hers. He drank the entire glass and took the strawberry into his mouth. Touching his lips to hers, he encouraged her to bite off half of the strawberry. Then he signaled her to do the same, offering a strawberry to him. After two glasses, she seemed to relax and he put them away.

Feather light at first, he nibbled at her lips. She sighed, reaching out to steady herself by placing her hands on his shoulders. Of their own volition, they crept to the back of his neck. He opened her mouth with his tongue and plunged inside, sparks of pure lightning streaking through his veins. He wanted to plunge his penis inside her so badly he could think of nothing else, except her fear. Which helped him keep his sanity.

Taking his hand, he undid the clasp at her neck. She gasped as the garment fell away and stiffened under his gaze. His lips trailed kisses all the way down her neck until she relaxed once again. He cupped her breast in his hand and teased the peak with his thumb. This time her gasp was one of excitement, not fear.

"You are incredibly beautiful."

His mouth followed his hand and he suckled each of her breasts in turn. Her hands kneaded the back of his neck and her gasps turned to moans of pleasure. Breaking away for a moment, Nicholai opened the tunic and ripped it over his head. He took her hands and placed them on his chest, savoring the exploring touch of her fingers. "So are you."

Breath flared through his nostrils and his chest heaved. His arms wound tight around her as he savaged her mouth. His hands lifted the back of her gown to stroke the flesh of the back of her leg. She met his kiss with a savagery of her own as her hand slipped between them. She molded his erection in her palm and he pushed against her with a cry of delight.

His hands left her back and pushed the rest of the garment from her hips. He caught her gaze and held it while he removed the buttons and pushed off his trousers. Her breath caught when she saw him and he heard the fear again. "Do not be afraid."

Stretching out his hand he took a chance. Would she put her palm in his? When she reached out a thrill of pure joy shot through him and he lifted her into his arms.

The dais was soft as down, like swimming in an ocean of velvet. That was what he imagined he'd feel when he was finally inside her. That was what he tasted as his tongue reached out to lathe her mouth as his finger entered her core.

Her back arched against his hand. Greedy little thing, he thought with a smile. No fear now, only feeling. And fire. Such heat, such promise. She was dripping and moist and as ready as she would ever be.

Moving between her legs, he rested his weight on his elbows. He used his arms to spread her open and lift her to get a better angle. Positioning the head of his penis at her core, he nudged just a bit so the tip gained entry. Then he stopped. "Look at me, Tara." Desire swam with fear. "Do not be afraid." He pushed in a bit more. Her body, smarter than her mind, shifted to allow him better access. "I will not hurt you." He slipped inside a little more and hit the barrier of her virginity. Releasing one hand for leverage, he bent down and kissed her lips. Soft and exploring, then harder until his tongue mimicked his need. As soon as she opened her mouth to accept him, he thrust, once, sharply.

She cried out and he spread kisses all over her face. Sweat broke out on his brow. Her heat was ten times better than he imagined. "Shh. Do not move. Get used to me first."

Again he kissed her. Fire swirled all around them as they let passion take the lead. He moved very slowly at first, a hell of its own as his body cried out for release. He even stopped and shuddered before gaining a modicum of control.

"Don't stop," she pleaded and he sensed she was searching for her own pleasure. She sounded stunned by the feeling and he knew that he could bring her to the ultimate, a hope he'd dared not even think about.

Withdrawing almost fully, Nicholai thrust deep. Again and again. She strained against him, her head thrashing from side to side in search of what he knew, and she was a moment from finding out. With his thumb, he reached down between then and touched the pinnacle of her core. She cried out and thrust against him harder and harder. He matched her rhythm and touched her again.

All of a sudden she screamed and he knew she was going to topple over the edge. He let go of his control and felt the pressure build inside. Capturing her mouth with his, he pushed into her again and again and again. He wanted release, sweet, sweet, release and as her body convulsed around his, he found it. Pumping, shooting, he thought his seed would never stop.

Coming back down to earth, his chest heaving for breath, Nicholai grinned. He opened his eyes to find her grinning back. "Did I hurt you?"

****

Hurt her? Her body felt magnificently different, languid. Complete. "Only a little. The end totally justified the means." The soreness was already disappearing between her legs.

"I am glad." He hesitated. "I was not sure you would be able to…I mean, be fulfilled. I worried that the pain might interfere."

Her nipples had tightened to hard pebbles,

attuned now to the touch of his hand and seeking more stimulation. Her skin rippled with the breeze, every sense alive with expectation. “You were worried? About me? About making love?”

“Yes.”

Wow. He cared. He’d asked if he’d hurt her. Stunned, she wasn’t sure what to think. But she knew how she felt. “You’ve taken the pain away.”

Withdrawing, he rolled to his side and tucked her head into the crook of his arm. “Pain?”

Would he understand? Could she explain the missing link he’d finally forged? “I grew up with Nuns. Proper ladies didn’t talk about sex.”

“I see.” He pulled her closer and she reveled in his care. “A stranger in a strange land.”

“That too, no doubt. But I always felt like I should never ask, you know what I mean? As long as I didn’t bother anyone, it was OK.”

He sighed, kissing the top of her head. “You learned to be self-sufficient at an early age?”

“Yes. Not that I’m complaining. They loved me, each in her own way. I guess a little knowledge would have gone a long way though. And not just hearsay from another teenager.”

He chuckled, kissed the top of her head again, and rose. Long and lean, he moved with the grace of one who knew his own power. For a moment she was envious. It would be nice to feel that complete.

“To the search for knowledge,” he toasted, after handing her a fresh glass of champagne.

“To the unending search for knowledge,” she replied with a grin.

He grinned back. “I will drink to that.”

His gaze roamed her face and body. She should have felt awkward. Instead, she lifted her head and straightened her shoulders with pride. He lifted his glass in salute. She returned the salute with a regal tilt of her head. “True Blood to True Blood.”

His smile couldn't have made her happier. They were communicating on a level they couldn't have achieved without making love. "Forever and always."

Did she dare? Why not? Her decision made, Tara reached out and took the glass from his hand. Setting the two glasses aside she reached out, grasped his hand, and pulled him towards the pool. She looked back over her shoulder to find a strange half-smile playing about his lips. He wanted her. That was evident. Very evident. Then what was up with the smile?

The warmth of the water contrasted the warmth of his gaze. She'd watched his eyes grow hard as steel when angry, now they were smoky, swirling with desire. Out of seemingly nowhere, he produced a small vial and poured out what looked like oil into his hands. Now she understood the smile.

Sensation upon sensation rocked her to the core. The silky feel of the water against her skin, the slippery sensuous touch of his hands. Each graze of skin against skin, lip upon lip, heightened the other's awareness. Tara ached for him to fill her again and this time felt safe enough to tell him so. "I want you inside me."

His nostrils flared as he sucked in a deep breath. But he shook his head. "Not yet."

He carried her over to the steps and set her on one so that she lay half in and half out of the water. Then he bent down with a devilish grin. Where was he going? His tongue. Making little swirls over her belly, causing shivers up and down her spine. Lower and lower—oh, dear. Tara didn't know a man could do that to a woman.

Streaks of lightning, bolts of thunder, and an incredible pressure building in her belly. Building, building. If he didn't stop soon—

All of a sudden he lifted his head. Pulling her hips forward, he positioned himself at her core and plunged inside. Tara screamed. Wave upon wave of incredible pleasure washed over her. No gentleness just pure need. His hips pumped frantically to match hers. Each time he pushed she heard soft grunts of helplessness. She couldn't believe she did that to him, reduced him to a point where he was no longer the almighty prince but simply a man, a man who needed her—well, at least her body.

Just as she thought she could stand no more, he reared back and cried out. Guttural, from the depths of his being, he pumped his seed into her as if there would be, no, could be, no future without their bodies joined this way. She joined his cry with hers as her body convulsed around him, pulsing, the pleasure so intense she thought for a moment she might pass out.

They both would have probably drowned if not for Nicholai's presence of mind. He withdrew, picked her up, and carried her to a chaise for two next to the pool. Lying next to her, his body heat warming her as the air cooled her wet skin, Tara didn't want to think of the future only the now. Questions bubbled through her. There was so much she wanted to know. "Is it always like this?"

He didn't respond right away and Tara feared she'd become too personal, although how much more personal they could become—

"No," he told her. "I am ashamed to admit that I have been engaged in the act and wished I was not. I see now that there have been times when I was most unfair."

Bewildered she asked, "Why would you do want to do that? I mean, shouldn't you want to make love before you make love?"

He laughed. "You wound with your innocence. But you are right. I should not have."

"I didn't mean—"

"I know. I have just found out how wrong it was.

And how right we are."

"Are we? I mean, I guess...I wonder what you feel. You know, when we're joined." She let her voice trail off. Maybe he didn't want to share, maybe it was too soon to ask.

"Hmm. How do I feel? That is a tough one."

Her face fell. "I shouldn't have asked."

He pulled her towards him and looked deep into her eyes. "Never. Do you understand? Never be afraid to ask. Anything. We are mates now. If we cannot share, we cannot become…I do not know how far you can go with this, Tara. You do not know me yet. Nor do I know you. But that does not negate the connection between us. Your blood flows in mine, mine in yours. Time will tell. In the meantime, I promised you honesty.

"What do I feel? Physically, I feel incredible heat. Like being in a velvet furnace. Every time you wrap yourself around me, it is all I can do to hold back. I want to take my time, savor every sensation, but you make me insane. I become like a greedy child. All I want is more, and more, and more." He looked down at her with a warmth she'd never thought she'd see. "I never want to hurt you, Tara. Never again." He paused. "Do you still hate me?"

Uncertainty? From the man who was king? He was as unsure about her as she was about him. Only on the physical plane did they communicate. And boy, could they hold a conversation.

"No."

"Just no?" he prompted, his body tensing next to hers.

He wanted more. She was certain he did. Deliberately vague she replied, "I'm not sure I understand what you're asking."

"I am asking if we can begin again. Perhaps build on the foundation we created tonight."

"Can two people build a relationship on just

sex?"

"This was not just sex and you know it."

She hid a smile. "If you say so."

"All right, since you know everything, what did you feel tonight?"

She thought about that for a moment. "I'm not sure I have the words to describe the feeling. I mean, I never knew two people could do these things." All right she was blushing. "How about better than a morning feed."

He laughed. "I would never have thought to put it like that. What else?"

"And give you a swelled head?"

"Did I not do the same for you?"

"Yes. Umm. Although it was uncomfortable at first, I mean, you didn't hurt me but I hadn't experienced anything like it before. Then I found myself reveling in your strength. The sensations, I just wanted to climb higher and higher. Then I realized how careful you were trying to be, how gentle. I want to—"

He put a finger on her lips. "No. Do not. We shared tonight. Perhaps we can build on this after all."

"If I'm not dead."

"Do not even think that!" he cried, his one hand gripping her arm so tight it hurt.

Tara frowned down at his hand until he loosened his hold on her. Pleased that he cared, she couldn't deny reality. She might not be around by this time tomorrow. So what the hell, why not enjoy what time she had? She bent her head and he devoured her lips. His hands cupped her breasts and made reality recede into the night.

When they finally came up for air, he whispered, "Rather than worry, let us make sure they have a reason to keep you alive."

Chapter Twelve

The Great Hall on the Hudson filled with Nobles in somber silence. Even the rich wood paneling seemed muted. The towering sconces seemed to absorb the light rather than reflect. Even the banners, which decreed each House hung without a whisper of movement. Was it a portent of things to come?

Each House stood in rank. Nicholai caught many glances as he stood as head of his House. Tara caught even more for few women were asked to attend. Only a handful knew why they'd been summoned. Now everyone there was about to find out.

Tara stood off to one side as a member of his House. She'd asked to stand alone. Nicholai suspected this was because of the danger she put him in. She wanted to accept the consequences by herself. What she didn't realize was she would never be alone again.

How regal her pose. Head up, shoulders back, dignified and proud. How different than when he'd first met her, so confused and human-like, so helpless in that hospital bed. Helpless? No, never that. Defensive, wary, vulnerable, but never helpless. His gaze caught hers. He nodded. She lifted her chin in answer. *Never helpless*, he repeated. And no matter what the outcome, she was his woman now. His mate.

Nicholai could not believe the ease with which she filled the role as his mate. As if she were destined to be there, always, by his side, his other half. She knew. She knew his pride for her. He could tell by the softening in those velvet brown eyes. She knew his desire for her. He caught the flame of need in her gaze and answered with his own. In spite of the gravity of their situation, her lips twitched. *Later, he promised. With or without a modicum of privacy.*

Nicholai shook his head to clear unwanted thoughts. He needed his wits about him, not his hormones. He watched as Tara did the same, stiffening under the weight of the stares she received. She threw them back showing no outward emotion but inside he knew she trembled. Alexi was right. They could turn on anyone like the pack of hyenas they were. And enjoy doing so.

He vowed once again not to let that happen. She was his mate with all that went with the title. Funny, but the word no longer scared him. He, Nicholai Valentin, terrified of being tied down to one person for life, accepted this woman without reservation. He saw her as an asset, a friend, someone to lean on, to help him carry the burden of responsibility. She'd earned the right to his respect, which he now gave unequivocally. She'd also earned the right to more.

In the midst of a crisis that could end both their lives, Nicholai wondered. Not about death, but about life. Could there be more between them than duty and honor? Could there be more than just unpaid debts? Could they share more than just the possible life growing inside her belly?

An elbow tapped him in the ribs. He tore his gaze away from her to find Alexi standing beside him. His heart swelled with pride. Alexi had shown disdain for the Nobility in the past, but there was no question of his loyalty when it came to family. He may not feel the depth of duty Nicholai did, but he knew this was something he had to do. Besides Alexi and Tara were bound together, ever since she brought him out of his coma. Should anything happen to Nicholai, Alexi would take care of her to his last breath.

How jealous they all were. He had Alexi by his side, Dmitri Borodkin guarding his flank, and other lesser houses surrounding him. Not many came so well prepared. But one House, he suspected, did. The House of Rhys-Jones was a formidable opponent. And would always be.

"Nicholai Valentin."

The High Council was already seated. So much for paying attention. "Aye."

Normally they would motion him forward as a chosen one, one being groomed for the High Council. Not this time. This time he was being summoned. So be it.

"Is this the woman who was made two weeks ago?"

Nicholai found himself bristling at their lack of respect. "Her name is Tamara."

Several members of the High Council were taken aback. They'd expected an ally, not an adversary. "We were given to believe that your brother was in a coma."

"I am perfectly well," Alexi called out, stepping from behind several members of their House. Nicholai watched him dare them to reprimand him for speaking out of turn.

"Yes, I can see that," came Han-Sing's droll reply. Alexi merely smiled and bowed with a flourish. Several coughs scattered through the room. "A pity," the man muttered.

"That's not what the lady said last night." Several chuckles, some hidden by coughs, came from the assembly.

"Have a care, young one. This is no game we play."

"Isn't it?" Alexi cried. Nicholai knew what his brother was trying to do and shook his head. He would only be able to divert their attention for so long.

"My Lords," Nicholai called out, forcing them to listen to him and not Alexi. "I believe an explanation is in order. Many do not know why they have been summoned to this meeting."

Not exactly true but a way to buy time and at least give a piece of their side of the story. "You are right," Ariel Gold agreed. "By all means, enlighten us. But be brief."

He did as requested and as he finished, he threw Tara a look. He sensed her anger and begged her to be patient. She was not a thing and they were treating her that way. Soon they would all know the difference.

"Tamara Duncan," Stefano Benedetti called. Duly noted and registered, old man. I never told you her last name. "Come forward."

"Say, please."

Nicholai had to stop himself from applauding. He caught a tiny smile on Ariel Gold's face before she spoke. "We meant no disrespect."

"I find that hard to believe."

"Do you know who you are?" Han-Sing cried out, his tone aggravated.

Stefano took charge. He inclined his head. "Please come forward, Ms. Duncan. We are not your enemy."

Tara walked forward to stand beside Nicholai.

Never before had he felt so proud.

"Oh no?" she challenged.

"We simply want to find the answers to some questions," Ariel continued.

"By talking about me as if I were a piece of furniture? I don't think so."

"There are rules here," Han-Sing declared. "Rules that will be followed."

He watched Tara smile. Uh-oh. "Petty Arthurian bullshit is more like it."

Stunned silence followed. Many were curious as to the outcome of this little battle, many probably agreed. Nicholai certainly did. There was nothing noble in the way they were handling this situation.

"Perhaps," Ariel continued. "Especially to one who has no real knowledge of the Nobility—our ways, our customs."

"And wants no part of them either," Tara declared, "if this is the way you conduct yourselves."

"Point taken, Ms. Duncan," Stefano replied. "Now, will you answer our questions or not?"

She nodded. He could see the weariness in her face. "Yes."

"Your memory. Has it returned?"

"Not completely."

"Do you have any idea how you were made?"

"No."

"Do you know who you are?"

She smiled. "Very definitely."

A confused murmur ran through the crowd. Only those who knew the truth were not surprised. Tara stepped forward towards the dais as he'd instructed. She lifted her hand aloft for all to see. Inside rested the Pendragon signet. "My name is not Tamara Duncan. Before you, you see the Pendragon signet. Mine by law and by birth. I am Tamara Pendragon."

Many gasped, more gaped in astonishment, but

most of the assembly stood in horrified silence believing she'd just signed her own death warrant.

"Do you realize what you are saying?"

Nicholai appreciated that at least one member of the High Council, Ariel Gold, was concerned for Tara's fate.

Tara laughed.

Good for you my darling, Nicholai said to her in his mind. *Show no fear.*

"Do you?" she asked, her tone confident.

Even Han-Sing had no answer. None of them did. There was only one true test.

Nicholai snared her gaze with his. *Now*, he told her. *You are a queen among the Nobility. Let them see you now as you truly are.*

With that she slipped the signet, now a ring, onto her finger.

****

Tara cried out as a flash of something she would never be able to describe, ran through her. All of a sudden she realized there was more to the Nobility than simple petty Arthurian bullshit. She felt as if the lives of all her ancestors right down to the very beginning of her line, were part of her life now. She staggered and sensed Nicholai reaching out. *No. I am all right.*

She had to do this alone. She had to keep them from taking over. With every ounce of willpower at her command, she fought for her sense of self. They put up a good fight. She guessed they had to. She had to be strong enough to bear the weight of them all. Once they decided she was worthy, they receded into the back of her consciousness. They would always be there if she needed them, especially the sense of her mother. Deep regret and pride. *Don't. I will always need you.* And to her grandfather Christian she vowed, *I will right the wrong done to our House.*

All of this took place in the time it took for her to straighten up. When she did, Tara also had her full memory back and the precious knowledge of the child growing inside her. She smiled, radiant, confident, a queen. That threw them even more.

"She must die," Charles Rhys-Jones snarled.

Tara flinched inside but did not let them see. Instead she caught Nicholai's gaze and thanked him for saving her life. For the moment, at least. He smiled back and she found herself drowning in the happiness her knowledge gave him. She hadn't been sure until now how he would react to the child.

"The Pendragon name is forfeit," someone else cried out.

"Traitors they are, traitors they will forever be."

"In the face of what treachery?" Alexi cried out.

"Hold!" Stefano thundered. "There will be order in this Hall or it will be cleared. Is that understood?" Silence met his question. "Now," he said, turning to Tara. "Do you know what you are being accused of?"

"All I know," she answered, her voice steady and calm, "is that my grandfather performed a great service to the Nobility and ended up accused of treason. All I know is that no one ever tried to find out the truth, all of you merely accepted his guilt because he lost a fight. A fight, for all I know, that may have been rigged."

Several rumbles of approval greeted her words and that pleased her no end. "All I know is that my mother died as the result of treachery and that I live because a servant woman remained loyal to my House. All I know," her tone became harder, clearer, each word more succinct. "Is that the only woman I have ever called mother, a saintly woman, a woman of God, was murdered because of who I am. When does this end? How many have died without due process? What gives you all the right to wipe out an entire family? How dare you even consider killing me? Haven't you all done enough already?"

That got to them. At least some of them.

"These are our traditions," Han-Sing answered, not one ounce of regret in his tone. That got to her. "They have been handed down for centuries."

Funny but all she felt was sorry for them. "You call yourselves the Nobility." She tried to keep the derision from her tone and failed. "But how noble are you? Death is not an answer. Certainly not now, not in this day and age. Keep this up and you'll tradition yourselves right into oblivion. Is that what you want?"

She had them thinking at least. But she feared the old ways would win no matter what she said. "Traditions can be changed. What worked in the past may not work for the future. I have been told the plight of the Nobility. Can you justify the loss of even one Noble when there are so few left? Can two wrongs possibly be right?"

"Your very existence breaks our laws," Ariel Gold replied with a gentleness she'd never expected.

"Then change the laws."

Ariel nodded and smiled back at her. "Well done." But the woman's gaze told her the argument might be futile.

She realized that futility as Han-Sing answered. "That would wipe out all that we were, all that we have ever been. I will never accept that as an excuse for the truth."

"But you'll accept a fight between two men as the truth," she spat back. "You don't want the truth," she told him letting her voice drip with disdain. "You never will. Not until you make the effort to find it."

"She's trying to save her own life," Charles Rhys-Jones cried. She is a Pendragon. She must die."

"Who among you..." Nicholai called out, his tone clear and true as he stepped forward to stand with her. “Who among you will cast the first stone?” When no one answered right away, she watched him nod, his demeanor that of an English barrister. “I thought not. Because you all know that Tara Pendragon’s death, here and now, would be meaningless, merely a gesture, a total waste.”

Rhys-Jones gave him a sly look. “You’re right, Valentin. I say put her on her back. One baby for each House. Let her atone for those we lost.”

Tara turned on the man. “Why you lecherous, sleazy, ball of hypocrisy. How dare you? Har—” A hand on her arm stopped her. *Not yet*, he told her. Shaken, Tara realized what she’d almost let slip. They hadn’t told that part of the story yet. “So, it’s all right to rape me. I mean, what the hell, it’s better than being dead, right?”

At least the asshole stood by his own convictions. “Yes,” he replied, his tone belligerent.

“My Lords,” Han-Sing called out. Obviously the man was not going to relent. “At the heart of this dilemma is all that we are. We struck the name Pendragon from our ranks. No matter how desperate we are, we cannot make exceptions to that which we have already done. Otherwise we’ve negated all those decisions made before us. No matter how distasteful, no matter how great our need, we cannot—we dare not—deviate from our laws. Tara Pendragon must die.”

A small murmur of assent ran through the assembly and Tara felt her heart sink. She’d hoped they would all agree with her, hear the truth of her words, not listen to the political correctness of their past.

All of a sudden she was glad they’d done what they’d done. In fact, she wanted to shout the words out loud, at the top of her lungs, that she was proud of whom she was—Pendragon and Valentin—and that she loved the child she carried.

Tara looked up to find Nicholai staring at her. *No longer afraid,* she told him. And I will never be alone again.

"My Lords," she cried, her call silencing the hall. "That will not be possible." She smiled at them all, then settled her gaze on the man she called mate. "You are already too late. You see, I am no longer Pendragon." She held up her arm and let her sleeve fall down so they could all see the mating scar.

Nicholai smiled back at her and the world went away. There were so many questions she wanted to ask him. Was he happy about the child? Frightened? Did they dare think of a future? Deep down she knew one thing—he would be an excellent father.

He lifted his arm and let his sleeve fall also. The two scars matched. They were mates and now they were one inside her belly. "Tamara Pendragon is now a member of the House of Valentin. I acknowledge her as mate and all that goes with that title. All that I have is hers, all that is hers is mine."

She thought Rhys-Jones would explode. His face turned purple with rage. Too bad he was a Noble. With blood pressure like that, he'd be dead if he were human. "You will both die!" he screamed.

His loss of control seemed to shock a few. Nicholai's calm demeanor won many votes. "I do not think so, Charles. Not this time."

Tara looked over to see the faces of the members of the High Council. She wanted to judge how they would vote. Ariel had a small smile playing about her lips. She seemed to be enjoying the spectacle. Han-Sing looked nearly as angry as Charles Rhys-Jones. He seemed to manage his emotions better. Stefano looked grave. Yet they were all processing, moving to the next step, and the next. They all knew they had a major problem on their hands.

Nicholai lowered his arm and she lowered hers. He caught her hand in his and brought the back up to his lips. The gesture only seemed to infuriate Rhys-Jones even more.

"You see," he continued. "The woman standing before you bears my heir. Touch one hair on her head and your next breath will be your last."

Chapter Thirteen

"That went well," Tara threw at him.

Nicholai fumed at their being taken by car, under guard, to an undetermined destination. He watched the cliffs of the Hudson speed by. Of course it didn't go well. Yet they were still alive, so well was a relative state. "I would say that depends on your definition of the word."

"Smoothly. With benefit to all involved."

A poker of white-hot anger shot through his insides. That they should do something like this. To *him*. "And your point is?"

"That we're fucked. Literally and figuratively."

"Perhaps." He flicked her a quick look of warning.

Easy does it, he thought. He'd told her to put on an act. No sense in overdoing things.

"Gee thanks," she replied, sarcasm evident in her tone. "Easy for you to say. This is my life—"

"You carry my heir," he interrupted.

"So at the end of nine months you both walk. What about me?"

"You worry without cause."

"Care to try trading places?" She really was making a good show of things. He'd never have thought—

"Hypothetically speaking?"

She looked shocked. "Why you smug, self-seeking, bastard. No, wait a minute. Let's use the right word here. Self-perpetuating is more like it."

"It is our nature."

"One more endearing trait. With your chock-full-of-goodness personality."

"We suit." He reached out and grazed her ear with his fingertip. She shivered. "You see?"

She turned to him, her gaze confused. Nicholai had anticipated the furor at the meeting but not the Council's decision to detain them. Using their psychic connection, he'd told her to act as if her world were about to cave in on her. Obviously she had no idea where he was going with this.

Nicholai let his finger trace her cheekbone, down her neck, only stopping when he reached the 'V' in her blouse. If he didn't come off as the vain, arrogant, selfish prince, his audience would wonder.

Yet the feelings between them were impossible to fake. She gasped as he undid one of the buttons and trailed his finger inside her bra. He hated having to use her desire for him, but he had no choice.

"Is that all you can think of?" she cried, slapping at his hand.

"Me? I can smell the heat coming off you in waves, woman."

"Bastard. That you could actually shove something I can't help back in my face."

He placed her hand on the tent in his pants. "Actually, I was thinking more along this line."

"I'll bite it off first."

He laughed out loud but inside he seethed. To have to stoop to this level of play-acting, especially for those two apes in the front of the car. "No, my darling, you will not. That would deprive you of the toy you love to play with."

"There are other toys."

He engulfed her mouth with his; cutting off anything she might say next. She reacted with surprise at first but couldn't contain the need she felt. He was grateful that she accepted the role without the bitterness he was feeling.

"Are there?" he asked as he lifted his head. He tried to tell her how he felt with his gaze.

"Hmm," she answered, the response both a question and a statement.

Nicholai couldn't resist. He trailed kisses up and down her neck and teased the shell of her ear with his tongue. What inner strength she had to put up with all this nonsense. Detained, he fumed again. How dare they. To have to lower himself to such a level. But that was just it. The truth stung. This was how they expected him to act.

"You see my dear? We suit very well."

They did. So the elaborate play-acting wasn't exactly a hardship. Still—

In the moment he tried to frame his next thought, Nicholai and Tara were both thrown forward out of their seats. Nicholai twisted his body to take the brunt of the fall, shielding her from harm as much as possible. The car doors were flung open as the car shuddered to a halt. Nicholai wrinkled his nose against the smell of burnt rubber and brake pads. He heard the men in the front seat get yanked out of the car then the dull thuds of their bodies as they crumpled to the ground. He smiled. They were going to have big time headaches when they woke up.

"You are late," he admonished Alexi.

"Traffic," his brother replied with a wink and a grin. He watched Alexi lift Tara off his body with a gentle grip. "Are you all right?"

"Fine," Nicholai answered with a frown. "Thank

you for asking."

"I wasn't."

"I know."

Tara laughed. As she did, Nicholai felt the simmering in his belly subside a bit. "Both of you stop," she cried.

Nicholai took her face in his hands. He wanted to explain how he felt, how awful he felt. "I am sorry. You should not have had to go through that."

She moved her head so she could kiss the palm of his right hand. "No, I shouldn't. And someone will pay dearly for that little debacle back there. But I don't blame you. Trust me."

He did. "My Lord," Sergei urged. "We must go."

He nodded, ushering Tara to an old but immaculate vehicle and climbing into the back beside her. He didn't want to let go of her. He, what? "Alexi?" His brother had climbed in beside him. Then he realized who was sitting behind the wheel. "Dmitri? Are you mad?"

"Maybe." Nicholai watched him put the car in gear and felt the car jerk forward as the petal hit the floor. "The Council is wrong in this."

Nicholai waited until the car stopped fishtailing to answer. "That does not mean you should put yourself in this kind of danger."

"You are my friend." His gaze lifted to the rear view mirror. "Yours also, madam."

He watched Tara incline her head. *God she was beautiful.*

"Thank you." Her mouth turned upward in a wry smile. "From both of us."

Nicholai looked down to see one of her hands covering her abdomen.

Wonder flooded his system. A child. He was going to be a father. He still couldn't believe it. He reached around her shoulders with his arm and pulled her close. He kissed the top of her head. "I fear I will have damned few by the end of this day. As always, I cannot thank you enough. But I still think you are crazy."

Dmitri laughed. So did Alexi. "You will never learn, will you? I'm not stupid. No one saw me. I will be questioned and when they realize I know nothing, I will give them a tirade they've never seen before." He pulled the car over to the side of the road a few moments later. Alexi got out and moved up to the front to drive. "There is a bus stop close by and my plane awaits. They will have to meet me on my own turf."

Nicholai chuckled. "A daunting experience."

"Nicholai?" Tara asked.

"I'll explain later."

He turned to his friend and lowered the window as Dmitri leaned against the car. "How is it you got so lucky?" Dmitri asked him.

Lucky? Nicholai wasn't so sure. At the moment he was fighting for his life. Then he looked down. Tara's hand had entwined with his and she was squeezing hard. "True Blood to True Blood."

Dmitri nodded in understanding. "Justice will prevail. Be careful."

Alexi shifted into gear and car started moving. Not long after they switched to another car, and another, until Nicholai was certain they were not being followed. Once they were on the highway and heading for an airport, Nicholai finally allowed himself to relax.

"Are you all right?" he asked Tara, his tone only loud enough for her to hear.

She smiled and he marveled at her strength. "Yes. I guess I didn't realize how angry I would be. I've never been on the wrong end of injustice before."

He lifted her hand to his lips. "We will win this together. I promise."

"I believe you."

Sergei, as always, had thought ahead. They were going to leave from a small out of the way airport and he'd found a restaurant that looked decent nearby.

Nicholai grinned when Tara placed her order. She was eating for two now.

"Will you gentlemen excuse me? I'd like to freshen up."

They all rose and when he sat back down, Nicholai's anger was hard to contain. "They will pay for this, I swear. I had to humiliate her to make them believe—"

"What a wonderful guy you are?" Alexi finished for him.

He hung his head. "Yes."

Alexi punched him in the shoulder. "Come on, Nico. You're really not *that* bad."

"Thanks."

"My Lord. The signet?" Sergei asked.

He didn't answer. He had a theory but wanted to wait until Tara returned to the table. When she did he asked, "Tara? The signet. Am I right in believing you have your full memory back?"

"Yes," she answered in amazement.

He threw her a quick look, which she understood. Bearing a signet was a huge responsibility and there were things about that responsibility that were best left unsaid. "What do you remember?"

"An estate sale."

"An estate sale?"

"Sure. It's how I make my living. You wouldn't believe what you can find in an old house."

Nicholai watched the color drain from her face. "Tara? Are you all right?"

"No, Nicholai," she answered, her tone scaring the hell out of him. "And neither are you."

****

"Please explain," Nicholai answered, his tone harsh and flat. She'd scared him, scared them all, with good reason.

"The estate sale...wasn't just an estate, I don't know how else to say this." She shuddered. "The house was evil. I know you don't believe me but it was. I sensed an old, festering hatred. I ignored it, I didn't want the feeling to stop me, so stupid."

"What happened?" Nicholai asked.

"I didn't realize what I was walking into. All I could think of was finding treasure. Hidden treasure. Every house has its secrets. Sometimes they're better off undisturbed. I didn't listen." She broke off, unable to continue.

This time Alexi urged her to continue. "Go on."

"There was a stairway. Very ingenious the way the device was camouflaged. Only someone looking for a key, or someone who knew it was there, would have been able to find it. I walked down and…" She choked, remembering the smell of decay all around her. "I should have listened to myself. One of these days I'm going to. I walked down the stairs in to a room that was positively opulent. Gorgeous. Decadent. I mean, from the crystal chandelier to the velvet furniture. It was self-indulgence to the max. I'd hit a jackpot. In my excitement I didn't feel the menace but all of a sudden, something was telling me to get out. Quick. I backed up, turned, and started towards the stairs when I bumped into a table."

"A table?"

"Yeah. I caught the table to keep it from falling, but I didn't realize there was some sort of box on it."

"A box, Lady?" Sergei questioned, his tone worried.

"Whatever it was, I tried to stop it and that's when the lights went out. All I remember after that is the hospital. And Nicholai."

"I was not kind to you that day. I am sorry."

Tara had already forgiven him. But a little squirm was definitely in order. "Really? The Inquisition would have been easier on me than you were."

Alexi laughed. Sergei, though, still looked worried. And Nicholai simply smiled. He already knew she was twisting his tail.

Their food arrived and Tara realized she was starving. She started to eat; with such gusto that it took a few minutes for her to realize Sergei had not touched his plate. "Sergei? Your food's getting cold."

He shook himself as if he'd been deep in thought. "Forgive me, lady." He made a half-hearted attempt to eat.

Dread seeped into her belly as she watched him fail. "All right." She put her fork down, her appetite suddenly deserting her. "What gives?"

"This box. Can you describe it?"

She shook her head, a bit puzzled by his request. "Not really. It was dark in the room and I only had a flashlight. I can't even tell you it *was* a box. I said box because that was a first impression."

"First impressions are usually correct," Sergei returned. "You are an astute observer. You make your livelihood doing so. I am inclined to believe my assumptions are correct."

"Sergei?" Nicholai questioned.

"In the late 1700's, early 1800's, furniture making was an art. For the rich, of course. One of our people, Thomas Fife, was an exceptionally talented woodworker, even for Noble standards. Our lives are a gift from God no matter what race we belong to."

Tara raised a brow. This from the man who would be her enemy? No, that wasn't right. A cautious man whose job it was to keep his family intact. And now that she was a member of the family, he would be her personal bull terrier too. Of course, that didn't excuse him from being needled either. "A man of God, Sergei? You surprise me."

"No madam, I do not." He cleared his throat.

Duly chastised and noted, she thought, enjoying the moment. "This young Noble took it upon himself to design a case, no one could ever call this casket a box," he continued, disdain clear in his tone, "for the Chalice."

"The Chalice?" she questioned.

"The vessel that holds the Water of Change."

"A cup?" OK, so she couldn't resist.

Sergei shuddered. "Would you call the Sistine Chapel just a painting?"

She laughed. "Lighten up, Sergei. Out of all of us, I think I have the most at stake here, don't you?"

He shook his head. "No, Lady." He addressed her but his gaze encompassed them all. "Not if what I surmise has happened."

They all sat up a bit straighter. "Explain," Nicholai commanded.

"The Council of that time decided to accept the "box" as the casket for the Chalice. Both were hidden as they are now and have always been, with the Council the only ones to know of their location. In the late 1800's someone tried to steal the Water of Change."

Nicholai leaned forward, his expression hardening. "Why was I not told this?"

"Because few know of it. The Council does, as do a few Stewards. I only know because my father passed this information along to me. Also because the thief was human without a trace of Noble blood. The robbery was deemed to be just that, happenstance; a thief who had no knowledge of how precious his booty really was. There was no way he could know. And yet, I now wonder."

"If he did?" she asked.

"Perhaps. Or if the robbery was orchestrated by someone who knew the value of the prize."

"But why?" Alexi asked, thinking out loud.

"I do not know, young one. Aside from birth, there has been only one way to create a Noble. The Water of Change. I believe this stolen box would also have that power which now makes my first statement incorrect. How else could you have been made, Lady?"

She didn't know. But his logic was impeccable. "Good question. And here's another. Who happened to end up with this so-called box before I stumbled into it?"

"It was never recovered, so I cannot say."

"Sergei," Nicholai questioned. "Does the High Council have any idea?"

"If they do," Alexi answered, "they certainly wouldn't tell any of the Houses. Unless leaking the information served their purpose." His tone dripped acid. "Let's not forget this is just a Good Old Boy's Network."

Tara watched Nicholai wince. But Alexi was right. The High Council appeared to take a great deal upon themselves. "We must go back to that house," she said. "There has to be a trail of some kind that we can follow."

"Or a trail someone wants us to follow," Nicholai added.

No one had an answer to that.

****

Plans within plans within plans. How predictable they were. One plan would have sufficed. Or would it? Better to be safe. Better to be smart. So much smarter. Better to be strong. So much stronger. Patience was a virtue.

And they had the nerve to call themselves the Nobility.

Did they know whom they were dealing with? A

question he could not fully answer. Hence the alternatives. Tweak the course of one life here; destroy another there. Plant the seeds and watch them grow. What joy to see the product of his labor finally begin to bear fruit.

They would never know his purpose until it was too late.

Plans within plans within plans. She was the one he couldn't read. Just another puppet, or so he hoped. But he did not like hoping. Strings were meant to be pulled, plucked, and played with a gentle finger. He couldn't enter her mind and that concerned him.

Not like her brother. Not like his wonderful Morgan.

He'd had another puppy before. A long time ago. Thomas.

Yes, Thomas was a beautiful young man. With only one little secret. He wanted other men in a world where such behavior was condemned. How easy to invade his dreams. How simple to give him all the pleasure he desired, night after night after night. A twist here, a turn there. Oh how close he'd come to his ultimate objective.

Plans within plans within plans. He'd made a mistake. He'd underestimated the power of fate. He hadn't planned. All he'd come away with was the holder, not the vessel. But even in this, he was able to salvage some of his work. And so he'd begun again. And this time, every alternative was covered.

Soon. Very soon. They would all die. Each and every one of them. And then he would savor the sweetness of his revenge.

Was revenge really a dish best served cold? Soon he would find out.

Chapter Fourteen

Swirling grey and white clouds covered the moon as they traveled sometimes allowing its light to shine through, sometimes not. At times the sky appeared to stand still, seeming to take a breath in anticipation. Then after a sigh, all would begin again.

Not the best night for secrecy, Nicholai thought. But one where he could teach Tara the use of her Noble blood powers. How to move without being seen. How to cover great distances without overtaxing her body. Especially now.

He hadn't wanted her to come. He wanted to protect her. She carried his child. She fought back with logic, of course. He didn't know the house, she did. He'd have no idea where other clues could be found; she might. Then Alexi got into the discussion and he put an end to the arguments. Three Nobles traipsing around an old deserted house in the middle of the night made absolutely no sense at all.

Nicholai drew up short. They were in a fairly remote area of the southern Jersey Shore. Smithville. A historic place where an estate like the one he faced could be welcome but not watched. He stopped just before the wrought iron gates that stood guarding the house, flinging an arm in front of her in caution. She stepped beside him whispering so low no human could hear. "You feel it too, don't you?"

He nodded. She had been unable to describe the smell of decay that filled his nostrils, the sense of foreboding sitting on the back of his neck, the uneasiness deep inside his bones. "We do not belong here."

She shivered in answer. As a human she might have sensed a tenth of what she sensed now. "I know. But we must."

"Wait here." She started to protest then acquiesced. He circled the property to inspect his options. He didn't want to touch anything he didn't have to, as if the disease that had destroyed the house might be contagious.

Along with the decline of the building, nature had tried to reclaim its own. The grounds were overgrown, a tangle of weeds and bushes, encroaching the fence but not going beyond. He understood why. Living things would know not to go near such evil.

About half way around he found an old tree. The tree hung into the yard just enough for them to get over the fence. Nicholai went back to Tara and helped her into the yard.

Once inside, he could only think about turning around. He chided himself for his fear then acknowledged that this was not simply fear. Fear he could handle. So could she. Yet he was infinitely glad when her hand crept into his and held on tight.

"This way," she whispered, pointing to the opposite side of the house.

Tara led him to a small door, somewhat like a servant's entrance once used in the early 1900's. Very narrow with several steps, the corridor led to a room that must have been a pantry or storage area for it was lined with shelves now covered with dust and cobwebs.

He took heart that at least the spiders weren't afraid. Indeed he felt better, not so oppressed by the—-yes, he had to call the house evil—in the truest sense of the word. He hadn't believed it possible. He did now for the house carried an essence of something terrible that kept on trying to wrap around him, smother him.

Tara hesitated, took a deep breath and letting the air out in a slow hiss, before she walked into what he assumed was the kitchen. Old porcelain appliances cringed in neglect and the counter tops looked like they were rotting from misuse. He felt an almost physical pain as he stood in the center of the room. The house cried out to him with the agony of such abuse.

But there was more. He could handle disrepair; he could handle the rot and the shame. People had died here. That was what he sensed; he sensed their demise and something told him they did not die well.

Nicholai followed Tara towards a center hallway. The walls seemed to close in on him. Was it an attempt to warn him to stop? Perhaps an attempt to cause more harm. They came to a halt before a long stairway. "I'm—I'm sorry. I cannot go on," she said.

Lord knew he understood. "Go outside. Wait for me."

She shook her head. "I must show you how to open the stairway." She shuddered. Even her whispered words seemed to die from the oppressive atmosphere. One stair at a time. He walked, she followed. He turned to see her struggle as if thousand pound weights were attached to her legs. His insides burned with anger that she had to go through this torture. What kind of—was there even a name for this? What manner of the universe could spawn such terror?

"Here," she said, her hand covering the top of the banister. She placed his finger on the release so he would know how to open the hidden doorway. As they touched, Nicholai knew they could surmount any obstacle as long as they were together. His gaze caught hers. He conveyed the strength and hope he felt, shared his courage and used hers in return. He pressed down on the imprint in the wood.

Of all his life's experiences, nothing had prepared him for this. He had to lock his knees in an effort not to flee as far away as possible. The air smelled of a hundred dead Nobles. The room screamed with the souls of a thousand more. Only the training, only the knowledge, the communal presence of his ancestors, all that made him a prince of his race, kept him still.

Although Nicholai had perfect night vision, nothing could penetrate the foul mist creeping up the stairway. They had prepared for this, purchasing a torch, not just a flashlight, from a hardware store. The light bounced off the mist for the most part creating a rather fog-like atmosphere. "Can you find the circuit breaker for the house? I saw that the power lines coming into the house were still intact."

"I'm not sure there's any power. I usually check out houses during the day. Besides getting a better feel for the place, I don't want to be mistaken as a burglar."

"The real estate agency is trying to sell the property, no? They would make sure there is power, would they not?" The task would get her out of this area, away from the terrible smell of—could he really be smelling burnt flesh—and at least make her feel useful. She deserved that in the face of such courage. "Go," he repeated, kissing her forehead. "See if you can get some light going. This torch is just about useless."

She stared at him without moving. "You're going down there, aren't you?"

"Yes."

"You don't need to. I told you what was down there."

"Just a quick look around. I promise."

"It's not necessary."

Touched, he used her caring as fuel for his already depleted reserves. "I am all right. I will be very careful. Meet me at the bottom of the stairs when you are done."

She turned and started down the first step then whirled, threw her arms around him, kissed him, and whirled back. Had the scene been any less dreadful, he would have smiled. She wasn't one for such displays.

He watched her all but run down the stairs and watched his courage fly away with her. Had Alexi really thought he wasn't afraid of anything? He was such an imposter. Looking down he watched his hands shake, trying in vain to will them to stop.

Then he turned. The landing at the top of the unhidden stairs served as the landing for the hidden stairs. The first step was the hardest. The anger that had bolstered his courage died a thousand deaths. Was it just his fear of the dark? No, this was too much like the dreams he'd had as a child, the ones where he would wake up in a cold sweat, his heart thundering in his chest, and lay there begging for the Sun to rise.

One more step. That awful odor growing stronger.

Had he known then? Had his dreams been prescient to this moment? *Another step.* Being a member of the Nobility meant being able to commune with all members of his race. Could that ability also pertain to time as well? *Another step.*

Nicholai reached deep inside his soul. He

pushed past the terror to search for the truth. Whatever frightened him had to be Noble born and bred. Nothing human could create such a sick feeling so deep in his bones. *Another step.* He could barely breathe as the stench made him want to retch until his guts came out.

And another.

A cloak of fetid decay washed over him joining the already unbearable smell of burnt flesh. Choking, he tried to draw a ragged breath. He couldn't see, couldn't breathe. Trapped, he realized the futility of Tara's errand. No light would penetrate this. Not only was this evil, it was evil incarnate, as if all the wrongs of all the Nobility had been captured in one place. The story of Dorian Grey entered his mind and would not leave. Was it possible? Had they been so fortunate for so long because they—

Nicholai reached the last step. No, evil and wrong, spite and greed, they were bad enough. But worse was the malevolence mixed in. Someone or something not only wanted to feed off all he'd thought a moment before, it wanted to suck him dry, stomp on him, smash him, beat him and pulverize him until no part of him remained. And then do it over and over again.

There was more here than any of them knew. As he lowered his foot to the floor, Nicholai was certain he was going to step in a pit of writhing snakes. His skin crawled while tiny shivers raced up and down his spine. He didn't want to move. Couldn't move. Nothing could be so important, finding out what was down there could never be so important, as to make him move.

In desperation, he tried to cut a swath through the fog by flipping the torch back and forth. For a moment the light illuminated, almost like seeing a spark. He did it again and got the same reaction.

Wondering what could possibly shine in this black pit of hell, Nicholai forced his feet to move towards the spot. He bumped into something solid and felt around. A table? Could it be the same one Tara mentioned?

He thought about that for a second. What else would have the power to cut through this darkness but its antithesis—The Water of Change? The Water of Life. Or in this instance, the case that held the Chalice.

Having already explored the edges, Nicholai slid his hand along the surface of the table. The middle thrummed under his palm. Yes, the casket of the Chalice had rested here. Each time he drew away, the darkness closed in on him again. Each time he neared the spot, his heart sang with hope.

If only he could figure out what happened to it.

He turned, intent on leaving as fast as he could. Black such as he'd never experienced tried to swallow him. Not just darkness, for he was able to penetrate that. This wall rendered him totally blind, took away all of his senses.

Screwed. Realization struck with a hammer's blow. He tried reaching out, but excruciating pain zapped his fingers. He tried to take a step, thousand pound chains held his feet in place. He was going to be killed, even worse, sucked dry as he'd imagined had happened to others before. Yet he would also remain alive, for the delight of his—

The table. Nicholai reached around. He centered his hand on the wood. The power of the Water gave him the ability to see just a tiny bit. The will to move was up to him. He pictured Tara's face before his eyes, as she looked when he gazed down at her, his body joined to hers. He had all the reasons in the world to live. One step. Then another. The weight of the world fell onto his shoulders. He staggered and sank to his knees. He didn't care. He, Nicholai

Valentin, prince of the House of Valentin, prince of the Nobility, crawled. And would do so over and over again. *For her.*

****

Light. Let there be light. Oh God, why hadn't she taken Shop instead of Home Economics in school. Circuit breakers. Basement. No basement. Pantry? Her flashlight seemed to be of little use. Wires. Follow the wires. What wires? Wait a minute. An electric meter. There had to be one outside.

Tara couldn't believe the freedom of being out of the house. She drew in deep draughts of air, letting them go with gusto. Her inner wire, the buzz in her veins that never left, revved her motor and gave her back her strength.

Nicholai. His name pounded inside her brain. He needed her. Turning, she was about to run back into the house when common sense prevailed. He needed light more. If the house seemed to be able to suck the very life out of her, she could only imagine how he was faring.

Instead she searched the perimeter of house until she found what she was looking for. She traced the wires back into what looked like a long side porch. Now where? The kitchen? Using the flashlight, she followed the path she thought the wires would follow. Reciting the Hail Mary, she stepped back into the house. For the first time in a long time, the words brought a measure of comfort.

Wait a minute. A closet was set back next to the pantry. Easy to miss if you were just walking through the room. She opened the door and a fog not of this world seeped out to surround her. Her fingers trembled. She reached out.

"Tara?"

She screamed and died a thousand deaths. Her heart threatened to explode in her chest. Tremors seized her. Then she realized who was speaking.

"Morgan?"

Scared the crap right out of her. "Oh my God, Morgan." She rubbed her face with hands that had Mexican jumping bean cream all over them.

He cocked his head and stared at her oblivious to her distress. "Tara?"

"Morgan." By saying his name, everything changed. He was her brother, her flesh, and her blood. By all rights he should carry the signet, not her. "I need your help."

"Help," he repeated.

"Light? Do you know how to turn on the lights?"

Comprehension dawned. He nodded and motioned for her to follow him. She'd been on the right track, just the wrong side of the wall. They had to go back through the pantry and into another tiny closet to find the breaker panel. She flipped every switch on the panel to "on." Nothing happened.

He cocked his head again, this time as if to say 'I could have told you that, all you had to do was ask.' It figured. "I have to go back inside."

"No. Bad." The fear in his gaze was all too real.

"Morgan, I have to go back. To the bad room. Nicholai is there."

He gave her a quizzical look as if to ask who Nicholai was, then shrugged. "No."

She turned and started walking. His hand grabbed her shoulder and spun her around. "Very bad man, very bad man," he chanted.

Morgan rarely showed emotion. He was visibly upset now. "Wait here."

"No."

That was odd. Morgan never argued. And she didn't have time to argue back. "Let go."

"No."

Wrong answer. She pushed him away. He ran a few steps to stand in front of her again. Was she missing something here? Was she going to have to use force to get around him? How could she use force? He was her brother.

Torn, Tara hesitated. She had to go back to Nicholai. But Morgan was her brother. He needed to know who and what he was.

No, Nicholai first. Tara pushed past Morgan into the center of the kitchen. She got a few steps further only to find Morgan blocking her way again. How'd he do that? "Morgan, please."

"Hurt you."

She didn't have time to explain. Reaching up she cupped her brother's cheeks with her hands. She had no idea the signet rotated on her finger. As she touched him, the signet pressed against the side of his face, just above Morgan's jaw. An amazed look came over his features. His eyes, normally half closed, widened in shock. His perpetual glazed-over gaze cleared. "Tara."

"I'm your sister, Morgan. You know who you are now."

"Yes."

"I must go to Nicholai."

"He'll hurt you, Tara. You're not powerful enough to stop him."

"Stop *who,* Morgan?"

He shuddered. "The oldest of the old."

Tara didn't understand and didn't have time to figure it out. "I have to get back to Nicholai. I love you." She kissed his cheek, let go, and ran around him, terribly grateful when he didn't follow her. She didn't want to fight him.

The center hallway seemed even darker than before. A black mist billowed from the opening at the top of the stairs. Panic tore through her when she didn't see her mate. She fought the mist and trudged up the steps as fast as her legs could carry her in this unearthly atmosphere. Coughing, choking, her eyes burning, she tried to find him. A cold dread seized her. She was too late. He wouldn't come out, couldn't come out.

Nicholai.

She screamed his name in her mind over and over again. Her heart, ready to thunder, nearly pounded out of her chest. *God, no!* Don't let me be too late.

A pair of hands came out of nowhere and pushed her aside. Stunned, she didn't know what was happening. Morgan?

He seemed unaffected by the foul fog. She watched him become enveloped by the deadly dark only to return moments later with Nicholai in his arms. He reached her, half carrying, half dragging her mate. She wanted to say a prayer in thanks but none of them was safe. "Outside. We must get him outside."

Morgan nodded in full understanding. Tara wondered for a brief moment if she would be able to get to know him as a sister should. She would like that, more than he would ever know.

Moonlight was better than none so she helped Morgan bring Nicholai to a clearing in the yard. She held her mate, cradling his head on her lap. Had she delayed too long? If only she'd realized. If only she hadn't stopped to help Morgan.

"Nico?" Tara had never used Alexi's endearment before. She rubbed his forehead, pushing his hair away, willing him to open his eyes.

"Tara?" Morgan was crouched on his haunches in front of her. Deep sadness filled her as she realized it was the same Morgan she'd always known. Gone was the comprehension, the knowledge, the Nobility.

"You did good, Morgan. Thank you."

Morgan cocked his head. Usually she would wonder if he got her message when he did that. This time she was certain he understood.

A deep, hacking, in-drawn breath drew her gaze down. “Nico. Please. I know you can hear me.”

Was that a twitch of his lips? She’d used his nickname again and decided it fit him, when he wasn’t being his usual pain-in-the ass princely self. “Speak to me, you pompous, obstinate pain.”

She ran out of words and didn’t know what else to do, so she started kissing him. That was when she realized his shoulders were shaking.

“A bit hard to do, my dear, when you’re sucking face with me.”

She didn’t respond. Not yet. Not when it felt so right to just keep on doing exactly that. She’d hit him later. “Thank you, God,” she whispered when she finally lifted her head.

“I have never associated with your religious beliefs, Tara. But tonight I will say the same and count myself very lucky. I was not sure I would ever speak with you again.”

Stricken, she wasn’t sure what to say. “Morgan saved you.” She lifted her head to acknowledge her brother only to find him gone. “He’s…gone.”

“It is all right,” he answered, squeezing her hand. He struggled to sit up and she helped him. “He knows what he did. I could feel the strength in him as he helped me up the stairs.”

She started trembling. She couldn’t help herself. “What was it, Nicholai?”

“Shorten my name,” he insisted.

Exasperated she said, “What?”

“Use my nickname. When we are together. Alone.”

“I don’t understand. You were almost destroyed and yet you want to discuss nicknames?”

He nodded, his countenance grave. “Because that is all I can speak of. I must deal in life right now for what I encountered, there are no words.” He reached out and held her tight. He, too, trembled.

"Say my name."

"Nico." He smiled.

"Morgan called what was up there the oldest of the old."

He nodded. "That would fit." He struggled once again only this time he was able to stand. "We must get out of here."

She helped him to walk, step by step, until they reached the tree they'd scaled before. Funny, but it seemed a lifetime ago. "Tara."

They whirled. Morgan approached and he was carrying a canvas sack. He'd reverted back to the old Morgan and sadness flooded her. She wondered if she could repeat the process with the signet.

"No, Tara," Nicholai told her. "You will not be able to help him."

"But—" She turned to plead with her brother. "Come with us, Morgan. I can help you. I can make you whole again."

He shook his head. "No, you can't."

"I'll take care of you, then."

He smiled. A smile of yearning for that which could never be. "He will know."

Nicholai reached out to clasp his shoulder. True Blood to True Blood. "I can protect you."

Morgan smiled. "No, you can't. Gone now but be very angry. Come back soon. Must go."

"What is it, Morgan? Who is it?" She had to know.

"Death."

She lifted her hands to his face. Such bright befuddled eyes filled with so much fear. "I love you." She lifted up on her toes and kissed his cheek.

"Yes." She let go and he turned and ran into the night.

Nicholai reached up and grabbed hold of a tree limb. He pulled himself to his feet, then into the tree itself. He reached down and helped lift her up.

"I'm scared for him, Nico. He's in danger."

"We all are."

Just as they were about to walk along the limb to get over the wall, they heard Morgan return. They stopped and he threw the canvas bag at them. Nicholai caught it easily. Just as quickly, her brother was gone again into the night. They left the property and ran to the car they'd hidden down the road. Nicholai handed her the sack and got in to drive.

As he floored the accelerator to get them far away as fast as possible, Tara gasped. "Oh my God," she whispered, opening the burlap. "There is no way you can call this a box."

Chapter Fifteen

Nicholai shivered as the cool pre-dawn mist shrouded his body. Or did he shiver from a world turned upside-down? He simply wasn't sure. He'd brought her back to her island, hoping a walk on the beach would soothe them both.

The steady cadence of the waves crashing upon the shore told him nothing had changed since the day before. The prescient knowledge that the Sun was about to rise told him a new day was about to begin. Both facts of nature, constants of life and reality—

Reality? Now that was a joke. Spoken by a man who'd just had his legs cut out from underneath him. All that he'd ever believed and trusted in was gone. All he could count on now was the woman standing in front of him. And his desire to protect his unborn child. The horror of the night still ravaged her face, causing a pang of deep regret within him. If *he* was having trouble—he couldn't imagine how she was faring. All he knew was that by holding her, together they might be able to survive the darkness. Perhaps the dawning of the Sun would be able to obliterate—no, nothing would do that. Her hand kept squeezing his. Her head never moved, her gaze remained fixed on the ocean. Watching the waves. Back and forth, back and forth. But her shoulders stayed ramrod straight. Not once did she bow her head in submission. She asked no quarter, expected no pity. She bore the mantle of her Nobility with pride and distinction, courageous in the face of the unexpected, defiant in spite of fate. God, she was incredible.

"Tara?"

Her hand squeezed his harder in answer. She seemed to absorb blow after blow unscathed, yet he knew her sadness. Morgan would never take his rightful place as heir to the House of Pendragon. He might never again be as lucid as she described to him, that one moment when the signet touched his cheek. He would understand yet never understand her love for him. He would never comprehend her need for a family to love, her desire to share as only a brother and sister can. Nicholai did. And he tried to soften those blows with his touch.

If only. Thank God the dawn was just moments away. The hum that signaled a morning feed thrummed deep inside his veins. No, the Sun would not obliterate the horror of the night. The High Council, those smug bastards, had much to answer for. He'd play by their rules, he'd prove to them how Tara was created, and get them to rescind their "house arrest." He might even give them insight into this thing and help them formulate a plan of action. Although, plans and rules were probably useless at this point. Whatever this thing was, it was too powerful to be defeated—unless the entire Nobility joined together to do so.

As faint pink stripes outlined the horizon and the thrum in his veins turned to a sizzle, Nicholai realized how much he needed Tara. His resolve hardened into steel. He vowed he would protect his family until his last breath.

Pulling her close against his body, he waited for

the Sun. His entire being was fused with hers. Mate to mate. True Blood to True Blood.

Nicholai lifted her arm to his lips. He traced the mating scar with his tongue. Her arm jerked with each spark he ignited. Placing his scar against hers he tried to tell her all he could not say in words. Together, they were the antithesis. Together, they were the essence of the Nobility. Together, they were light within light. Together, they would conquer the darkness.

A slow burn ignited in his belly. There could be no mistaking his arousal. The first rays of the Sun danced along his skin lighting tiny fires he could not extinguish.

He turned her around to face him. Did she understand? This wasn't simply sex. This wasn't in answer to a night gone mad. He wanted her. Craved her. Needed to become her. Needed her to become him. He wanted to crawl inside her head, find out everything she knew and use that knowledge to give her all of himself. He wanted to become one, not just flesh inside flesh, but one being, one entity, joined forever.

Nothing like this had ever happened to him before. In recognizing his own bewilderment, he recognized hers. This need for each other was new to her as well. Under other circumstances, he was certain they would both be scared. But not now. Not after— He would never hurt her and knew she would never hurt him.

He bent his head down and tasted her lips. She turned in his arms and wound her hands in his hair as she opened her mouth to allow him full entry. Her breath caught as she realized he held nothing back. Then she gave him all of herself and he found her need just as great as his.

Her hand slipped down his belly and slid inside his boxers. Between the heat of her hand and the cool of the air, he thought he was going to die.

"Bitch," he whispered into her mouth. She smiled. Until she realized two could play the same game. She screamed as his fingers found her heat. He swallowed her scream by pouring his tongue down her throat. She was wet, hot, and totally ready for him.

But now they faced a dilemma. A public beach was still public even if it was dawn and Nicholai had no desire to end up in anyone's jail. Even though he saw no one, he would have to do this carefully. He turned her around and asked her to bend over. When she did, he pushed aside her clothing and slid inside her. He was certain he was going to come right then and there. Instead, he lifted her back up against him so that hopefully no one would see they were joined.

One problem solved, another created. He dared not move. Sweat broke out on his brow from the exquisite torture. She began using her internal muscles, squeeze, release, squeeze, release, and while his body fed in the deepening sunlight, he grew. Thick, huge, ready to explode.

While one arm held her in place, he used his other hand to return the torture. He played with her folds until he was certain she was ready to peak. His hips jerked involuntarily as they both neared the edge.

He didn't care who saw them. He withdrew until only the head of his erection remained inside her then thrust into her with all his might. His fingers found her nub and she exploded all around him. He followed in huge, hot, shuddering waves. Long seconds passed before he could breathe normally again.

He slipped out of her and adjusted their clothes. He led her up to the dunes where they'd left the rest of their things. Picking them up, he shook out the sand and handed them to her. He smiled as she tried to dress and found she couldn't because her fingers wouldn't quite work right. Their encounter had moved her just as much as it had moved him.

As soon as they were presentable, they left the beach and walked to the main street. He clasped her hand in his, vowing once again never to let go.

"That was unexpected," she quipped.

"I needed you," he confessed.

"I know," she replied, her tone serious. "I needed you too."

They walked a few more moments in silence then he added, "We celebrated life. At the moment, I think that is all we can do."

She shook her head. "I'm not so sure. There has to be a way to fight this thing."

She sounded as though she were trying to convince him as well as herself. He could feel the uncertainty in her and tried to comfort them both. "Then we'll find it together. I promise."

They walked some more. "Morgan called it death."

He shuddered. He needed no reminders. "Worse."

"I'm scared, Nico." Her hand covered her belly.

"I know. We have much to live for. Do not give up yet, Tara. We can stop this thing. We *will* stop this thing."

****

Why did she get the feeling he was trying to convince himself, not just her? This was not good, not good at all. "What are we going to do?"

"Follow our original plan. The High Council knows where you live. That was why I wished to check into a motel and not go back to your house. Is Jeri on her way?"

"She should be."

"Good. No one will know she has the case. I do

not trust the Council."

"About damned time," she declared.

"Or anyone else right now," he was quick to add.

"Even me?"

He swung her around to face him, grabbed her cheeks with his hands, and kissed the hell out of her. "Does that answer your question?"

"Yes." The kiss had also forced her to lock her knees so she could remain upright. "What about Alexi?" she asked, trying to gather her wits about her.

"He and Sergei are going to gather the Houses in secret. The Stewards will help. They must know they are in danger, even if some will not believe what we have found out."

"They'd better."

He turned, headed for their motel again. "If my guess is right, this *thing* has only been able to cause strife within individual Houses. All planned towards a specific goal—our ultimate destruction. My hope is that it does not expect a united front. We have been bickering amongst ourselves for so long, we may have led it to believe we cannot work together."

"Can we?" Skepticism razed her tone.

"Yes, we can. And we will. But first I must clear your name and restore your House. The debt must be repaid."

Tara, walking beside him, whirled away in disgust. "Debts. Honor. Payments. My God, Nico. You sound like a bad Arthurian novel. I'm not important. My name is not important. My House is not important. *This* is important." She brought his hand to her belly. "People are important. Life is important. Making sure our child and our people survive is important. Don't you get it?"

He grabbed her hand and yanked her hard against his body. Bending his head, she tasted his heart and soul on his lips.

"Yes," he said, finally letting go. "I do. But I cannot let go of the traditions that have molded our race. Change takes time—"

"Change takes survival," she interrupted.

He nodded. "True. But to do that, I still have to work within the system."

Was he right? "Do you?" she questioned. "I'm not so sure. Especially not when the system needs a total overhaul."

He smiled. "Patience, oh headstrong one. One problem at a time." Kissing her forehead, he let her go. "Come. I do not like feeling exposed."

"Could've fooled me," she quipped, referring to their open-air exhibition a short time before.

He laughed. Tara found she liked the sound. She wanted to hear it more often. For a bleak second, she wondered if she would. "Shall I repeat the process?"

That got her out of her funk in a hurry. "Any time you like," she challenged.

His gaze darkened. "Too many people. What I have in mind is private."

The shiver up her back lit a fire in her belly, which warmed to a red-hot glow by the time they reached the motel. Jeri wasn't there yet. Funny how great minds thought alike. As soon as the door shut behind them, his mouth was on hers. The kiss was all lust. This was going to be hard and fast, just the way she wanted.

All right, she still figured she was a novice at sex. She didn't really know hard and fast—yet. But she wondered for a moment if everyone felt this way, the intense yearning, the giving into sensation, and the need for completion. His mouth was grinding down on hers. Instead of feeling pain she savored the act. His hips banged against hers in a simulation of their coupling. She wanted more.

She simply couldn't get enough of him. Her hands ripped at his shirt, kneading the skin of his chest with her fingers. She wanted him inside her even though they were both fully clothed. But not for long, for as he finally let go of her mouth and started trailing kisses down her neck, his fingers undid both her outer shirt and the underwear beneath.

The layers fell away as he pulled back. His gaze raked the length of her, hot and hard. Her nipples pointed straight at him begging for his tongue. He complied, biting down with just enough force to cause molten lava to pour through her core.

She grabbed his head in between both her hands and pushed him even harder against her chest. She didn't even recognize herself as she squirmed, begged and pleaded for more. He lifted her up for just the time it took to free the rest of her clothes from her body, pulled off the remnants of his shirt, then made to remove his pants. She pushed his hands away. This was her job and she was going to enjoy every moment.

Pushing his boxers down she gripped the length of him, marveling at how soft yet how hard he felt. She inhaled the musky male scent of him and her hormones responded. Still, no matter how badly she wanted him, her touch was exquisitely slow. He growled deep in his throat at her torture and she smiled. Two could play the game.

The next thing she knew, she was flat on her back on the bed. He pulled her legs to the edge, positioned himself, and rammed home. He put his arms on either side of her, pulled out almost all the way, then thrust into her as hard as he could.

Her cries started in the back of her throat. The sound begged for something more. She wanted him to thrust into her, again and again, harder and harder. Sensing her need he complied, and in doing so, fueled his own desire. He plunged in and out, growling, biting, and laving the hurts with his tongue.

Just when Tara was certain she could stand no more, just when she felt him grow to incredible proportions, he paused. A split second, no more. He shouted her name and rammed into her for all he was worth. Tara screamed as the world exploded. Wave upon wave of pleasure coursed through her body as hot jets spurted into her womb. On and on as if he'd never stop coming.

All right, her experience up until now had come from books. She'd read about *la petite mort* but never really believed it was possible. She did now. She lost track of time, space and feeling. When she "came to" she read concern all over his face.

"Did I hurt you?" he asked in between gasps for air.

She reached up to caress his face. He'd collapsed on top of her and she enjoyed the feeling of his length on hers. But her true focus, the one that mattered, centered on the pulsating shock waves between her legs. "No."

She closed her eyes. Her breathing was just as labored as his. "Are you certain?" She smiled at the alarm in his tone.

"No." He made a move to withdraw and she cried out. "No."

He settled back down but kept most of his weight off of her. "We can't stay like this forever."

"Damn," she sighed, snuggling into his neck. "That was—incredible," she told him, the wonder of their encounter resonating through her tone.

He chuckled. "Yes."

She pulled in a breath with gusto. "Jeri will be here soon." Letting the air out she added, "I guess we have to clean up." She could feel his half-hard erection still inside her. Had they not been so sated, she was certain they'd have gone another round. But that wasn't what was so important. She savored the intimacy and when he finally rolled off her, she felt bereft as if a part of her had gone with him.

"Come." He rose and pulled her up with him. They took a shower together, sharing an ease she'd never thought possible. They played with the soap, laughed, and kept touching each other. In spite of their trouble, Tara relaxed.

She heard a knock at the door just as she finished drying her hair. "Jeri," she cried, running to hug her friend.

"Hi, baby. Glad to see you're back." Tara shook her head with an affectionate smile. Leave it to her best bud to know she had regained her memory, and tease her with her use of language at the same time.

"Thank you for coming," Nicholai added, leading the woman to a chair and making her comfortable.

All of a sudden, Tara noticed Jeri was, well, sniffing the air. Then a huge grin split the woman's face. "I do believe we had some early morning loving going on in here."

She looked over at Nicholai and to her utter delight, found he was blushing. "More than that," she answered.

Jeri frowned for a minute. "Don't follow you, babe."

"I'm, well, um—pregnant Jer."

Jeri sat in stunned silence for a second then cried out in delight. "Why that's wonderful. I'm so happy for you both." Then she turned in Nicholai's direction and teased, "Fast worker, aren't you?"

Tara burst out laughing then sobered. "There was a reason, Jer."

Nicholai rose and came to stand beside her. "Hmm. Temp around here just dropped about twenty degrees. I guess you'd both better tell me what's going on."

Tara began the story with Nicholai adding comments as they continued. "So I guess you could say," she ended, "that we know what's going on and yet we don't."

Nicholai nodded in agreement. "That is also why the casket is so important. My guess is that this—entity—was waiting to use the case. I'm not sure why yet. Using the case or using the Water of Change, or the Chalice, is still only a one at a time proposition. No matter what gets used, it only works on one Noble at a time. The entity I encountered would not have the patience to destroy us like that."

Jeri shuddered. "I don't like any of this. Not one bit. Especially your distrust of the High Council. How can anyone possibly fight this thing if no one trusts each other?"

"I know." Nicholai rose. He reached out to squeeze Jeri's shoulder in comfort. "Do not give up hope. There are many who are already working to fight this terror. Together."

Jeri reached down and felt around until she found her bag. "I brought the camera as you asked."

"Thank you." Nicholai unwrapped the canvas bag with care and began taking pictures of the casket. He hesitated before wrapping the case back up again. "You face a tough decision, Jeri. One I would not want. If you touch the case you may cure your blindness. Or you may die. I ask only that you decide after your task is ended. We need you right now."

A surge of hope shot through Tara only to end in fear. "Ah God, Jer. I'm selfish. I want you around to be godmother to our daughter."

"Son," Nicholai corrected. "Sons, actually."

Jeri laughed. Tara marveled that she didn't seem the least bit concerned with the dilemma that faced her. "And I'm beginning to love you too, you arrogant pain in the ass," Jeri said before she turned towards Tara. "Sometimes I wish to see a sunrise with every cell in my body. Just one. But that's not a reason to put my life in jeopardy. Now, that doesn't mean I might not change my mind. And when I do, you'll both be the first to know. But for now, un-huh."

Nicholai covered the case carefully and handed it to Jeri. "You will not know they are there, but you will be guarded night and day. Just go about your normal routine as if nothing has changed."

"Gotcha."

"When I am certain that it is safe," Nicholai continued. "I will send for you and the case. Until then, hide in plain sight."

She nodded. "You can count on me."

"If you believe you are in danger or that the case is at risk and my people are not present, call this cell number. There is only one man besides my brother and my Steward that I trust. Dmitri will tell you what to do and take care of you, or die trying."

The silence that followed slammed into her. "We're all at risk here." No more games, no more talk. Tara's hand slipped to her belly without thought. "But even more is the next generation. We can and will win. For her sake. And all those not yet born."

"His. Theirs," Nicholai corrected with a smile, showing her what was really important and what was not.

Chapter Sixteen

Nicholai stood before Ariel Gold, his heart beating faster than he would have liked. Tiny, dark haired, full of incredible energy, she held an enormous amount of power for one so small. Would she help him? She owed him no loyalty. He'd gone renegade as far as she was concerned. His very presence put her in conflict with her position.

"You believe this is how your mate was made?" she asked, her shrewd gaze catching and holding his.

Damn if he didn't feel like a young pup all over again. "Yes," he replied, marveling at her stature. She looked like royalty sitting in her high-backed chair set behind a large ornate desk.

The Nobility had amassed wealth throughout the ages. Although Nicholai had no desire to be dubbed as *noveau riche*, Ariel Gold didn't seem to have a problem with that. Her mansion sat on the cliffs of the Hudson in one of the wealthiest sections of New Jersey that reeked of new money, and though the outside fit in quite well, the inside was rich, old, and rather intimidating.

Ariel had used some of the most expensive decorators in New York and her walls were adorned with incredible works of art from painters like Degas and Renoir. A huge stone fireplace took up an entire wall of her living room. Rather than carpet, expensive Persian rugs covered different areas of the room. There was not one ounce of chrome, no stark white walls; none of her rooms could be called cold. Yet he still felt uncomfortable.

"Interesting," she murmured. After long moments of silence, she threw the photos he'd handed her onto the desktop and stood. "Were I dealing with anyone else, Valentin, I would believe this to be an exquisite forgery."

"The case was thought to be lost a long time ago. Dare I presume that the members of the High Council believed it passed out of existence?" he asked, his tone sarcastic.

She whipped off her glasses, glared at him, then rubbed the bridge of her nose. "Snide doesn't suit you." She held up her hand, weariness reflected in her face. "I know you don't give a damn." She put her glasses back on. "The case was presumed lost because we lost our connection with it. We couldn't figure out who or what would have the power to do that, but we were certain it was safe."

"Safe?"

"In the sense that the casket had not been destroyed. You cannot destroy something that is an absolute part of you. Every Noble would have known."

Stunned he asked, "Then you knew the casket had the power to change a Noble into a True Noble?"

"Not exactly."

Confused, Nicholai simply stared. "I am sorry. I do not quite follow."

"Remember your history. The case was stolen three times before it was lost forever. Each time the guardian of the case was found dead. Murdered, we believe, by the thief. And every one of the thieves was a full-blooded human. Ask yourself why."

"Because a full-blooded human would not be affected by the case, would have no knowledge of what it truly was."

"Exactly."

"But the last time the case was not found. Just the body."

"A puzzle, no? The casket was ornate, indeed worth quite a sum, but we would have found it eventually if a human had simply stolen it."

"The High Councils of the past thought a Noble was behind the theft?"

"What else was there to think? But how to probe and how to accuse without blowing up our entire society? That was the tricky part. Can you imagine the hornets nest a few well-placed questions would have stirred up?"

She walked over to a polished oak side bar gilded with gold trim, and held up a very expensive bottle of cognac. "Will you join me?"

He needed one. "Yes, thank you."

"Sometimes being a member of this Council means patience beyond endurance. The one advantage we have is that we have long lives."

"Not when they are cut short."

She walked back carrying two snifters and handed him one. "*L'chaim.*"

The irony of her toast was not lost on either of them. "I hope so," he replied quietly.

"Something tells me there's more to this story than just the casket."

"I am not sure how to explain this, but what if something Noble yet not Noble stole the casket? Wouldn't that sever our connection?"

"Very likely. Would you care to elaborate?"

He shook his head. "Not yet."

"All right. We all have our secrets." She took another sip of her drink. "Then perhaps you'll answer another question. Why me? Or better yet, why not Stefano?"

A hard question, but a fair one. Stefano was, is, God, he wished he knew, his mentor.

"Stefano will act in the best interest of the Nobility according to his assessment of the facts. If necessary, he will adjust as he goes along. I have no wish to die before the right questions get asked."

"What if I just turn you in?"

"You will not."

She laughed. "You're either terribly naive, incredibly arrogant, or the best judge of character I've ever met."

"The latter. You prize the truth above all."

"Very astute," she replied, her tone impressed. "I also abhor injustice. And frankly the attempt they made to incarcerate you, if you get my meaning, reeks."

"I thought so too."

"All right, you have my attention. What else?"

"There may be more to all of this than even I can handle."

"How so?"

"One part I cannot talk about, not until I know more. The other has to do with my mate. The House of Pendragon was called traitor in error."

"Are you sure of that?"

"Very sure." He took a deep breath. "And a member of the High Council may have been an accomplice."

She sucked in a deep breath. "You had better leave now."

"Not yet."

"You dare to sit in judgment of those who have lived only to serve?"

"No. Never," he replied, his tone full of passion and pride. "But what of those who made judgments in the name of the greater good only to realize the error of their decisions later on? To cover up the truth is to lie no matter what words are used in disguise. Christian Pendragon was framed and the perpetrator could not have framed him without help. No one else knew what his true purpose was except the members of the High Council. Someone else found out."

"Can you prove that?"

"When the time comes, yes."

She snorted in disbelief. "No offense, young one, but Trial by Combat is only fifty-fifty odds."

"That is the other reason I am here. I have been blind to many things especially my people as a race. We let ourselves believe we were above reproach. I plan on being around to rectify this situation. But just in case, I want my mate and my heir protected."

"And my role in this is?"

"Call a meeting of the entire Nobility. Show the High Council the pictures. Tell them I have the casket. We make a trade. The life of my mate and my child for the case. They are not to be touched. Ever. And they retain all rights within my House."

"They'll want this kept private. Especially Han-Sing."

Nicholai just smiled. Her eyes widened for a split second then she nodded. "Impossible. The casket must be returned to the entire assembly. That way they cannot renege on the deal."

"They'll buy that," she agreed, seeming to be thinking out loud. "They'll think you quite shrewd."

"Frankly, I don't give a damn what they think. Compromises were made in the name of integrity. That was a terrible error in judgment and must now be paid for."

Astounded, she merely looked at him for a long moment. "You're going to teach them? You're going to exact justice?"

"No," he replied, his tone even but the horror of what he'd been through written clearly on his face.

"Something I have no name for will do that."

****

The Great Hall was not her favorite place. Somehow, Tara thought to herself, it felt even colder and less inviting this time. Of course much of her unease stemmed from Nicholai's plan. Men, she thought with disgust. As long as they could perform their macho deeds everything would turn out hunky-dory. So what if the setup had more holes in it than a piece of Jarlsburg Swiss. *We are men. We get to beat our chests and prove how wonderful we are. Until we die.*

"You're frowning," Alexi commented, interrupting her thoughts.

"Give me one reason not to."

"The baby."

Tara turned; ready to heap her frustrations all over his head. He gave her a wry, knowing look. "Not fair," she bit out.

"Never said I was," he replied with a smile. "I wasn't sure you cared."

"Nicholai is the father of my child." She stopped. Was there a deeper reason than even *she* cared to admit? A reason she didn't want to recognize?

He nodded. His gaze told her not to lie to herself. "Don't worry. Nico'll be fine. He's really, really pissed."

"Anger makes people make mistakes," she said with a frown.

"Not my brother. He gets razor sharp when he gets angry. Believe me, I know."

Her brows drew even further together until they almost touched. "How comforting," she muttered, falling silent as the High Council entered.

Once the formalities were dispensed with, Dmitri Borodkin walked to the center of the hall. "I ask that fair trial be given to Nicholai Valentin.

"He's renegade," a member of the Rhys-Jones

family called out. "And that one," the man pointed straight at her. "Must die."

"Hold!" Stefano thundered. "You do not have the floor."

As he glared out at the crowd, she had to admit the old guy had balls. And the power to keep order. "Dmitri. Continue," Stefano ordered.

Dmitri cleared his throat and resumed his speech. "I ask that the members of the Nobility listen to the facts before they try to condemn a man who is a prince among us. Nicholai Valentin has spent his life serving our people and his own. His mate has done nothing but be a pawn in a game she had no idea existed. Indeed, she never even knew she was a Noble until she was made. And last, the House of Pendragon has been a scapegoat, the victim of fate and perhaps even deceit."

"She should be dead," a voice called out.

"The name Pendragon is traitor," cried another.

Tara could stand no more. "No...it...is...not!" she called out, her tone scathing. "And—" She never continued. Dmitri's fierce look and Alexi's grip on her arm told her to hold her tongue.

"The name of Pendragon," Dmitri continued, settling the crowd by gathering their attention to him, "forfeited all its rights during Trial by Combat. That is our way. Sometimes, though, a defeat is not indicative of the truth. We all know this." A few heads nodded in agreement. "However, that is our law. Just as the Water of Change is forbidden. Yet the woman before you stands accused of using it. I suggest she did not."

"Can you bring proof of this to the Council?" Stefano asked Dmitri.

Alexi stepped forward. In his arms he carried a canvas bag. He walked to the center of the room holding the casket with reverence. As soon as he stood before the High Council, he unwrapped the material. A collective gasp ran through the room. "This has been lost to us for a long time. I suggest this has more than enough power to change a Noble into a True Noble."

"But...but—," Han-Sing stammered. "How did you come by it?"

Alexi held the casket aloft asking for silence. "I ask that Tara Pendragon, now of the House of Valentin, tell her story."

An alleyway parted for her to step to the center of the hall. Heart pounding, all eyes upon her, Tara walked forward. Her life depended on her answer and with so many staring at her; she had to wonder whether they all wanted her dead or not. She took a long look around the room. "Story? You want a story? You don't care about stories. All you want is blood. And more blood. And more blood."

No one knew how to answer. They'd expected her to grovel; they hadn't expected derision. "Nobles. You all make me laugh. You want to murder an innocent woman, deprive a child of its mother, all in the name of honor. And family. And face." A hot sliver of anger burned in the pit of her belly. "Tell me. All of you. Where is your Nobility now?"

"Get to the point, woman," Han-Sing demanded, his tone disgusted, telling her how dare she, a mere woman, berate the Council.

Tara whirled to face the man. "You already know the point, old man." She turned back slowly. Funny, but they were actually listening to her. Maybe there was hope after all. "We're all pawns in some sort of plan. Someone is a master manipulator among you. I was used first. This case was planted at an estate sale. Whoever planted it there knew I would touch it and be made. They had to know. Antiques are my livelihood." She stared out at the crowd trying to discern who was traitor and who was not. "Whether or not I died made no difference. The key was to begin the destruction of another House."

"Another House?" Dmitri asked.

"Yes. The first was my House, the House of Pendragon."

"Impossible," a voice answered.

"Sheer fantasy," called out another.

"Oh really?" she asked, her tone so bitter the room fell silent. "Is that because you all love each other so much you won't let it happen?"

"You show spunk, woman," Han-Sing replied, holding up his hand so as not to be interrupted. "But the Council will not be deceived. You are merely trying to deflect the real issue, that of your guilt. How do we know you didn't steal the case in the first place? How do we know you're not the master manipulator, as you put it?"

"Because if I had, I'd be pretty stupid to bring it to you now."

"Not if you were trying to use it to save your life."

She nodded. "Not a bad idea. But where's my ace in the hole, then? By bringing the casket here, you have me and you have the prize." She shook her head, her smile gentle in its certainty. "No, you've already made it clear that after my child is born, I'm history. So tell me, all you super smart Nobles. Why would I walk back into the lion's den?"

A clear voice, one she knew so well, rang out from the back of the hall. "To see justice served."

****

Surrounded by the Stewards of every House in the Nobility, Nicholai walked toward the front of the hall. "What is the meaning of this, Valentin?" Stefano asked.

Nicholai said to himself. *Not Han-Sing? Interesting.*

"Your pardon, my Lords," he mocked with a bow. "But I fear this farce must end. Now."

"Farce?" Stefano questioned. "Perhaps I have misjudged your use of the word. The only farce I see is a group of Stewards who have forgotten their place."

"I beg to differ, my Lord," Sergei bristled. "We may swear fealty to our House but we also live to serve the Nobility. Perhaps it is the High Council that has forgotten *its* place."

"We need no Steward reprimanding us," Han-Sing cried out. "How dare you!"

"We dare nothing," Connor, rightful Steward to the House of Pendragon answered, his tone soft but made of steel. "We come in the name of justice. We come because some in this room have forgotten their honor."

"We've forgotten nothing," Stefano replied, his anger apparent to all.

"No?" Nicholai asked, commanding the room to silence. "I did," he continued, his gaze locked on Tara's. She bowed her head a bit in acknowledgment. "I forgot who I was and why I was placed on this earth." He turned, scanning the room. "What has happened to us? When did we lose all that we are, our very essence, our Nobility?"

"We haven't lost anything. Perhaps you have, Nicholai," his mentor suggested, speaking to his recent actions.

Nicholai shook his head a great sadness filling him. "Is the greater good worth the price of integrity?"

He watched Stefano wince, but the man, to his credit, answered with unwavering honesty. "Yes."

"Then what I have lost, my old friend, is my innocence. Innocence lost can never be reclaimed. I ask again. What have we done to ourselves?"

The Hall fell silent. Nicholai could see most of them had no clue what he was talking about. "Forgive us, Nicholai," Dmitri Borodkin began. "We do not understand. For many, you speak in riddles."

"Then answer this one," he called out to all of them. "Why make a True Noble female if your intent is only to kill her?"

No one could. "Again, Valentin," Han-Sing replied. "You speak in riddles."

He shook his head. "One among you, perhaps more, knows exactly what I am speaking of." He waited a moment for his words to sink in. "My mate, Tara, was made on purpose. The casket that carried the Water of Change was placed where she would find it and be made. I was asked to find out how and why. Knowing me, knowing who I am, that person knew I would be bound to protect her when I found out she was Pendragon. My father swore a life oath on it. By following that oath, I put myself and my House in jeopardy before you all, right here and right now. I had to protect her. There was only one way to do so."

"Guilty out of his own mouth," Charles Rhys-Jones cried out.

Nicholai held up his hand for silence. "I would not gloat too much, Charles. No one has heard the end of the story yet."

"Then you admit," Han-Sing asked, his tone a bit too bloodthirsty for Nicholai's liking, "that you deliberately impregnated this woman to save her life?"

"Absolutely. And would a hundred times over. She is my mate."

The members of the High Council looked at each other not knowing exactly what to do. "Be careful, Valentin," Ariel Gold warned. "You're incriminating yourself."

Nicholai smiled, his demeanor totally unconcerned. "My Lords. Ladies. Members of my esteemed race. I ask your indulgence. I stand accused of that which is not a crime but to prove that, I must go back into the past and answer with a story."

"You're going to let him spew this drivel?" Charles croaked.

"Silence," Stefano thundered. "Nicholai Valentin, by right of birth, can answer any way he chooses. That is our law." He looked straight at Nicholai, his gaze telling Nico he was terrified for his protégé. "Continue."

Nicholai felt a shiver of relief flow through him. Stefano might know some of the facts, but he was not privy to the crime. Someone was manipulating the Council as well. "During World War Two Christian Pendragon was asked to perform a service for the Nobility. He was asked to infiltrate the Third Reich High Command."

"No one ever denied that," Stefano replied. "It was kept secret to keep him safe. But he turned traitor."

"No, Stefano, he did not."

"Can you prove that?"

"Yes."

"But how? The High Council at the time tried and failed."

"He was set up. Framed."

"Forgive me, but we would have known that."

"Would you?" Nicholai asked, his tone quiet but full of certainty. "That would have been impossible because the casket was lost to us."

"The casket?"

"Yes. Someone used the casket to create an Aryan, Albert Manneheim. They tested him, to see if he was indeed a Nazi Noble, by forcing Christian Pendragon into a corner where he would have had no choice but to seek Trial by Combat. They, not Pendragon, promised Hitler a race of Nazi Nobles. Only the High Council thought someone had gotten to the Water of Change. They were wrong. You see, they forgot the existence of the casket."

"Impossible. They didn't forget. It was gone," Han-Sing answered. "No Noble had seen it for centuries."

"Not true. I ask that Connor, rightful Steward to the House of Pendragon come forward and tell his story."

Nicholai watched the Steward bow. "My Lords. My grandfather, Nelson, was Steward to the House of Pendragon at that time. He set to my father, who in turn, set to me a legacy—to prove our House innocent. I now have that proof.

"After Christian Pendragon was killed, my grandfather took his body to the car. Grieving, he watched Edward Rhys-Jones get into his car. All he wanted in that moment was for God to serve justice. He knew the whole meeting was a setup, knew his leader had died for no reason, knew the word honor would only hold bitterness for him for the rest of his life. He would also have to try to explain to Sarah Pendragon why her mate had died—before he tried to figure out how to save her life and the lives of her twins."

"My family had nothing to do with that," Charles Rhys-Jones defended. "We were asked to be there when it happened."

"Then what was your grandfather carrying, Charles?" Connor Pendragon asked. "What was he smiling about as he got into that car? Because my grandfather wrote in his diary all that transpired. Then he just happened to meet an untimely death. Of course my father, being a young man, held his suspicions. Until he, too, tried to find out more. Then he was also killed."

"Your father died in an explosion."

"Which I later found out was proven to be arson." Nicholai felt Connor's grief as a living thing. They all did. "My father left to me all his information in a safe place. It wasn't until Tara was made into a True Noble that I knew their suspicions were correct." He reached into his jacket pocket and withdrew a small notebook and a sheaf of papers. "My grandfather's diary, the information my father gathered pertaining to my grandfather's death and the arson report on the building fire that took my father's life."

"This is ridiculous," Charles called out.

"An incredible fabrication," Han-Sing agreed.

"Really?" Nicholai returned, his tone a slice of steel.

"Yes, really," Charles sneered back. "Why would my grandfather want to risk his own death to destroy a House?"

Nicholai paused and turned to be heard by the entire assembly. "To Rule the Nobility."

Chapter Seventeen

Oh God, she thought, her stomach plummeting. Of all the damned, pigheaded, macho— She bit her lip as she ran out of expletives. He was going to do it anyway. *Be careful, Nico.*

A bark of derisive laughter rang through the room. "My Lords. Nicholai Valentin, to *save* his own skin, has just come up with the biggest piece of bullshit ever to grace this hallowed hall." Charles Rhys-Jones stood in the center of the crowd facing her mate.

Funny, Tara thought, as she scanned the room she noted more Nobles than not were silent.

"Gee, *Chuck*," Nicholai mocked. "Your fan club membership seems to be way down these days. I wonder why. Could it be that the members of this august body understand that your family is capable of this kind of treachery?"

Rhys-Jones scowled. "I'm not going to lower myself to answer that."

"My Lords," Nicholai said. "Is it not possible that over the years, perhaps even centuries, because of our nature, because of how our traditions have been built, that we have all been used? Do we not quarrel over the smallest of slights? Do we not bear grudges for centuries? Does it not take the tiniest amount of provocation before we mistrust each other? Now add an unexplained death. A mating gone sour. Unexplained missing finances. We manage to do the rest quite well."

Tara watched as light bulbs started popping on. "Why accuse Christian Pendragon of treason?" Nicholai continued. "To bring down his House. Why accuse me of treason? To bring down my House. Who's next? Where will this end?"

No one answered. Nicholai's logic, actually her own, was impeccable.

"Now I am forced to defend my honor. I have no wish to fight, but I see no other way to clear my name and defend the honor of the Nobility. My word against his."

"You are still traitor," Charles hammered home. "I call for trial by combat."

At first there was silence. Then a voice called out, "Aye."

"Aye." More voices joined the first.

Although he clearly wanted to defend himself, Tara could tell Nicholai didn't want to fight. "I declare my brother Alexi my second."

Charles responded. "I have the right to a champion."

"You do," Stefano affirmed.

"I choose Gunner Manneheim as my champion."

Nicholai didn't seem surprised and as Tara looked around, not many did either. "History repeating itself, *Chuck*?"

"I'm not doing anything wrong."

"How did Albert find time to mate? Why didn't the assembly know you had taken the Manneheim's into your House?" Nicholai swept his arm wide to include everyone in the hall. "A well kept secret, no? And consider this—Albert Manneheim, if he was *bred* for the very purpose of destruction, wouldn't he have had to mate before his *assignment.* Nothing is ever guaranteed."

An angry rumble ran through the hall. Those assembled were beginning to piece things together and were finding them a bit too coincidental not to have been planned. Even Tara found it hard to keep silent. But a hand gripped her arm. She looked up to see Dmitri Borodkin shaking his head. He was right. Now was not the time to interfere.

"You should have been a novelist," Rhys-Jones scoffed. "This is quite a story."

Nicholai paused as he lifted his shirt off, holding the fabric in his hands. Her heart quickened at the sight of his lean body, a body she wanted very much alive.

"You are right, *Chuck,* this is some story. Imagine, finding out your sworn enemy is in a vulnerable position because someone on the High Council leaked that information. Imagine a member of the High Council seeing that he could pit two Houses against each other, watch them destroy one another, then be around to pick up the pieces. Imagine, a member of the High Council, once this occurred and seeing the ease with which it was done, figuring the same could be done again. And again. And again. No, Charles. Not hard to write this story at all."

A collective gasp rippled through the room.

"Prove it," he cried.

"I intend to. But first you and I have some unfinished business. Honor first, traitors second."

"We'll see about that."

Gunner Manneheim looked like a man bred to fight. Tall, well-defined muscles, he stood square and ready to battle. Tara's stomach plummeted. She watched the men square off against one another and prayed for her mate. A thin-bladed knife meant for killing was placed between the two men. Then their arms were held out and crossed and tied with a thong of leather around the wrists. Then each man's wrists were tied together with another small piece of leather. Just enough room to maneuver but none to win. The knife held the key. Whoever cut their bindings first would have a distinct advantage over the other.

Manneheim had not spoken a word. He didn't have to. Tara read the hatred in his gaze. Born and bred to total loyalty and unquestioning devotion. A true Nazi Noble. Terror gripped her heart.

All of a sudden, even though he was across the room, Tara sensed Alexi. She'd forgotten their connection. She didn't dare distract Nicholai, but she needed a shoulder to lean on right now. Alexi gave her a calm she needed to hold on to.

"This will be a fight to the death. Trial by Combat. Charles Rhys-Jones has chosen a champion, as is his right. As the defendant, he has chosen to fight in the old way of our people. Do you accept, Nicholai Valentin?"

"I do."

"On the count of ten the fight will begin. Are you ready?"

"Aye."

Manneheim nodded. "No mercy," Rhys-Jones called out to his champion.

Nicholai didn't flinch. He looked perfectly calm, almost detached. Tara couldn't figure out why. Then she realized he was seeking aid from his ancestors. To that end, she too went into a semi-trance. She called on her past family to help her mate and clear her name. The eagerness she sensed from her grandfather's spirit gave her a small measure of peace.

Both men were circling each other as she came out of her daze, testing their bindings and looking for an opening of some kind. Then Manneheim struck, falling backwards and rolling on his back, pulling Nicholai forward. Nicholai simply went with the motion and rolled over in a somersault, landing on his feet easily behind the Aryan. Then they turned and started again.

Manneheim snarled as Nicholai gave him a small smile. As he fell, he tried to pull Nicholai to the side and grab for the knife. But something was wrong, Tara thought. The Aryan was not Nicholai's major focus. He seemed to be preoccupied and that scared her half to death. What the devil was he doing?

Manneheim charged like a caged bull, but Nicholai jumped to the side, only to be charged again. But this time he tried to slide tackle Nicholai. At the last second Nicholai jumped and landed on his feet, but he didn't try to pull his opponent any closer to the knife and Tara couldn't figure out why. What the devil was he doing?

At last she realized. As Manneheim charged again, this time trying to wrestle her mate to the ground, Nicholai let him. He took the brunt of the fall, grunting in pain, but as he hit the ground his hands came free. He rolled Manneheim off him and jumped to his feet.

The knife! she thought. *Get the knife!*

Every muscle in her body tensed as the silence in the room roared in her ears. Manneheim dropped and rolled, beating her mate to the weapon. He cut his bindings and slashed at Nicholai. Nicholai jumped back and Manneheim lunged again. Each time the man attacked her heart stopped. Each time he missed, it started again. Nicholai seemed to be losing ground with each step. He would parry with his arm, catch the knife hand and then get pushed away. But looks were deceiving, as the more Manneheim missed, the more he became enraged.

Then suddenly Tara realized the man's

weakness. Nicholai hadn't missed the knife at all, he'd deliberately let the Aryan have it so he could do exactly what he was doing right now—wear himself out. Nicholai was using the man's emotions against him.

God, she thought. If he lives through this, I'm going to kill him.

Both men drew back, continued to circle one another, each trying to catch their breath. Tara thought Manneheim looked less exhausted than her mate and that worried her. Still, Nicholai continued with his tactic. He razzed the man in an ancient Cossack dialect. Manneheim screamed vitriol in German right back.

Just as Tara thought she might be able to take a breath, the Aryan lunged at Nicholai. Nicholai jumped sideways to avoid the rush and his foot slipped. He staggered and Mannheim charged, the knife raised in his hand, a blood-curdling scream accompanying his killing blow.

An answering scream built deep in Tara's throat as she stared at the knife aimed straight at her mate's heart. But Nicholai wasn't there. At the last possible second he'd twisted and ducked to avoid the arc of the blade. Manneheim went flying, falling hard onto the stone floor. The knife skittered into the crowd. Nicholai leapt to his feet, wiping the sweat off his upper lip with the back of his hand.

"Now we fight fair, Nazi."

Manneheim nodded savagely. "I will enjoy snapping your neck like a chicken." His hands mimicked the act.

"There is a phrase about counting eggs, Nazi," Nicholai warned.

Manneheim simply laughed and that was another weakness, Tara discovered. He truly did not think he could be defeated. Born and bred to this moment, defeat had never entered his mind. What arrogance, she thought, from an arrogant race. How hard the mighty will fall.

They circled each other again, this time in what seemed to be a cross between wrestling and boxing. Then Nicholai swung his fist and the Aryan grabbed it, twisting it behind his back until she thought Nicholai's shoulder would be torn in two. Nicholai whirled around, getting the other man in a headlock. Nicholai fell to one knee and used Manneheim's own force against him only to have the man wriggle free. Then they started again and again and again.

Tara's fear grew. Nicholai was older and not as strong as Manneheim. Suddenly, Manneheim jumped Nicholai from behind, his hands in a death-grip around his neck. Nicholai turned redder and redder, fighting for air. He tried in vain to pry the man's fingers apart. Then Tara watched as her mate shifted his weight and stomped down on the Aryan's foot. Manneheim grunted in pain and surprise as his hold loosened just enough for Nicholai to wrench free. He fell to one knee, grabbing his neck, gasping for air.

Manneheim, seeing his opponent down, lunged for the kill. But Nicholai was far from through. As the Aryan swung his arms to chop Nicholai across the back, Nicholai's fist drove into the man's solar plexus, the air whooshing out in a rush. Tara watched a surprised look come over his face as Nicholai drove another punch into Manneheim's face, the Aryan's head snapping back from the force of the blow.

More blows followed and Manneheim stumbled, dazed but not down yet. He regrouped and caught Nicholai in the gut with a solid punch and he grunted in pain as Manneheim crowed with delight. "Hurts, doesn't it old man?" the Aryan said, sending Nicholai to one knee with a nasty uppercut.

Tara didn't even acknowledge her fear,

absorbing her mate's pain.

"Get up, coward," the Aryan snarled again.

Nicholai swayed, trying to stand as Manneheim moved in, gloating. As the Aryan drew near, her mate rose and threw a vicious uppercut into the man's chin. Manneheim staggered backwards, Nicholai following with a vicious rain of punches to his head and midsection. Tara gasped; never before had she seen Nicholai's eyes blaze with such clarity of purpose, and she knew there would be no defeat now. Manneheim swayed like a drunkard, each blow knocking him back but not off his feet.

With every gaze in the building locked on the battle, Tara looked away to see Charles Rhys-Jones edging through the crowd. Not trusting the man, she slipped away from Dmitri Borodkin and circled around to where her enemy was standing. She watched him bend down, rise, and smile. Everyone had forgotten the knife. He was going for the knife!

Rhys-Jones edged to the front of the circle where Nicholai had now stopped pummeling his opponent and stood waiting for the man to fall. She would have to mirror his movements from behind. She slipped several rows back then sidestepped until she was directly behind the man with only one person between them. He edged forward, so did she until now she was directly behind him. Then she tapped him on the shoulder.

Rhys-Jones whirled and she grabbed the knife. She missed the handle but caught the blade, the sharpened edge cutting into her flesh as she turned the point towards the man.

"Move," she hissed. "And you die."

Funny, but she didn't feel any pain. Her blood dripped onto the floor and she could care less. All she knew was that Nicholai was not going to end up with a knife in his back.

All of a sudden she felt the blade turn. A roar

rang through the crowd. Nicholai must have won. She barely registered the thought before another occurred to her—Charles Rhys-Jones was stronger than she. Tara put her other hand on the blade to keep from getting skewered.

Problem was, she wasn't going to win this one. With a quick side step, she released her grip and tried to jump out of the way. Rhys-Jones rushed forward with the force of his momentum. She wasn't fast enough. The knife caught her in the side, driving deep. At first, she was pissed at herself for getting caught. Then she curled inside herself to make sure the baby was all right. Then she felt the streak of lightning and fire run through her side. And that was when she heard Alexi call out, "Tara—no!"

****

Nicholai heard the words from a great distance. His heart hammered in his ears. He drank in great draughts of air causing a wind tunnel to whirl in his ears. His foe lay beaten on the floor at his feet. Did someone say Tara? *Tara!* What the devil was wrong with Tara?

Nico.

The crowd parted. Tara lay on the floor covered in blood. He was at her side in an instant. Then he fell to his knees as his legs refused to hold his weight. "Tara? Oh God, Tara? What have you done?"

"Saved your life, you ungrateful wretch."

That she could answer helped him to breathe again. "What happened? What is going on here?"

Nicholai looked up and saw Alexi and Dmitri Borodkin holding onto Charles Rhys-Jones. "Sergei," he cried. "Quickly." His Steward rushed forward to help.

"He was going to kill you while no one was watching," Tara whispered.

Nicholai looked back down and ran a gentle

finger down the side of her cheek. “For me?” he asked her.

She gave a slight nod. “I seem to need you around.”

Sergei bent down and examined the wound. “It is not mortal, my Lord. She will be all right.”

“I wasn’t fast enough,” she told him as he gazed down at her.

He rose and a red haze began to form around his eyesight.

“She came at me with the knife,” Rhys-Jones counter-attacked.

“Hold him. I will deal with him in a moment. Sergei?”

“I have already stopped the bleeding.”

He walked to the center of the hall. Gunner Manneheim lay unconscious near his feet. “How long?” he roared. “How long must we go on destroying ourselves before we learn?”

“Nicholai,” Stefano reminded him. “You have your duty to perform.”

“No,” he replied, shaking his head. “I will not. No more lost lives, no more blood shed. We need every Noble we can get our hands on.”

“You’re not going to kill him?” Han-Sing queried, his tone both stunned and concerned.

“No, I am not. Instead, I am going to let the assembly rule. Manneheim was a champion and had no part in this betrayal other than to be a puppet. Charles Rhys-Jones was a pawn in a game started by his grandfather. It ends now. I ask that they both be spared in spite of all the treachery. Both must be banished and the House of Rhys-Jones must be disbanded and assimilated into the other Houses so as not to try this treachery again. What say you all?”

The punishment spared their lives but merited most of the crimes. A collective “Aye,” rang through the room.

"No one would blame you for calling the man out," Dmitri Borodkin told him.

Nicholai looked over at Tara. She shook her head. He nodded, knowing he had a lifetime of learning to experience with her. "No. Banishment will be punishment enough." He walked over to Charles Rhys-Jones and stood in front of him. He nodded to Alexi and Dmitri to let go of the man's arms. "However, no one in the room is going to mind if I—" Nicholai never finished his sentence. Instead, he pulled his right arm through the air as hard as he could and smashed his fist right in Charles's face. His hand hurt like hell, but he grinned from ear to ear. "Do this."

Turning, he walked back over to his mate and knelt down. "Thank you for trying to save my life." His gaze could not capture enough of her to his heart.

She laughed, lifting her hand and tapping the heel to her forehead. "What was I thinking?"

He smiled even though he thought he might cry. "Someday I will get used to your teasing."

"She may be moved now, my Lord. A morning feed or two and she'll be good as new. Purely a flesh wound. Nothing more. And the babe is fine."

He shuddered with reaction. He hadn't even thought of the baby. "Alexi and Sergei will take you to an apartment we keep nearby. I will join you shortly." He bent down and kissed her forehead.

"I won't break."

Her lips tasted sweeter than the best of his wines. "I will join you shortly."

"No revenge, Nico. Please."

He shook his head. "You have taught me well, love. No revenge."

She started at the use of his endearment, but that would need to be discussed later.

Nicholai acknowledged. "We will talk. After I

beat you for taking such a risk."

"Hmm. I might like that."

He didn't know how to answer. He just rose and motioned his head in the direction of the doorway to get her out of there. Once they were gone, the assembly moved back to their regular places. Only Dmitri Borodkin remained by his side. "He'll try to kill you, Nicholai."

"I promised my mate. I will not break that promise."

Stefano called the room to order. "We have decided. Charles Rhys-Jones, you are hereby banished from the Nobility."

"Better that you should kill me now."

"Will you seek revenge?" Ariel Gold asked.

"With every breath in my body."

"We cannot afford to lose one more Noble, Charles. Even though you tried to murder my mate, I will not kill you. We face an even greater danger than your treachery. And you may get your wish sooner than you think."

Many in the crowd began to mutter. Nicholai could hear questions in the background.

"So you have said before," Stefano answered. "Now you must explain. You have accused the High Council of treason. That you must also explain."

Nicholai took a deep breath, the horror of what he'd seen showing clearly on his face.

"I have seen death and we must do something to save ourselves from it."

Chapter Eighteen

Standing before the mirror, he drew the mist back unto himself. Terrible in his beauty, the evil one smiled. Crystal eyes of ice tinged with blue, so cold even he shivered to look at them. Midnight black hair, the mark of their kind. Only his hair absorbed all the light around him. His aura was of the dead, due to all the souls he'd sucked into his body to feed off of until they were drained dry.

He was the antithesis of the Nobles, the dark one. Whereas their kind fed off light, he could not. Even the light of the moon hurt him beyond a thousand deaths. How he suffered through each passing day, the Sun always there, always painful. Each passing night, the moon, only bearable in its tiniest portion. Trapped in a frozen coffin. Century upon century without end. Always sensing them. The life inside them. He wanted, begged, *pleaded for escape from his icy prison.*

They would suffer the agonies of hell for his torture. Such joy to watch them die in bewilderment and fear. Oh, the sweet taste of fear. The after-dinner cordial they called their souls, sip by sip, vanquishing the goodness inside until naught was left but the shell.

His plan was working to perfection. He made sure no more births occurred. He made sure they would keep on destroying each other, piece by piece, bit by bit. Except for the one.

How had that happened? The woman had survived the change; therefore he'd used her as the catalyst to destroy another House. How had they created a child? While not a catastrophe, it was a definite setback. Certainly not part of the plan. But that was the sweet beauty of it all. Plans could change. Why not? He had all the time in the world. Why even his faithful puppy Morgan did not know he'd been used.

All leading to the ultimate prize, The Water. He would find the Water and he would destroy it. No new children. No hope of Change. They would grow old and die. One by one. Until only he remained.

****

Nicholai told his story in a detached monotone. He had to in order to separate himself from the horror he'd experienced.

"I need answers," he told them as he finished.

"I second," Dmitri Borodkin called out.

Could they have deceived us all along? Nicholai wondered.

Stefano sat without giving an iota of his feelings away. Han-Sing looked a bit uncomfortable. Ariel Gold sat with a tiny smile playing about her lips as if she'd already seen this moment. Used. She'd used him too. He'd become the catalyst. That she'd needed? For a moment he wondered if she ran the Council and not Stefano.

"Are you sure of what you encountered?" the man in his thoughts asked.

Nicholai shook his head. "I am not sure of anything. What I encountered scared me nearly to death. Isn't *that* enough to convince you?"

They put their heads together and whispered

amongst themselves for a moment. "Clear the room," Han-Sing ordered.

"We have the right to know what is going on," a voice called out from the back.

"I second."

Stefano motioned him forward to the dais. "The last thing we need is a panic."

Nicholai nodded. "I agree. But they need to know what is going on. I say they stay."

Dmitri had drawn forward just behind him. "I agree."

Stefano clearly did not like this decision, but Nicholai knew the time for secrets was over. "We will have order in this Hall. You will all return to your stations and wait until you are acknowledged before speaking. Charles Rhys-Jones and Gunner Manneheim, you will both be set outside this room never to return."

"No," Nicholai cried. "Have you heard nothing I've said? We need all the help we can get."

"I will not accept pity," Rhys-Jones countered.

"Then stay and fight as a warrior should, for if we do not stand together, we may all fall. What say you?" Nicholai cried out to the assembly.

A chorus of "ayes" reverberated through the room. "Now," Nicholai continued. "We need some answers."

Ariel Gold spoke, reciting in the dialect of The Nobility. "There were two and would always be two. One good. One evil. The Mother knew. The evil would destroy the good. She took the evil one away, never to be heard from again."

Nicholai frowned. "Always two?"

"Twins," Stefano replied.

"The Mother?" Dmitri asked.

"The one who made us all," Ariel answered. "You see, we began as humans." Ariel went on to tell the story of Mur and Og and the ancient ones.

The cave lay shrouded in mist. A chill ran up her spine as Mur gathered her things. She'd hidden them, piece by piece, so Og would not know her plans. She'd kept her mind blank, focusing only on the child she would never know.

She knew the legacy now, knew that there would always be twins born first within the clan. Always male children. And the blood within her child would create a new race.

Og's blood too, a tiny voice whispered to her.

He'd kept the stone for his own. He would never know that the very thing he craved would cause his destruction. The Water was power and, as the keeper of the Water, made him very powerful. But power begets jealousy and greed, opening the wounds in which to grow the seeds of dissention. With great good, so was there great evil.

I am sorry, she told the people, saying farewell to her home. I should never have touched the stone.

Heartbroken, Mur set out for the north. And her death. Not only did she have to destroy her child, she knew she could not stop the events already set in motion. But if, by her death, she could redeem the future, then she was willing to sacrifice herself gladly. Only she would never know the outcome. Who would be stronger? Who would be victorious? Good or evil?

"We have always just accepted that the Water existed," Nicholai commented.

Ariel answered. "Because we never wanted to accept that the evil one existed. But the story has been passed down from Council to Council."

Nicholai stared at the three people sitting on the dais then locked gazes with his mentor. "The evil one lives."

"From your story and other facts, we fear that it

is so."

"My God," Dmitri whispered. So did many others.

Nicholai began pacing in thought, playing the recent and the historical events over and over in his mind. "He has been playing with us. Setting House against House. He created Albert Manneheim just as he created Tara Pendragon."

"We believe so."

"You knew and yet you let The House of Pendragon be destroyed?" Nicholai raged.

"We forgot about the casket until it was too late. By then, what was done could not be undone."

"But you continued the farce. What about the innocents? The rest of the family?"

"The Council at that time had no idea who the traitor was. Pendragon could have planned the entire scheme himself. There was no way of knowing."

"And yet there was always the suspicion of the evil one."

"You accuse without cause, Valentin," Han-Sing answered. "We sense it then we do not. Not one Council could be sure it would awaken in their lifetime. We all prayed it never would."

"The evil one is as powerful as we were in the beginning."

"Perhaps, perhaps not. Maybe it made a mistake with Morgan," Nicholai retorted.

"And maybe it didn't," Stefano answered.

"Why now?" Dmitri asked, the question in Nicholai's mind as well.

Ariel Gold spoke first. "We believe the evil one has been buried in the ice until modern times. Perhaps global warming is at fault? Who can say? But the mischief it brings began only recently."

"Would we not have known, though?" Nicholai asked. "I mean, we are all connected, aren't we?"

"Yes. But the re-birth must have taken place slowly," she replied. "Rest assured, Nicholai. What we are dealing with is very powerful. I have the truest sense of him. That is why I am the first female to ever grace The High Council."

"And your point is?"

"That he has learned all manner of things and the more he learns, the more dangerous he becomes."

"So have I. I have learned that the people I have trusted, indeed, the very faith I built my life upon, was built on a lie." And in that moment he knew exactly how Tara had felt. Shame mixed with the bitter bile of betrayal in his mouth. "You would have sacrificed my House also if it would have kept this thing at bay."

"You were willing to make a bargain to save your mate and your child, Nicholai Valentin," Ariel Gold reminded him. "We made a similar bargain. You did what you thought you had to in order to save your family. We did what we thought we had to in order to save our race."

Fury boiled in his blood then he looked over at his friend Dmitri. Disgust marred his features, and those faces of many others around the room. There was no traitor in the High Council; the entire Council was traitor. Yet not traitor. Yet he read fear in many gazes as well.

"Then perhaps it is time to outfox the fox."

"Do you have a plan, Valentin?" Han-Sing asked.

"No, but so far we have been the puppets to his puppeteer. I would like to see this thing make a mistake. I want him to know he can be wrong and can be wrong more than once."

"This man, Morgan. Would he help us?" Stefan continued.

"I think so. But I do not believe he gave us the

case of his own accord. He is damaged enough to have gotten the suggestion from his master then thought the idea was his own." Nicholai paused a moment. "And yet I sensed no evil within him."

"Then perhaps we can use him and the casket to draw our adversary out." Stefano outlined his plan. They would return the casket using Charles Rhys-Jones as their ambassador. Nicholai would then become a spy. While not brilliant, it would probably be worth a try even though the plan might put Morgan at risk.

"At least let me speak with Tara first. It is her brother we are putting in danger."

The Assembly agreed. They would reconvene in two days. Until then, each and every one of them would not be getting much rest.

****

So beautiful, Nicholai thought, watching the woman in his bed sleep. So innocent, her hand curled under her chin. For a moment a picture formed, one of her as a child. The same pose but a teddy bear tucked tightly in the crook of her arm. How alone she must have felt back then. Then the picture transposed to what he imagined their children would look like. He vowed the babies would never know that kind of loneliness. Yet what if something happened to him, to both of them?

Shuddering, Nicholai shook his head. Tara must have felt his distress for she moaned and turned over onto her side to face him. A piece of her nightgown fell away, baring the milky globe of her breast to his gaze. As always he responded, only this time he was grateful for the distraction. He could not stop the emotions running through his mind.

Seeking additional distraction, Nicholai studied her. Wonderment filled his soul. Gone was the she-devil who graced his bed. Gone was the proud cynic who hid her feelings behind her razor sharp tongue.

Gone was the fierce yet loyal warrior who'd saved his life and would always remain by his side. What was left was a woman. His other half. His mate.

For a moment Nicholai wondered what he'd done to deserve such beauty. A woman like this should stand beside a king. She was a queen and in her presence, he felt like her humble servant. If he told her that, she'd look at him sideways then laugh. He was the prince, the champion; he'd just fought for her and restored her honor. Yet he knew he paled by comparison. She'd earned her stature the hard way, through life.

Now he was going to ask something even harder of her. And he didn't want to ask. He didn't want her to hurt any more. He wanted to protect her, cherish her—

"Nico?"

He moved to her bedside and sat down. He took both her hands in his, kissed both palms, then rubbed his cheeks against them. "You saved my life." The awe in his tone said what words could not. "I don't know how to—"

She placed a finger on his lips. "Mostly luck. I just happened to catch Rhys-Jones moving out of the corner of my eye." She stared at him, trying to read his thoughts. "You wouldn't let them kill him."

Her tone was more statement than question. "No."

She relaxed against the pillows. "That is my reward."

Funny, but he understood. This wasn't about Charles; she wanted to make sure he did the right thing. "I fear we will need every warrior who can fight before this ordeal is over."

"Then I was right."

"Yes." He went on to explain what happened at the Council meeting.

Her gaze grew sad and frightened. "Poor

Morgan. Trapped in his own innocence. I could feel his confusion. He didn't understand that he'd done wrong. Once he did, he didn't understand why this—I don't even know what to call it—made him do wrong. He was so lonely. I suppose he was trying to make amends with the casket."

Nicholai shook his head, hating to make her believe the worst. "No one can be sure, not even you. His actions might have been part of the master plot."

Her gaze grew even sadder and more frightened. "What are we going to do, Nico?" Her hand slid to her belly. His followed. "The child I carry now becomes even more important, doesn't it?"

He nodded. "We are not finished yet, love. Do not give up hope."

"Give up? Me? Never." She grinned then turned serious. "Do you remember when we first met? I called you Elrond. From *The Lord of the Rings*."

"I remember."

"Middle Earth was on the brink of destruction. The Dark Lord had put his plan into effect and grown strong; he seemed invincible. Yet one small Hobbit had the courage to change the course of history."

"With a little help."

"Yes," she agreed. "With a little help." She squeezed the hand resting on her belly. "He didn't want the responsibility, never asked for it, had no clue what he was getting himself into. Yet when he found out, he refused to give up. He did what was right, not for himself but for everyone else. Can we do any less?"

"No." Nicholai tried to remember the book, how he felt while reading the story. Funny, but he never felt the quest was hopeless. No matter how many times they seemed on the brink of failure. Was that the lesson she wanted him to learn? "Do you think you can convince Morgan to help us?"

She shook her head. "I'm not sure we should."

He frowned. "What do you mean?"

"We need to play the same game that's being played with us. But in reverse."

"That could backfire."

"True, but he would also be more realistic."

"And more unpredictable."

"I think we can work around that. My major concern is Rhys-Jones. I am not sure he'll cooperate. Better yet, he might try to turn traitor."

"The Council, I'm sure, is well aware of that possibility. I'm also certain they'll make sure he doesn't."

She didn't seem convinced. "He hates us, most of all you. He might just decide that bringing you down is worth destroying The Nobility."

Nicholai shook his head. "I don't think so. Turning traitor at this point wouldn't be worth the risk. The ancient one is too unpredictable. Besides, Charles has more to gain staying with us. He might just be able to restore his House. And you know how important *that* is to a Noble."

She chuckled. "Yes, I know."

Nicholai fell silent. His gaze traveled over her face. "How do you feel?" He still couldn't get over the awe he felt. That she had put herself in harm's way—to save him.

"A little sore but for the most part, fine."

"Your hand has healed already."

"So has my side. Sergei said the healing might be faster because of the baby."

"Then you must rest." He made to rise and a strong hand stopped him.

"Where do you think you're going?"

"To the couch. You need to get some more sleep."

She grinned, that little half-grin he loved so much. "Not on your life, buster."

"*Buster*?"

****

God, she loved to tease him. Tara was certain she'd never get enough of seeing *that I can't believe you just said that to me* look of his. Of course, she loved seeing that "I can't believe you just did that to me "look," either. So when she put his hand on her breast, she ended up getting both.

"Are you sure?"

She smiled. He was cute when he was uncertain. Almost boyish. But there was nothing boyish about the fire in his gaze. "As long as you're careful."

He cocked his head. "Hmm. I think that can be arranged."

He leaned down and grazed her lips with his. Just a graze, a light touch, no more. She shivered. "I won't break," she gasped.

He nuzzled her cheek, just a whisper of his hot breath across the shell of her ear. "*Nico*!"

"Yes, love?" Damn the man, he sounded way too innocent. She tried to capture his face with her hands and kiss him, but he moved away to leave a trail of incendiaries down her throat.

He was going to end up killing her with kindness. "Isn't there a law against torturing your wife?"

"Not that I know of," he replied, continuing in the same vein.

His hands held hers at her sides as he continued to work his way down to her breasts. Her nipples were harder than steel and begging for his touch and yet he kept circling, circling. "You know what they say about pay backs," she strangled out.

"Yes, dear." That was it. She was going to kill him. If he didn't end up killing her first.

Finally, his teeth closed over her nipple, worrying the appendage gently. She whimpered, finding that what she wanted most wasn't what she needed at all. Her hips twisted, searching for his.

She wanted hard and fast. He wouldn't let go of her hands, so she couldn't reach out for him. "Nico, please," she begged.

Lifting both hands over her head, he followed with her nightgown. Then he rose up on his knees and straddled her chest, careful not to put too much weight on her. She was still caught, her arms useless as his legs created an exquisite prison. He undid the buttons on his shirt with the practiced ease of stripper. How she longed to run her hands over his well-muscled chest. He knew.

Next he tarried with his belt, taking his time. Her mouth literally watered at the thought of him inside. Each notch of his zipper echoed through her brain. One inch closer, closer. She could smell his musky scent. Finally, his erection stood naked and proud before her. He leaned in allowing her to taste just the tip. His face tightened and she knew he wanted this just as much as she did.

Now the crown. She licked the salty fluid off and teased him with her tongue. He moaned as he pushed as far as he dared. She took all of his length, then he moved back, in and out, as he would in a few moments to her core.

All of a sudden, he rose. He lifted off the bed, shucked his clothes, and lay down next to her. Before she had a chance to put her arms down, he held them prisoner again in one hand. He didn't say a word, didn't have to. He merely touched her core. Tara moaned.

"You are so hot I might burn up in there."

"What a way to go," she choked out.

One finger, two. She was going to explode in a moment if he didn't stop. He seemed to know exactly when that was, for he stopped just long enough for her to calm down.

"Nico?" All right, she was pleading, beyond just begging.

"Yes, dear?"

"Nice is not going to cut it."

"Are you sure?"

Damn the man, why did he have to keep asking? "If you don't start doing something right now—"

"Mmm. Threats. I like threats. They turn me on."

His finger was working its way inside her again. She screamed. Epithets. Promises. All she wanted was more.

Still being careful of how he handled her, Nicholai turned her over onto her stomach. He lifted her hips, slid his thighs tight behind hers, and bent her over. She couldn't believe how he filled her as he slid inside. She was so hot, so wet; he kept sliding in and out without any friction at all.

"I want you," he whispered in her ear. "I want you to know all of me inside of you. Every inch."

She did. She could feel him. His tongue laved the skin of her back, he nipped at the back of her neck, his hands took her nipples and squeezed until shots of fire ran back to her core. Then he straightened. His hands held her hips and he began to thrust. Not thrust, not push, pound. This was what she'd wanted, craved.

"Nico, please," she begged.

He was ready. One hand slid off her hip and down to her nub. He massaged and teased and the world began to tilt. He was pounding into her for all he was worth when the universe imploded. This wasn't just reaching a crest, this was skydiving; she was screaming at the top of her lungs and didn't care. He was crying out just as loud. They fell together into the aftermath and Tara knew she'd just experienced the ultimate.

Still he was careful, although at this point it didn't matter. Instead of collapsing on top of her, he fell back on his haunches and rested against her back until he could breathe again. “Happy now?”

She turned on her side to lie next to him. “Not fair.”

“All’s fair in love.”

She grinned. “I’ll remember that.”

He captured her lips with his before finally coming up for air. He was growing against her side again.

“What was that about paybacks?”

Chapter Nineteen

Charles Rhys-Jones surveyed his domain with a grim sense of self-deprecation. The paint seemed to peel from the walls with too much enthusiasm. The rust stains in the plumbing added to the richness of the decor. But it was his sense of smell that took the brunt of these offensive surroundings. He couldn't get the scent of stale urine out of his nostrils no matter how hard he tried.

How the mighty have fallen.

A knock on the door drew him out of his self-pity, at least for the moment. He swung the portal wide, not surprised by the man standing before him. "Have you come to gloat?"

The look of distaste was evident on his enemy's face. Nicholai Valentin walked into the hotel room, his keen glance surveying his surroundings. "Nice digs."

A bitter burn of hatred ran through Charles' stomach. "Not much left when you have no home, no family, no identity—" He let his voice trail off. What was the use anyway? He'd made his bed. Now he had to lie in it.

"You can change that if you wish," his opponent replied.

Charles stared hard into a steel gray gaze thanking the heavens that he read no pity there. "I'm not into charity."

"Do you still believe death is the better alternative?"

"Yes," he whispered from the depths of his being.

"Then you are a fool. You know as well as I that your grandfather's schemes would never come to fruition."

"We are all bound by duty. And honor."

"Be honest. Just once. Did you really want to kill my mate?"

Charles laughed, with such bitterness even Valentin seemed taken aback. "If I'd wanted to kill her, she'd be dead right now."

"So would you."

Charles nodded. Fair was fair. An eye for an eye and all that. "So we understand one another."

"Not quite," Nicholai replied. He leveled his gaze at Charles trying to read him. Good luck. "There is something I really do not understand. How could you not know your strings were being pulled?"

"I knew."

"And you thought you could outsmart everyone, including a being more powerful than you and I combined?"

Charles still wondered if the whole plan had been worth the price. He slapped his forehead with the heel of his hand. "What was I thinking?"

God, he hated this. Nicholai Valentin was standing before him looking at him as if he were a child, a very petulant, recalcitrant, and not the least, dumb child. "I cannot imagine."

Charles spun away and threw himself onto the mattress that served as a bed. He crossed his hands behind his head, trying to look nonchalant. "You should have just killed me."

He could tell the decision had been a hard one. "I promised my mate I would not."

"A pity."

The next thing Charles knew, he was being lifted up by his shirtfront and Valentin's face was inches from his. "Let's get one thing straight. Only a promise keeps you alive."

"Do it," he begged.

His head hit the wall as he was thrown away. "Quit tempting me."

Charles rubbed the back of his head then settled back into the mattress again. "I think you've overstayed your welcome. Don't let the door hit you in the ass on the way out."

"I would like nothing better but I cannot."

With a frown, Charles wondered what the hell that meant. "All right, I admit it. I'm confused."

"The High Council."

That said a lot but not quite enough. "And your point is?"

"We need your help."

For one split second a surge of hope flowed through his body. Then he leaned back and roared with laughter. When he finally caught his breath, he noticed his enemy was not amused. "How's it feel, lackey boy?"

Nicholai grew rigid and Charles was amazed at the man's control. "Be very careful, Charles. Promises have a way of changing." Valentin crossed his arms over his chest and Charles knew the action was to keep them off him. "We need to know how the ancient one contacted you."

"You would." He crossed his legs and started playing with a piece of string hanging from a ragged pillowcase.

"This is not a game," Valentin bit out.

"Never said it was," Charles replied, dusting his hands off on his shirt. "Are we bargaining here?"

"Reinstatement. Nothing more. You are a proven traitor."

Charles shook his head. Although the bargain was fair he didn't like the taste a compromise left in his mouth. "More charity."

"No," Nicholai countered. "A chance at redemption."

"You're all dead anyway."

Nicholai shook his head. "Not yet, Charles. We know the why, just not the how."

"You've always been so smart. Be smart now."

"Because you walked in my shadow?"

That hurt. But only because he'd failed. "We're not children anymore."

"That is the first thing you have said that makes sense."

Charles sighed. "What do you need me to do?"

"Accept the mission first then I will explain. I do not want you to pull a Benedict Arnold on us."

So they really didn't have any trust left. Charles took a moment to self-assess. Was his pride worth a lifetime of loneliness? "I'll take your terms."

"Smart choice."

"Depends on your point of view. So tell me, what is it you need me to do?"

"Contact this thing."

That part wasn't hard to figure. "And?"

"Tell it you have defeated me and destroyed my House. Tell it the plan is working."

"What plan?"

"The one where you become dictator over the Nobility."

"Oh, yeah, right. That one."

"Return the casket."

"A nice gesture."

"Use what or whomever you have to. Even Morgan."

"And do—" All of a sudden a light bulb went on

in his head. "You don't know, do you? You have no idea what it wants. I'm your fishing expedition."

"That is correct."

He snorted in disbelief. "Good grief. My son, if I had one could do a better job—"

"Oh really?" Valentin asked, cutting him off. "This from the man smart enough to screw himself over completely?"

Damn, he had a point. "Yeah, well, we all make mistakes."

"No, not anymore. We cannot afford a mistake now. We need to know how this thing is going to accomplish whatever it is planning."

"Underestimating it might not be a good idea."

"Agreed. But it also might not be using the best judgment either. Revenge and hatred have a way of clouding one's sense of reason."

Boy, didn't he know that one well.

****

Tara unlocked the door to her townhouse. A surge of child-like delight ran through her as she threw it open. Stepping into the foyer, she twirled around several times, arms held wide. "It is soooo good to be home."

She slowed and came to a full stop as she caught the bemused frown on her husband's face. "Come on, Nico. I love your home. I just love mine better."

His bark of laughter made her realize that didn't quite come out right. To make amends, she took him by the hand and showed him her most favorite artifacts and collectibles. Then she picked up a small figurine. As she did, her sense of peace and security fled.

"I preferred your smile," Nicholai chided gently.

"I know," she replied, trying to recapture the mood.

"Every time you doubt, he wins."

"I know," she cried, slamming the piece down on

the table. For some unknown reason, the figurine didn't break. "I found that at the estate of an old woman. She was very rich and very alone. No heirs, no friends to give her prized possessions to, no one. Is this the legacy we're going to leave our child? Or her child? Or her child's child?"

"I do not understand."

"What happens when only one remains?"

In an instant, Tara found herself wrapped in his protective embrace. "Never give up hope," he whispered into her hair.

"I haven't. I just can't stand this cat and mouse game. I'm not subtle like you. I want this over and done with. Now."

"Fair enough. But something tells me that is not the only thorn in your side." He kissed her forehead then looked deep into her eyes. "Now tell me. What is really bothering you?"

"Jeri. That," she answered, pointing to the canvas bag he'd placed on the coffee table in her living room.

"She asked us to bring the casket, remember?"

"Yes." Tara paused. "What if I pushed her into making that decision?"

He tilted his head and threw her a look. "You? Push Jeri? Really."

"Arrgghh," she cried, pulling away. "Some day you're going to stop being so damned condescending."

"I really would prefer you to watch your language. Otherwise our sons are going to have some problems when they—"

"Daughters," Tara interrupted.

"Right. When they go to—"

"Shall I tell you which?" asked a voice from the hallway.

"By the way, the door was open."

"Jeri," Tara cried, as they both turned in the

direction of her voice. Tara ran to give her friend a hug.

"And spoil the surprise?" Nicholai answered, his tone droll. "Think of all the fights we have not had yet."

Jeri threw back her head and roared. "You know, Nicholai, I'm getting to like you more and more."

He bowed even though Jeri couldn't see. He knew Jeri could sense his action and Tara's eyes filled at his respect for her friend.

"Don't mind him," she said, swallowing her tears. "He's just a know-it-all Noble. And a conceited one at that."

"They go hand in hand, Tara," Jeri replied. "But you already know that."

"Ouch," she said, letting go.

Jeri hooked an arm with one of hers and started walking towards the table that held the casket. "I have one more duty to perform."

Tara stopped dead in her tracks. "Duty?"

"All right," her friend replied. "Call it destiny then."

"To regain your eyesight?"

Jeri simply chuckled. "There are times, child," she said, shaking her head. "If I'd wanted to do that, why would we be here now? I'd have done that when I had the casket the first time, no?"

Tara frowned. "OK, I get the 'duh.' But—"

"I could die?"

"Duhhhh," Tara answered with emphasis.

"Grow up, Tara. Didn't it occur to you that there's more at stake here than one old woman or her dreams?"

That stung. "Yes. No." She hesitated a moment. "I can't just stop loving you, can I?"

"Of course not." Jeri reached out to give her shoulder a hard, swift, squeeze. Then she let go and started walking towards the table again.

"You need not do this," Nicholai agreed.

"We all have our parts to play. This is mine."

Jeri sat down and Tara sat next to her. "I won't let you do this alone," she declared.

"Nor will I," Nicholai added, sitting on Jeri's other side.

Jeri smiled. How Tara loved to see that smile. "I was hoping you'd say that. Both of you. Because I'm going to need your help."

Although she knew Jeri couldn't see, her friend knew exactly where the casket was. Most blind people compensated for their loss by developing their other senses. Perhaps because of her gift, perhaps because of her skill, Jeri's senses were magnified many times greater than those of normal human beings. "I'm not sure why and it probably doesn't matter now, but I seem to have a handle on this thing. I realized that the first time I came in contact with the casket even though I only touched the bag it was wrapped in. There is a chance that I can connect with this whatever-you-want-to-call-it. Maybe get a sense of where it is hiding. Or not hiding, if you get my meaning."

"If you sense it," Nicholai warned. "It will be able to sense you."

"If it does," Tara continued. "You could, oh God, I don't even want to think of that possibility."

"I know," Jeri replied with a nod. "Give me thirty seconds. No more. Otherwise I might end up with too much feedback."

"What if this so-called feedback is only what it wants us to know?" Tara questioned.

"I might still be able to get a sense of where it is."

"That would mean we could still use Rhys-Jones as bait," Nicholai added.

"I don't like this at all," Tara stated for the

record, knowing full well her protest would go unheeded.

Jeri leaned her head into Tara's shoulder and put one arm around her back to give her a squeeze. "Thank you. But try to understand that we don't have much choice. Vulnerability is a state of mind."

Nicholai agreed. "This thing thinks it has us up against the ropes. We need a sucker punch. We need to make it realize we are not stupid and then we need to plant a seed of doubt. Once it thinks its plan has a flaw or a possible flaw—"

"So much for going on record," Tara grumbled. *Plan*, she thought. We don't even know if it has a plan. It just wants us all dead. "What do you need me to do?"

"As soon as I touch the casket, each of you must grab one of my wrists. Don't forget. Thirty seconds. If I can't break the contact, you'll have to do it for me."

"Jeri, I—" She reached out for her friend one more time.

"I know child. I love you too."

Nicholai peeled back the canvas. "Our people owe you a debt they will never be able to repay."

Jeri nodded. "Don't forget. Thirty seconds."

Tara watched as her friend took several deep breaths. Everything seemed to be moving in slow motion. "Here goes nothing." Then Jeri placed her palms on top of the casket.

****

Black is a state of mind. Jeri had lived with that all her life. Darkness was only the absence of light, not even an obstacle anymore. Because of her gift or in spite of it, she didn't know; her senses were magnified. She was able to sense the shape of things, feel their outline. She might not know a sidewalk from a patch of grass unless she was barefoot, but she knew a curb when she saw one. No pun intended, of course.

As soon as she touched the casket, two things occurred. A tingle ran up her arms as if she'd touched a live wire. That was to be expected. But the second frightened her. The darkness changed. All her life, the darkness had been simply an obstacle, a cloud or a curtain. Now the darkness felt dirty, oily, a substance she neither wanted to be near or touch.

Black is a color truly known only to the blind. After a time, black becomes a friend, a comfort, a part of the way things are. What greeted her now alienated her. Whatever she'd stepped into wanted to draw her in, absorb her, and make her dirty too.

Jeri remembered a prank some children played on her one day. She'd reached for something. Lord, she didn't even remember what now. As she put her hand down, her fingers touched something slimy, cold, and ugly. She never forgot that feeling of terror, of losing the rightness of her world, even after she found out it was only mushed up Jell-O. She knew it was a joke; she was never hurt, she felt no pain. Only the pain in her heart, the loss of integrity. That loss terrified her because it could happen again.

It was happening now.

Every fiber of her being wanted to withdraw. A pair of hands wouldn't let her. She'd known this would happen. She was just a chicken at heart.

Their nemesis knew it too.

Forewarned is forearmed, the saying goes. But that doesn't always assuage the fear. She'd seen pieces of this event and her terror only increased. So far there was only darkness. Yet the more she delved, the worse her fear became. Until she realized that *he was* the darkness.

A scream built in the back of her throat. What was she doing here? How could she have possibly thought she was a match for something this evil?

Jeri tried to steady herself. That was when she sensed she was not alone. She heard cries, the plaintive wails of those this thing had engulfed. Her heart broke for the souls of those it had destroyed. They were trapped.

So was she.

All of a sudden, Jeri knew what she had to do. This thing, this evil incarnate that had taken the form of a human man, was playing with her. She was his toy. He was going to lead her on, show her a glimmer of hope, acknowledge her relief and then slam the door in her face. Over and over again until no hope remained. This was what he fed off of, delighted in.

Not this time, Jack.

Jeri concentrated on the touch of her two friends. Tara's energy was brighter, faster, a bit like quicksilver. Nicholai's was steady, heavier, like a protective blanket or a net she could fall into if the time came.

She'd need them both before the ordeal was over.

Without thought, Jeri charged into the web he'd created. That seemed to startle him for she was able to cut a swath straight to what she realized was his inner sanctum.

He was terrible in his beauty. Unbearable to look at for his gaze tore into the depths of one's soul and never let go. For one instant, though, she reached out. He laughed, seemingly unperturbed, as if a child had protested his path. His face held an indulgent smile, but his eyes burned with the fire of revenge.

He lifted a hand to destroy her and Jeri quailed inside. She couldn't move. She'd failed in her quest. Then she felt another life force. Tiny, sweet, full of goodness and hope and innocence. The antithesis of darkness.

The baby.

He seemed as stunned as she was and that was her cue to get the hell out of there. She followed Tara's beacon, as she would have the light of Galadriel. She, too, had drawn the same parallels.

Back, back, she clawed her way to the very edge of its consciousness. In that moment when he let his guard down, she was able to flee to safety. She used Nicholai's essence as her net and jumped towards the light they both shared, still amazed at the turn of events.

Because of one tiny life not yet born, he'd betrayed himself. Jeri knew where he was and what he planned to do. At least enough for her to know how to fight him because plans could always be changed.

Jeri opened her eyes and *saw them*, saw the concerned faces of her friends staring down at her. She didn't have much time; her life force had been drained. "Geneva," she whispered. "The League of Nations."

Then the world went black.

Chapter Twenty

Nicholai watched his mate with growing concern. One moment she seemed bound and determined to wear a hole in the rug, the next, she would stop and stare out of the window at the lights on the bay. "Your behavior is not going to bring Jeri back to consciousness."

"Too bad."

Such spite. Still, he tried to commiserate. He'd grown up in a loving family, albeit a strict one. When he lost his parents he had Alexi and Sergei along with many others to lean on. Tara had never had a real family, at least not in the traditional sense. And now she seemed on the verge of losing not one, but two surrogate mothers.

"Here," he said, handing her a small snifter of brandy. "Drink this."

She turned from the window, stared at the glass, turned up her nose, and went back to staring out the window. Nicholai was at a complete loss as to how to deal with her.

"Do you refuse the drink because the liquor will serve no purpose or are you being deliberately rude?"

Silence. She wasn't even listening. About to repeat himself, Nicholai was interrupted by a question. "I'm pregnant," she mumbled.

"What?" He shook his head. "Woman, you have the ability to wring the very last ounce of patience out of me." She didn't answer and that got to him. He had no way to assuage his own feelings of helplessness. How the hell was he going to assuage hers? "I told you before. There is nothing you can do for her now."

"Not good enough."

As if a declaration can change fate. "Tara, we did our best. We brought her back from the brink. She has to do the rest on her own. And in her own time."

"I'll go talk to her again."

He shrugged. "As you wish."

She whirled, advancing on him, her gaze aflame. "How dare you be so condescending. She put her life on the line for you."

"No, Tara," he refuted gently. "She did it for *you*."

She stopped in front of him, her face frozen with hurt. "Bastard." She attacked, her anger and frustration lending strength to her blows. But Nicholai knew she needed a release. He took her punches without uttering a word all the while wishing he could do more. Then as he stood there, with the slow dawning of a man newly awakened, Nicholai realized the truth. He'd go to the very end of Hell, face every demon ever known, if she asked.

He loved her.

How he wanted to wipe away her pain. He wanted to right her world, and reunite her with her friend. Instead he waited for the fight to drain out of her. With her emotions spent, she leaned against him for comfort, and began to sob.

Nicholai lifted her into his arms. He walked over to the couch, sat down, and cradled her on his lap. His gentle rocking soothed them both.

"I'm sorry, Nico," she said at last.

"You need not apologize."

She swiped at her cheeks, as would a child, with the back of her hand. It was an honest action, not bound by the dictates of popular society. She didn't need to be chic. She blew them all away with her regal dignity. A dignity she'd earned just as she'd earned the right to her sorrow.

"Why do you put up with me?"

He let out a short bark of laughter. "Ask me an easy question."

She sighed and his heart ached. "You don't have to, you know."

He shook his head. "We are mates. We have gone beyond the handshake and kiss-on-the-cheek stage, don't you think?"

"Of course, it's just that I—"

"Ah, Tara love, I do understand. And I am not expecting you to reciprocate my feelings. But you have to know." He lifted her head off his shoulder to look deep into her eyes. "I love you. Beyond life. Beyond the Nobility. Beyond imagination. You. No one else. Not even our child."

She didn't answer right away. He didn't expect her to. "Tara," he continued. "Do not put words into your mouth that are not there. I believe you have a heart big enough to love, big enough to love a whole lot of people, even if you do not. You have an incredible passion."

She blushed. "There is that."

"That is not what I meant," he countered. "Not sex. A passion for life, a passion for whatever task lies at hand, a passion for the people you care about." He paused to nuzzle her cheek. "You just do not know how to trust in love. You have been hurt, abandoned, forced to fend for yourself for most of your life. I am not stupid, you know. I know a shield when I encounter one. Hell, I have built my own. But

I want you to remember one thing. I am here. I will always be here, with you, by your side, whenever you need me. I am your mate."

"Nico, I—I can't answer you."

"Shh," he told her. "What we have together, right here and right now, is more that I could ever have asked for. I have only one request."

"Anything."

"Never lie to me. I do not think I could stand that." He kissed her forehead. "And if you never say the words, I will not be disappointed. Can you understand that?"

She nodded. "Yes."

He put her head back against his shoulder. "Good, because right now, I need you. Your strength, your faith, all that you are." He held her for a long time. "Tomorrow we must meet the High Council."

"What are you going to tell them?"

"I do not know. I am not sure what Jeri was trying to tell us."

"That this entity, this destroyer, is in Geneva, Switzerland."

Nicholai chewed on that possibility one more time, as he had when he first heard Jeri's words. "I do not think so."

Tara leaned back to look at him with a quizzical frown. "Why not?"

"I am not sure." Strangely enough, he wasn't. Because he had to doubt this thing's every motive? The truth was hard to find when the foundation for seeking it was built on lies.

"Then go with your gut."

That wasn't him. But he was learning. And she was his teacher. "If I have to."

Her arms closed around his neck and that gave him comfort. "If it's any consolation, I've lived my entire life using my gut."

He hugged her back. "I know."

She didn't reply right away then asked, "That isn't going to help us with the High Council, though, is it?"

He shook his head. "I cannot simply go to them with a hunch. I'm afraid we are going to have to use Rhys-Jones."

"He'll turn on us."

Nicholai thought that one over once again. "I do not think so." Welcome to the wonderful world of trying to walk on quicksand. "But what if I am wrong?"

"Then we find another way."

Her words, no, her belief in him, filled the hole inside his stomach with hope. Where there was a will, there would be a way to win. He tucked her into his chest and held on for dear life.

"Do not ever leave me."

He could feel her shoulders shake with laughter as she answered, "Not even in your next lifetime."

****

The meeting with the High Council was short and to the point. Tara was glad for that. She wanted to get back home to take care of Jeri. The elder woman was resting easier but still had not awakened. She wondered, not for the thousandth time, if she should try to make contact again. Only, and this was the real kicker, her stomach wasn't talking to her.

"Charles Rhys-Jones," Stefano called out. "Do you understand the terms as they have been given? Reinstatement into the Nobility. Return to your House in five years provided—"

"I can come back alive," he answered.

"Yes," Stefano replied, his tone grave. "You will never again hold title, though."

Tara felt a shaft of pity for the man. She could see the pride ingrained in him. But everyone had to learn there was a consequence to their actions. Even she. For if she tried to contact Jeri, she could kill her friend.

"Here is the casket." Rhys-Jones stepped forward to accept the piece.

"Nicholai Valentin."

"Aye," her mate answered.

"You will be Rhys-Jones' contact."

Ariel Gold spoke. "He is somewhere nearby."

"In the city?" Nicholai asked.

"I'm not sure he could manage the night life in New York," she replied, her tone derisive. "Don't forget. He is our antithesis. We feed off the light. He feeds off the darkness. He is more powerful than we are, young though he is old, whereas our powers wane with every generation."

"But we have had centuries to acclimate ourselves to this world."

"And he has not," Stefano agreed. "Therefore, we must use these weaknesses against him, draw him out, meet him on our terms, not his." He looked at both men, his features grave. "On your shoulders rests the fate of the Nobility. We will aid you in every way we can. May your purpose and your hearts be true."

As they filed out of the hall, Charles Rhys-Jones stopped beside her. "You seem no worse for wear."

Tara couldn't believe her ears. Had she really felt sorry for this asshole? She caught his gaze, stunned by the arrogance she read there. As if he were daring her to punish him.

"Gee, I'm sorry," she sneered, "I tried to kill you." When he didn't respond, she continued. "Man, I really screwed up."

His chin lifted ever so slightly in answer. She hit her forehead with the heel of her hand. "What was I thinking?" Tara continued. "Your mate would have killed me in a heartbeat if I hadn't stopped him."

Tara paused expecting a reply. When she got

none, she got mad. "Oh, that's right. I didn't really want to hurt you. I just lost my head." She paused again. Only this time she did see a flicker of something cross his face. "You mean you forgive me? Why, I'm stunned by your generosity. After all, you weren't the only one I was trying to kill."

"Enough."

Tara spun around to see Nicholai coming towards her. "I was just getting started."

"I agree, Valentin," Rhys-Jones chimed in. "Let her go on. She's doing a fantastic job."

Nicholai shook his head. "By whatever twist of fate or happenstance, I do not know what to call this agreement. You are alive and we need your help. Do not press your luck."

Charles shrugged as if he couldn't care less. That got to her.

"I saved your life, brainiac. A simple thank you will do."

She got the surprise of her life when he answered, "Thank you."

Only the answer she received was drowning in bitterness. "You'd be hanging by your balls right now if I, no we, hadn't refused to take revenge."

The man shuddered but his words still mocked her. "Perish the thought."

"How dare you," she replied, her tone full of dignity. "You had options. You could have killed yourself if you'd wanted. *Seppuku* is a path of honor among the Japanese."

She caught a glimpse of his inner agony as he replied, "Too much of a coward."

Damn the man. Why did she feel sorry for him? "I have no mother, no father, no family because of you and yours."

"Neither do I."

She could go tit for tat all night. No one would win. At least he'd tasted a portion of her life.

Loneliness was a bitter pill. Outcast even worse. "I have only one person left and he barely knows who he is let alone who I am. So now I'm going to make you repay a portion of your debt."

Her nemesis looked at her with the first spark of hope she'd seen in his gaze. She wondered once again if she was going to hate herself in the morning for doing this. Then she thought of all the pain and suffering from the past. "I charge you with protecting my brother Morgan."

"What about him?" He pointed at Nicholai.

"That goes without saying. I want additional insurance."

Charles seemed to mull that over in his mind for a moment. "Go on."

"Morgan has no idea what this thing is, I'm almost positive of this. But even if he does, he has no grasp of the danger he's in. I know he can't comprehend what this thing will do to us all, not even what it can do to himself. Or you, for that matter."

Hmm, she thought. Not so sure of yourself now, are you? "There's going to come a time, Charles Rhys-Jones, when you're going to have to put another life above your own. Make it my brother's and the feud ends this second."

"Tara," Nicholai warned. "Once a snake, always a snake."

Charles bowed to her mate. "Thank you for your belief in my integrity."

That was the question now, wasn't it, she thought? Did Charles have any left?

"It's a deal," he replied. He held out his hand.

Tara looked at the appendage, looked him straight in the eye, turned on her heel and left the room

****

The silence between them had turned deadly

hours ago, but Nicholai dared not speak. Not yet. Aside from trying to figure out where they were going, he also wanted to try to figure out his new ally. Why did it have to be Charles Rhys-Jones, of all people, who knew where this thing was?

North. Always North. A flight to Boston and now this interminable car ride. They'd crossed into Maine an hour ago. The forest continued to get thicker, deeper, and the night only got darker. Nicholai guessed that was the point. In the middle of absolutely nowhere, Rhys-Jones finally stopped the car.

They'd come to the end of a very rough dirt track, not even something he would call a road. Nicholai pulled his coat closer to his neck after a gust of chill air went down his back. But his senses? Even the hairs on his arms would pass inspection, let alone the ones on the back of his neck. Their nemesis had been here and could still be nearby.

He tapped on Charles' shoulder. Using hand signals, he motioned to the tall bank of trees in front of them. Charles nodded then gave the signal to be quiet. As if he didn't get that.

What Nicholai didn't expect was the panorama that panned out in front of him as they made their way through the trees. The forest was simply a cover for as they broke through its edge, they ran into a solid wall of rock. Large, not quite a mountain, but not what he could call a hill either.

Not even the most discerning Noble, knowing what he was looking for, would have found the entrance. But as Charles made his way along the rock face, he simply disappeared. So did Nicholai as he followed.

They were standing in a cave, though it wasn't simply a cave that was for sure. More like a tunnel. Water dripped down the rock walls, the sound nearly deafening in the eerie silence. A fog swirled around their feet, much like the one he'd encountered at the house. He jerked his head around at the sound of something slithering across the dirt floor.

Demon-made, Nicholai thought. The area they were standing in stank just like the house in New Jersey—of malice aforethought.

How were they ever going to defeat this thing? he asked himself.

In the false darkness, Nicholai's courage fled. The previous encounter had left him scarred and feeling terribly alone. Their enemy was smart in that respect; it knew one's weakness and expounded on it.

Nicholai drew in a deep breath to regain his determination. That was when he realized the twin was gone, not long gone though, by the stench of its evil. Had Charles planned it this way? The idea made sense since the two of them were no match against its power. Besides, they wanted to catch Morgan alone, perhaps learn something of its intent—

"Ahhhhh!" came a banshee-like scream.

Nicholai barely had time to get himself out of the way in time. *Morgan*. He caught a glimmer of something in the false darkness. A knife? His second thought was that Morgan went after him, not Charles. Did that mean Charles was playing both sides?

The man in his thoughts stepped out of the way and stood by watching. Nicholai glared at him but wasn't sure if Charles could see in the dank darkness. Even with his exceptional senses, Nicholai could only make out shapes.

Morgan tried again. Nicholai could only defend against the attacks by pushing the man away as he charged and blocking the blows with his arms. He dared not hurt the man or face his mate's wrath.

"A little help would be greatly appreciated," he

hissed through clenched teeth as the knife just missed again.

Charles' muted chuckle sounded eerie in the dead darkness. "You're doing a fine job."

"I do not want to hurt him."

"Can't say the same about him, though, can you?"

"You made a promise."

"I'll keep it. In my own good time."

Nicholai growled. When he was done with his first problem, Rhys-Jones was going to taste his fist. Several times. Morgan charged again and Nicholai took a guess as to where he was. He stuck his leg out and the man went down with a grunt of pain. Nicholai couldn't be sure but he hoped the knife fell from Morgan's grasp. He charged, lifting the man by the shirt collar so his feet no longer touched the floor. Morgan struggled mightily, but to no avail. Nicholai was too strong for him.

Once Nicholai had Morgan's upper body locked in his arms and under control, Charles saw fit to help. Charles approached and Morgan stopped struggling as if he sensed a friend.

"It's all right, Morgan. We won't hurt you," Nicholai whispered in his ear.

The next thing he knew, Charles was doubled over and moaning in pain. He almost laughed as he realized that Morgan's leg had shot out with a ferocious kick, catching Charles right in the balls. Funny how fate had a way of evening the score.

Charles was none too pleased as they tied Tara's brother's hands and legs. "Little bastard," he muttered.

"Take it easy, *Chuck*," Nicholai replied, laughter still riding his tone. God knew how Charles hated the shortening of his name. "He did not mean it."

"Bullshit."

Now for the sixty-four thousand dollar question.

"What do we do now? You've been here before."

"Only this far. And not for more than a minute or two."

That made sense. He decided to try Morgan first. He leaned the man up against the wall of the cave so he could sit up.

"Morgan? Do you recognize me? Tara? Nicholai? I am your sister's mate."

Nicholai wasn't sure if they should turn on a flashlight, but he was tired of not being able to see. "Now you know why I stopped at that Home Depot."

The extra heavy-duty flashlight barely cut through the dense fog.

"Morgan," Charles said, kneeling down next to the man. "I've brought the casket back. For the Master."

Morgan nodded then struggled against his bonds. "Need casket. Hurry."

Nicholai looked over at Charles. The man shrugged. "Untie his wrists. But only his wrists." He grinned as Charles threw him a look.

Morgan twisted over onto his stomach and began crawling towards the casket. "Morgan, wait. I'll bring it to you."

Charles walked over to where they'd placed the box and picked it up. Nicholai lifted Morgan up and leaned him back against the wall of the cave. He still didn't want to let go of the man's legs. Not just yet. Even though the first time was fun to watch.

Once Charles placed the casket on Morgan's lap, he quieted. He stroked the burlap as a human would stroke a pet, over and over again.

"Now what do we do?" Nicholai asked.

"We wait."

Nicholai wasn't sure how Charles knew, but after a short while, Morgan began to unwrap the burlap. When he touched the wood, Morgan made the act a caress, just his fingertips at first. Like a lover he stroked the wood, over and over again, until finally he placed both palms against the casket.

Even in the dim swirling light, Morgan's countenance was one to behold. Beatific. He portrayed the face of a man in the throes of ecstasy.

Nicholai looked at Charles who stared right back at him. They were both at a loss until Morgan began to speak. "You must hurry. The Master approaches. He senses you here, will know you've been here."

Nicholai couldn't believe his ears. Morgan's voice had deepened. His words were clear, his thoughts coherent. "I have done this before, brother. But each time leaves me weaker in the mind. And the effects do not last as long anymore."

"I am sorry, Morgan. But I must ask. What does he want?"

"You know the answer to that already."

"How, then? How does he want to destroy us?"

"I do not know."

"Do you have any sense of where he goes next?"

"If I probe, he will know who I really am."

"Can you tell us anything?"

Already, Nicholai could see Morgan was fading. "I…am…"

"Tara loves you, Morgan."

He nodded. "Life…life…life…"

Chapter Twenty-one

They gathered in secret at the home of Ariel Gold. The muted opulence seemed superfluous now. What they needed were decisions. Stefano, Han-Sing, Nicholai, Tara, and Charles Rhys-Jones. Sergei remained at Tara's house with Jeri who still walked paths unknown.

For the first time since Tara had met him, Nicholai looked unkempt. Each time she observed her mate, her heart went out to him. He behaved so very unlike himself, almost on the verge of defeat. He continued to berate himself for leaving Morgan behind to face the consequences alone. He had to know there'd been no other choice. She'd only told him so a hundred times.

Her hand reached for his and she squeezed. He looked up, gave her a weak smile, then went back to brooding. "Is there nothing else you can tell us?" Ariel Gold asked Nicholai. He shook his head.

"And you, Charles?"

"I did what you asked," Rhys-Jones replied.

"Could have cared less," Nicholai muttered.

"Did you expect me to stay?" Charles shot back.

"I expected you to take your job seriously," Nicholai countered.

"Enough!" Stefano roared. "This bickering gets us nowhere." He turned and the Triad, as Tara liked to call the members of the High Council, whispered to each other. Then Stefano turned back. "Charles Rhys-Jones, you are hereby banished by the Nobility until five years pass, as decreed."

The man laughed. "If there is a Nobility when the five years have passed." He sobered giving them all a knowing nod. "I put your odds at, oh I don't know, a hundred to one."

"Why not a thousand," Tara shot back, his attitude chafing her. "Or ten thousand?"

She watched Charles rub his chin as if to make them believe he was deep in thought. But Tara knew better. He was playing with them all. Still a game, eh, *Chuck*, she thought.

"I honestly don't know, except you may have something to do with it," Rhys-Jones said.

"Me?" That caught her by surprise. "What do you mean?"

He bowed, giving her an enigmatic smile. "You are one hell of a woman."

"What does that mean?" she called out, but Charles simply continued walking out of the room. "Hey, wait a minute. You can't just let him go." She looked around to the others. "Get him back. He meant something. I know he did. Make him explain." She looked at her mate but he simply shrugged and retreated inside himself again.

Ariel Gold sighed. "You are reading too much into his words, child."

Tara lifted her chin several notches. "I am not a child. I've survived by existing on my instincts. He meant something by that."

"All right, then, what?" Han-Sing challenged.

"I—I'm not sure." She paused. "Yet."

Stefano held up his hand for silence. "Keep thinking," he told her. "In the meantime, we must concentrate on what transpired in this cave, as you call it."

"More like a tunnel," her mate answered.

"You keep saying," Stefano began, almost thinking out loud. "That this man, Morgan, if he is to be trusted—"

"He's my brother."

"And damaged," Stefano replied.

"Yes," she answered, the truth a wound that would always hurt her.

"Morgan kept repeating one word and only this one word. Life. Over and over again. Is this correct?"

"Aye," Nicholai responded.

"I wonder why."

Tara did too. "The obvious answer is that we represent the antithesis and this thing wants to destroy us."

Her answer seemed to spark something in Ariel Gold. "Us?" she questioned, looking directly at Tara.

Tara clutched her belly. *Her baby, babies?* The thought made her blood run cold. "Oh, no. That's impossible."

"Think this out for a moment," Han-Sing urged. As she did her gaze caught Nicholai's. The truth was there for her to see. Now she knew why he seems so—decimated. "You have to admit it makes sense."

"We can't rule out any possibility," Ariel added, her tone gentle. "Your babies will be the first True Nobles conceived in this generation."

"No. No. And no," she repeated, as if repeating the word would make it a fact.

"Tara, love," Nicholai whispered as he came to her. "Have faith."

Where's yours? She wanted to ask. But she couldn't add to his pain. "I refuse to believe—"

"Refusal gets us nowhere!" her mate exploded. "She needs to be protected at all cost."

The Triad nodded in agreement. "I open my

home to both of you," Ariel finally said.

"My sense of him is greatest, so you can both think of me as an early warning system, if you like." Her smile didn't quite meet her eyes but Tara hadn't expected it to do so. "He will not look for you here, at least not right away. That will give us time to make safer arrangements."

Each of them knew that those would be futile in the end also but no one spoke their thoughts out loud.

"Are we agreed?" Stefano asked.

"I thank you, Ariel Gold, for your hospitality," Nicholai replied.

Tara nodded in agreement. "Yes. Thank you."

"Many of our youth," Stefano added, "if you can call them that, wish to be of service. I cannot say I blame them. They will provide round—the-clock protection for what it's worth."

"My respect and gratitude," Tara answered.

"Mine also," Nicholai agreed.

"Then we will continue to work on finding answers," the elder man continued. He rose and Han-Sing rose also. They accompanied both men to the foyer where they bid them good evening.

After they'd left, Ariel offered them both a drink. Tara accepted a half glass of wine, her first since becoming pregnant. Normally she wouldn't, but under the circumstances she felt the need.

"My cook is excellent. I hope you both have at least a small appetite," Ariel said, interrupting her thoughts.

Nicholai laughed. Swinging around, Tara shot him a look.

"Nico?"

He came over to her and gave her a light kiss on the lips. He seemed normal, himself. "I am sorry, love. Ariel and I thought it best that Stefano and Han-Sing think I am greatly disturbed by recent events."

More intrigue? God, she hated games within games. "Why?"

"Two reasons, actually," Ariel replied. "One is that Nicholai has been relied on too heavily these past few days. We both thought it would be better if he were free to move about without the direction of the Council."

That made sense. "And the second?"

"Neither of us," Nicholai told her, "is certain of anyone anymore."

"That's just great!" she exploded. "So why should I trust you?" she asked the elder woman.

"You shouldn't."

Now she really felt comfortable.

"Tara, you must trust yourself. Do you really believe I would do anything to harm you or the babe? We simply can't be too careful," Nicholai said.

"Then you both think this thing is really after the children."

Her mate nodded, his visage grave. "But only in addition to, if you get my meaning."

"Not really."

"Do not underestimate our opponent, my dear," Ariel answered. "Your pregnancy was not part of his original plan and will have to be dealt with. But you and the babe are not the primary targets."

"Then why did you make Stefano and Han-Sing believe I was?"

"To buy more time. To try to figure out his master plan."

"That's easy," she replied. "Our annihilation."

"Yes," Ariel agreed. "But how?"

The elder woman's butler took that moment to interrupt and announce dinner was served. Surprised, Tara found she was hungry. Even Nicholai was hungry, matching her course for course.

"My cook will be well pleased. I don't entertain often enough for him. Nor do my guests take such pleasure in their food."

After dinner, Ariel and Nicholai each had a brandy and they all gathered in front of a huge fireplace. Tara declined a libation and wondered how such a wonderful evening could occur under such difficult circumstances.

"Take pleasure in the small things in life, Tara," Ariel told her as if reading her mind.

"I'm trying."

Nicholai reclined on the couch next to her and gave her hand a squeeze of encouragement. Just as she had for him. Deciding to get comfortable, she slid down and sat on the rug between his knees. His hand stroked her hair. The rug was a soft cushion beneath her. The fire a warm blanket to cover her. Mesmerized by the flames, Tara felt her mind wander. Something she'd done often as a child, and she had stacks of washed dishes to prove it.

The light of the fire reminded her of the Sun and her body's constant need to feed. The babies, she thought, her heart overflowing. She basked in the glow of the fire and her thoughts until she noticed that the picture before her eyes had darkened. Thinking nothing unusual, she assumed she was falling asleep.

But this was no ordinary darkness. The mass swirled and shifted, unsettled, doubt gnawing always at his mind. Somehow she'd connected with their enemy.

Where was her terror? Why was she not afraid? At first, she didn't understand. Then she realized she hadn't connected with this thing but rather had stepped into his dream.

He was searching for her that was plain to see. And if he sensed her, he would find her, dream or no dream. She needed to escape. Now. Before it was too late.

In her haste to claw her way out of the darkness, Tara almost missed the punch line. She slowed down for a moment and concentrated. The baby, babies? A question to be answered later on. Then what?

No sense pressing your luck, she told herself. Better to withdraw while still intact. As she did, a picture formed in front of her eyes. Stunned by its incredible beauty, she almost stopped again. *The Chalice.*

The silver metal radiated light and intense power. Inlaid lettering in their ancient tongue reiterated their most powerful words, True Blood to True Blood. A sword, point down, formed the figure of a cross. The handle bore the richness of the time in which it was wrought. Right and Might. A feeling of goodness and well-being flooded her. She could almost taste the Water of Change, but more than that, she realized what the Water of Change meant, not only to the Nobility, but also to all who inhabited the Earth.

All of a sudden, Tara knew exactly what was going to happen.

****

Her hand held his with all the power of the gods. Pain ripped through his arm. He would have laughed had his flesh not hurt so badly. He cried out but dared not move. Whatever was happening, he knew he could not interrupt.

Ariel Gold sat on the edge of her chair, her gaze too intense. He looked at her and begged for release. She gave him a quick, sharp, shake of her head. Whatever was occurring had to happen in its own time and he had to do his part.

Tara was not in this realm that was for sure. Where she was, he dreaded to think. All along Ariel had told him she was the key that was why he trusted her. He thought so too. There'd been too much coincidence in all the events leading up to this moment. Only the pregnancy had been unplanned. And his love for her.

He used that love to give her strength. His love for her worked for she broke her grip and pitched forward. He caught her, lifted her into his arms, rose, and placed her on the couch. Terrified that she'd tried to take on the creature by herself, Nicholai reached out to make contact with her.

"Don't," Ariel cried, placing a hand on his shoulder and whirling him around. "She has to come out of this by herself."

Agonized, he didn't know what to do. "Look at her face, Valentin. Does she look as though she's seen the devil?"

No, he thought to himself. There was even a smile on her face. An "I know something you don't know" smile. Instead, he did what he always wanted to do—he kissed her.

She stirred and with hope filling his heart, he kissed her again. He started when her hands looped around his head to keep him there. "Tara?" he asked, breaking off.

She let go, took a deep breath, exhaled and whispered, "Umm. Care for a rematch?"

Nicholai wasn't sure if he wanted to hug her or beat her. "Later," he growled. "Are you all right? Did he hurt you? Did you touch him?"

"Easy, Nico," she interrupted. "I'm fine."

"But—"

She smiled and her smile radiated confidence. "We're going to be OK. I promise. I'm just so tired. I need a few moments to rest."

She closed her eyes and Nicholai nearly screamed in frustration. He caught his hostess' gaze and she seemed ready to pounce. Only extreme will power held them both back.

"All in good time, Valentin. I believe she has the answers that we need. But now she must rest." The woman turned and took a healthy draught of her drink. "Take her to the guest room. When she awakens we will have what we desire. A few hours won't make that much difference."

He nodded but didn't agree. Still, he had a mate to care for. And a child. More than one. That put his needs at the bottom of the list. "I will call you when she is ready."

Placing her on the bed, Nicholai debated whether or not to lie down with her, or sit in a chair next to the bed. He opted for pacing first, his gaze constantly returning to his mate. What did she know, he wondered? Why did she seem so confident?

"Damn," he muttered, not knowing what to do with himself.

He sat down only to rise moments later. No help. Perhaps touching her, sharing himself with her, would help. As soon as he tucked her next to his body he knew he'd made the right decision. He could only hope she did the same.

Time passed slowly, the minutes dragging like hours. He even dozed for a few moments, the stress of the last few days finally catching up with him. He awoke to the shaking of her shoulders. *Laughter? At a time like this?* "What is so funny?"

"Hmm. Testy. Not a good sign."

He was in no mood for her teasing. "Sign? For what?"

She wiggled her derriere up against his groin. OK. So he had some nerve. Could he help it if he had no control? She was the culprit here, not him. "Farthest thing from my mind."

"Ha!" she cried.

"I am not kidding," he protested.

She was laughing again. The entire bed was shaking now as she tried to hold it inside.

"Tell that to him," she answered.

"Tara—"

"All right," she relented, turning over to face him. "I'll behave. But an hour or two probably won't make a difference."

What? She had to be kidding. "You are joking, right?" Only he wasn't amused. "The fate of the entire Nobility rests on a razor's edge and you say time will not make a difference?"

"That's right."

Totally bewildered, Nicholai asked, "Tell me what happened." Maybe her answer might shed some light on her behavior.

She shuddered. "I'd rather not."

"Then tell me what you know."

"I'd rather wait for Ariel and the Council."

Exasperated, he leaned back so he could look her right in the eyes. "Is there something you would rather do?"

"I thought you'd never ask." The next thing he knew, her lips were planted firmly on his.

He responded. God knew he was only capable of so much will power. But his mind wouldn't let him go. He broke away, gasping for breath. "Tara, I—"

She smiled, her smile the same as before—impish, confident, serene. "Morgan was right."

He only thought he was confused before. "I do not understand."

"Life, Nicholai. Life. Don't you see?"

"No, love. I am sorry. I do not."

Patiently, as if teaching a child, she explained. "Our nemesis is our antithesis. We feed off light. He feeds off darkness. We are alive. He wants us dead. Each time we give in, each time we allow the evil inside us to get out, we give him fuel. That's why he set House against House. Death is only the culmination. Think of all the nasty, juicy tidbits he fed off while my family and others were being destroyed."

Nicholai didn't answer right away because a light bulb just went off inside his head.

"The Nobility has been going downhill, for lack of a better word, for a long time," she continued.

"Yes."

"Appetizers for the main course."

Nicholai thought about that for a long moment. The Nobility at its best was argumentative, distrustful, and selfish. Not exactly a model race. Now add a natural arrogance because of their physical and mental superiority— "I am not one to believe in God, though I know you do. It would seem he has decided to take us down a peg or two."

"I suppose," she answered. "Or maybe this is his way of giving us a wake-up call." Her fingers trailed down his face, her touch gentle, full of hope, full of love. "No matter how you want to describe the reason, we have to stop giving this thing what he wants."

"How?"

She chuckled. "I thought you'd never ask," came her repeated reply.

"Making love?"

"No, Nico, not just making love. Making life. Celebrating life. How do we recreate life? Through the most intimate, most incredible act. Think of the power we hold."

"But we are only one couple, one set of mates."

"And there are those without mates and we all can't go around trying to multiply like bunnies," she answered. "I get the message. But the power of goodness exists everywhere and can be reinforced in a hundred million ways. Making love just happens to be the most powerful weapon we have at the moment."

Bending down to press his lips against hers he muttered, "Who am I to argue?"

However, Tara put her finger on them before he could start.

She shook her head and pressed him onto his back on the bed with her hands. She undid the buttons on his shirt with the leisure of a woman who had all the time in the world. His rock hard nipples were the end result. As her fingers caressed his skin, the fine hairs on his chest stood at attentions awaiting her command. She undid the buckle of his belt with practiced ease, removed his pants, and finally the last barrier until he lay naked before her.

Was this what she wanted? His hands gripped the bed covers as his mouth watered to taste hers. He was vulnerable, his anatomy standing stiff and straight, begging for her touch.

Thank God she needed him as much as he needed her. He didn't really see her clothes follow his. All he knew was that the flesh of one of her breasts required oral attention and that her warm moist heat engulfed his erection.

Not once did he take. He gave and gave. She rode him, controlling the pace. He thrust and thrust, holding back until she built for a second time. Then he unleashed his need. And as he reached the pinnacle, as they both cried out in ecstasy together, he understood exactly what she meant.

"I think we need to save our race more often, love," he quipped as his heartbeat finally returned to normal.

She laughed and Nicholai couldn't believe how wonderful the sound was. "That's a lot of saving, Nico. Sure you're up to the task?"

"This is one time when 'try, try again' will become my motto."

"Each and every one a valiant effort?"

"Always," he answered, his tone reverent.

She hugged him and they both rose. So beautiful, he marveled. She turned and he saw the already, very slight rounding of her belly. He couldn't help himself as he walked up behind her and covered their child with his hands.

"Yes, Nico, that's what I meant. Life, love, joy. Happiness, sharing, caring. All the things he is not."

"Then we must teach our people." He kissed the back of her neck and realized how much *he* had changed. "If I can learn, so can they."

They took a quick shower, dressed, and walked back out into Ariel's living room. Nicholai was surprised to see Stefano had returned. "Where is Han-Sing?"

"We were unable to reach him," his mentor answered.

Nicholai lifted an eyebrow. Deliberate? He might never know. "I see."

"I am well enough to answer your questions now," his mate told the others. "I seem to have been able to step into his dream."

Ariel and Stefano nodded. Her words made sense. "We are all connected," Ariel answered. "But I am also confused. When you collapsed, I sensed fear in him for the first time."

"That is because I know what he is planning to do."

Nicholai reached out and took hold of her hand in a gesture of comfort. What he got was a picture of what she saw. Amazed, he couldn't even speak. There were legends about its beauty, but the Chalice was beyond the stuff of legends.

"We know that our nemesis is planning to destroy us but we don't know how. Now I do and the answer is so simple, I can't believe we didn't see it," Tara continued. "No new births, no True Nobles. Taint the Water of Change, make the Water of Life as evil as itself, totally untouchable, and the Nobility dies. Not all together, not all at once. Slowly, generation upon generation. Just as this thing's soul died ever so slowly under the ice."

"Then we would become human again," Stefano replied.

"True. And you're thinking, well, we'd still be alive, right?"

"Yes," he nodded.

"Think again," she replied. "The human race is next."

Chapter Twenty-two

The Heads of the Houses had been summoned. Not all could get to the hall in time for the meeting. Those that were assembled looked grave, even a bit frightened as they listened to Stefano speak.

Tara knew they would rise to the occasion so to speak but would they work together? Even now, in the face of this kind of danger, some glared at others, always watching, always waiting for treachery. Finally, she could stand no more.

"Listen to me, all of you," she cried. "You are falling right into his trap. Generation upon generation, feeding him with mistrust, envy, hatred. Don't you understand?"

Nicholai, sensing her frustration, continued. "If you will not listen to my mate, then listen to me. There is only one way to face this enemy and that is together. We must become a team. We must join forces to fight an enemy too powerful for one House to stand up to. If we do not, we doom our race to a very ugly demise."

Most nodded, too many didn't. Tara wanted to rail and cry, anything to get them to understand.

"The child, children, I carry, they're a mistake as far as he is concerned. I should never have conceived. Do you wish to see my children dead before they even have a chance to live? Think of your people. Think of your children's children's children. Who among you wishes their House to be the last? Think of the loneliness. Think of having to watch all those before you die and not be reborn. Simple, you say? We'll simply become human? Before our race has a chance to mingle with the humans enough to become human, he will destroy us. I have seen his plan." With all the strength she had, Tara planted the picture of what she'd seen in all their minds.

No one spoke. At first, no one even looked at her. Then Noble by Noble, House by House, each man straightened his shoulders, stood erect, wrapped their pride around them like a shield until they all made their choice.

"I will die fighting!" one cried.

"I am with you," cried another, until a chorus of voices rang in agreement.

Tara took a deep breath. Nicholai stared at her, his concern plain to read. "I need to sit down."

He guided her over to the edge of the dais away from the crowd. "Are you sure you are all right?"

She nodded. Then she watched as they tried to work out a plan. "We must protect the Chalice at all cost," Dmitri Borodkin told them.

"The Chalice is hidden. If we move to protect it, we'll lead our enemy right to the hiding place," Stefano replied.

"Our enemy is not stupid," Ariel countered. "He senses the Water is nearby, knows we meet here, watches us all. Sooner than later the secret will no longer be secret."

As the debate raged, Tara watched. Something didn't quite ring true. "Nico?"

He turned to her. "Yes, love?"

She shook her head. "They're not telling the

truth. Look at Ariel and Stefano. They're frightened."

He nodded in agreement. "Do you believe Han-Sing has gone traitor?"

She thought long and hard. "I'm not sure. His attitude was always belligerent and he seemed high strung, but not a traitor."

"OK. Then what do you think?" He stopped. "Han-Sing has always been the most emotional, wouldn't you say even nervous, of the three?"

"Yeah," she agreed, reading his thoughts. "What better way to hide a secret than to only have one member of the Council keep it?"

"And if something happens to that person?"

"They'd have to have some sort of a backup plan, right? Directions that can only be opened in an emergency."

"That makes the rest of this make sense. Han-Sing knows where the Chalice is and he's running for his life right now. Or he's following a pre-set backup plan."

"Then we have to find out where he is."

"Yes."

As they sat in silence, the conversation in the hall filtered into her brain.

"We are agreed, then," Stefano called out. "We surround the United Nations with a full contingent of the Nobility. Twenty-four hours a day."

"The United Nations? Does that make sense to you?"

"No. Not unless this is some sort of decoy." He paused for a moment then bent down over her. "Double over as if you're in pain." She was about to protest when he gave her a sharp shake of his head. "Clutch your belly like you're having cramps. Cry out."

She looked him straight in the eye, a thousand questions on the tip of her tongue.

"Trust me," he continued.

She did with every fiber of her being. She even collapsed to make it look better.

Dmitri Borodkin was by them in an instant. "Nicholai? Tara? What happened?"

What a superb actor, she thought. Even she believed him for a moment.

"I do not know. I must get her to Sergei. Our enemy may be trying to rid her of the children. I will join you all as soon as I can."

Dmitri led them out to the car, helping Nicholai carry her.

"Go with God, Tara," Dmitri told her as he and Nicholai tucked her into the back seat. Touched, she reached up and gave him a quick kiss on the cheek. Then she doubled over and moaned again.

Nicholai jumped behind the steering wheel in seconds flat. He didn't stop the car until they were miles and miles away. "You can get up now."

"Phew," she said. "Thank goodness. I was starting to get car sick."

"At a time like this?"

Men, she thought. Someday, somehow, they were going to learn the meaning of pregnancy. "You go walking around with a baby, babies, in your belly and see how you feel," she groused.

He gave her a grin. "No, thanks."

"Come on up here with me. We can talk while we drive."

She did and they started back down the highway towards New York City. She watched the trees fly by, almost becoming mesmerized by them, and thoughts of Jeri simply popped into her head. "Nicholai, stop the car. Please. This instant. We're going the wrong way."

He slammed on the brakes, the car squealing to a stop. "What are you talking about?"

"They're using the United Nations as a decoy,

right?"

"Of course, we both know that."

"But if you're going to lie, have a ring of truth inside to make the story more believable, right?"

He smiled. "I suppose so. What are you getting at?"

"The United Nations. I was just thinking of Jeri and her words struck me. She talked about the League of Nations. Before there was a United Nations, there was a League of Nations. And where do you think that was? Geneva, Switzerland."

"And your point is?"

"That the United States became the most powerful nation on earth, New York the greatest city. My guess is that they'd kept the Chalice in the League of Nations for the length of time of its existence but were afraid to continue the practice, especially with the knowledge that the first city to be destroyed by a nuclear weapon would be New York."

"Hmm. Interesting. And very possible. But if not in New York City, where?"

"Geneva."

"I'll have to stop to call for the plane."

She started laughing and had a hard time stopping, the relief of the stress of the last few days finally catching up with her. "Sorry. But you've got it wrong, love. Not Geneva Switzerland. Geneva, New York."

****

Nicholai wasn't sure what got to him more, her laughter or that she'd said the word love. "Say it again," he commanded.

"Geneva, New York," she replied, her tone bewildered.

"Not that."

He looked over to see her smile. "Oh, you mean that little word at the end?"

"If you do not stop teasing me this instant," he

threatened.

"You'll what?" she dared him.

"I have no idea."

She leaned closer and he raised his arm so she could sit against his shoulder. "This wasn't exactly the way I planned on telling you."

At his wits end, he almost stopped the car. "I do not care."

Her voice grave she said, "I love you."

His heart skipped several beats. "You...are sure?"

"Very sure."

He couldn't help asking. "How? When did you know?"

"Aren't we supposed to be talking about important stuff? Like demons and people being in danger?"

"Say it again." OK, so maybe he was acting a little childish. *Too bad.*

"I love you."

He let out the breath he seemed to have held onto forever. "Always?"

"And forever."

"God, I want to kiss you. Come closer." She leaned over the console as far as she could and he turned his head as far as he dared. He thought about stopping the car. Especially when he was only able to kiss her for a second or two.

"Not satisfying at all." She slipped back into her seat but rested her head against his shoulder. "Damn bucket seats."

"Indeed. Then next time we rent a car—"

She nodded, caressing his arm. "An old fashioned Cadillac."

"Agreed." He changed the subject with reluctance. "We'll need to get a map. All I know is that Geneva is somewhere near Rochester."

"Sure." She was silent for a moment and he

wondered why. "You know, I was just thinking."

"Dangerous," he teased, trying to lighten the mood a bit.

She punched his arm. "Be serious."

He gave her his best stern yet attentive look. "I am."

"Would you have ever guessed that Morgan and Jeri would solve the puzzle?"

He countered with a question of his own. "Three months ago, would you have expected to be here with me, with our children growing in your belly?"

"No."

"Are you sorry, Tara?" he asked, not sure he wanted to hear the answer.

"Sorry about what?"

"Becoming a Noble, becoming my mate, becoming a part of this mess?"

"You're joking, right?"

He shook his head. "No, I was being very serious."

She didn't answer right away and his stomach fell. "No," she said, her tone and the hesitation telling him she was trying to find the words to answer with. "No," she repeated, with conviction. "I am not sorry. But before, I was only responsible for me. You know what I mean? Now I have you, the babies—the game's changed. At first I didn't want new rules. I wanted to be back where I was comfortable, where I only had to worry about myself. Now I wouldn't change a thing. I love you, Nicholai. You are my heart."

His own nearly swelled out of his chest. For a moment he couldn't breathe, then the world fell into place. All the doubt, the fear of never hearing her say the words washed away. "And you are mine."

"If the sacrifice were only mine, I wouldn't hesitate. Still, I suppose I don't have a choice."

He shuddered. "I cannot, no, I will not let you

sacrifice yourself or the babe."

"What difference does it make? Now or later? You can't ask me to simply cower in a corner and hide until no one is left. I won't do that."

"Never," he answered vehemently.

"So what are we going to do?"

"First we find the Chalice. Then you go back and stay with Sergei and Jeri."

"Before the pregnancy I would have called you a male chauvinist, but now I think that might be a good idea." She paused then asked, "Any clues as to how we find it?"

"We will figure something out."

"Glad you think so." She took a deep breath and sighed. "OK, so we find the Chalice. What the hell do we do with it once we find it?"

"Hide it again."

"And leave another generation with the same problem? Not nice."

"I do not know!" he cried. "Our only certain path is to destroy this thing."

"I hate to play devil's advocate here but again, how?"

"With every ounce of hope and belief we have."

"I didn't mean to suggest we wouldn't."

"I know, you are not being negative, you are being realistic. But you have to believe. Deep in my heart I am certain we will win. I do not know how, do not know why, I just know. Can you hold onto that?"

"He can't fight my love for you, Nico. So yes, I believe you and I'll hold onto that."

"Good."

They reached the Thruway and headed north. She rested her head against his shoulder and he held her hand. "You should try to sleep."

His beloved chuckled, her shoulder shaking against his arm once more. "Not happening. I'm starving. No, make that, we're starving."

"All right. We will stop at the next rest stop."

"No."

"Excuse me?"

"I said no. These kids are particular about their fast food. I'll tell you when."

All Nicholai could do was roll his eyes and keep on driving. They stopped for gas and he purchased a map. That was easy. The food—who would have thought there would be such a difference between tasteless and barely edible?

Once they were on the road again, Tara dozed for which he was extremely grateful. She did that for most of the rest of the trip.

When they finally reached Geneva, the Sun had set hours ago. Nicholai found a chain store pharmacy that was still open. They had no clothes or anything else with them so he purchased what he could. In asking questions during their rest stop, he found there were bed and breakfast's available in the town. He opted for a larger hotel instead, deciding a semi-crowded hotel would be safer. Besides, the hotel had a restaurant and room service was about all he could manage.

After dinner Tara said, "We should go out, explore."

"No," he replied, shaking his head. "This is his time. He is strongest at night. We will wait until tomorrow."

She grinned. "Any plans for this evening, then?"

"Would you be disappointed if I said no? I am tired from driving."

"Of course not. Well, if that's the case, I'm going to take a nice long hot soak in the tub."

Now that's helpful, he told himself, listening to the water run. I want to sleep and she's taking a bath. Pictures formed in his mind. Pictures totally non-conducive to slumber. "Dammit. This is not going to work."

He swung the door to the bathroom wide open, startling the heck out of her. His mouth was on hers before she could draw another breath. "Like hell I am going to sleep."

"There isn't room in the tub for both of us."

He grinned and started taking off his clothes. "Trust me. Where there is a will, there is a way."

An hour or so later he walked out of the bathroom with a towel draped across his shoulders and a smile on his face. He stretched out on the bed waiting for her to join him. He didn't speak when she did, didn't need to. Not long after he listened to her gentle snores.

Tomorrow would bring them to the brink. Of salvation or disaster? He didn't know. He could only hope they would be ready to face any challenge thrown at them.

Chapter Twenty-three

Tara awoke with a start. Lifting her head she looked around, not recognizing her surroundings. Reality hit her like a ton of bricks. She was about to plunge headlong into the path of a monster—then try to destroy it.

A fine tingling like ants crawling up and down under her skin told her the dawn approached. But the scene outside the window of the hotel seemed too dark, too barren, and too empty. Even with the love of her life lying next to her and a child growing in her belly, Tara felt alone.

You've always been alone, she said to herself. This is nothing new.

She put her head back down on the pillow and tried to go back to sleep. She'd awoken and found a hole in her soul.

Him.

How did one find the strength to combat such evil? She reached out and touched Nicholai and he stirred and turned over. With love? With hope? They were just words in the deep of the night. A race she didn't really know depended on her for its very survival. A child she wanted to see grow to adulthood was about to charge into the path of destruction through no fault of its own except that the babe rested in her womb.

You're falling into his trap, you know. Doubt yourself and he wins.

Easy words to say, so much harder to do, she countered.

As if in answer, Nicholai reached out for her. His arm circled her waist and he shifted closer to share his warmth. He seemed to be saying *believe in me, believe in us, believe in life not death. We'll win.*

Tara dozed, safe for now in her mate's embrace. And when she got up with him for their morning feed, she pushed her fears where they could not reach her. "He's nearby."

"I know. I feel the Sun as if the day were clear yet it is not."

They dressed, their mood somber. Funny, she wasn't hungry. Nicholai noticed as she picked at her breakfast in the hotel restaurant. "You still need to eat. You need the energy."

"You're right. Maybe it's this pall hanging over us. I just don't feel like doing much of anything."

"That is what he wants."

As if she didn't know. She tried to take a few more bites of toast, but they tasted like morsels made of sawdust. "I can't," she told him, pushing her plate away.

He reached out and squeezed her hand with his. "I asked at the front desk. There are two Roman Catholic churches in town. St. Francis De Sales and St. Stephens."

"We'll have to split up."

"Are you sure we will not miss anything here? I mean, why not Presbyterian or Lutheran? It is not like the High Council has ever had any ties to a certain religion."

"Because a Catholic church will use an ornate Chalice. The more ornate, the richer looking, the better. And a Presbyterian or a Lutheran church won't. Don't you remember, hide in plain sight? My guess is they probably bring the damned thing out on High Holy days for show."

"If you say so."

She nodded. "You know, I think I remember seeing that De Sales Church as we came in off the highway. No, wait a minute. It was a sign for a school. That must mean there's a church and a school. Maybe I should go there. There'll be more people around and I can always ask for help if I need it."

"A human will not be able to help. Still, I will feel better." He took a last sip from his coffee cup. "You have your story straight? I am at St. Stephen's etc, etc."

"Yes, dear," she told him, a tad exasperated. "We're moving into the area, you're checking out St. Stephen's, I'm checking out St.—what was it again?"

"Francis."

"Right. We use the 'friendly' rivalry and tell them we're checking both parishes out. That way they'll let us look around in places they normally wouldn't. I've got it, Nico."

"OK." He rose, paid the bill and they got into the car. "If you feel any danger at all, you will call for me."

"I'll call for you," she repeated.

St. Francis DeSale's church was older, made of brick, forthright in its simplicity. The brochures she picked up at the hotel told her this was a seasonal area so the church wasn't very large, but seemed large enough to hold an influx of holiday or summer visitors. A few concrete steps, large wooden doors, she'd forgotten what walking into a church felt like.

The holy water felt right on her fingertips. To genuflect, to kneel to honor Christ no longer felt like a symbol. All of a sudden, Tara knew what was missing. Her faith. She stepped into a pew, leaned her head against the pew in front of her, and prayed.

She wasn't sure how long she stayed that way. Tara rose with the thought that she would like Nicholai to come to church with her someday. Perhaps share the peace she now felt. She was about to make her way to the rectory office when she saw a priest cross in front of the altar.

"Excuse me, Father?" She walked towards him.

He stopped. "Hi. Can I help you?"

"My name is Valentin. Tamara Valentin." Funny, she liked the sound of that now. Liked it a lot.

"I'm Father Jim." He held out his hand and they shook.

"My husband and I are moving to the area. We're looking to join a congregation."

"That's wonderful," he beamed.

"Would you be able to take a moment and show me around the church? Nicholai is over at St. Stephens—" He stopped beaming as she let her voice trail off.

"You don't want to go there now, child. Believe me. We have a school and a family association, a wonderful atmosphere for the baby."

Taken aback she asked, "Possibly more than one. How did you know?"

"Too many years as a priest."

She laughed. "Father Duncan always knew too."

"Your pastor?"

She nodded. "From a long time ago. In New Jersey. Would you mind showing me around?"

"I'd be delighted."

She'd been right. The walls were simply painted with only a few stained glass windows. The pews were older, not ornate by any standards, but gleamed with fresh polish. A simple step up to the altar, a plain wooden crucifix—funny but she realized there wasn't a need to dress up a church. Here, the meaning of Christ came through with the love she felt inside.

A page over the intercom halted their tour. "I'm sorry," Father Jim apologized. "As you can tell I have an important phone call. Probably my mother." They both laughed. "Why don't you come on over to the rectory with me? After the call, I can show you the school."

"I don't want to be a bother. Besides, I'd like to stay a moment if you don't mind. Why don't I go over and see the school and meet you there in, say, half an hour. Nicholai should be back to talk to you by then anyway."

"If I'm not available, please wait. Rita can fill you in on any details, but I would like to meet your husband."

Tara smiled. "Thank you, Father. You've been very kind. I'll make sure we wait."

"Wonderful." They shook hands again and he left.

As soon as he was gone, Tara walked towards the Sacristy. Throughout this entire mess, Nicholai had continually told her 'hide in plain sight.' Where better to hide an ornate Chalice than in a Sacristy? At the Retreat they'd kept the more ornate, more expensive pieces in a cabinet with a lock. She'd heard other churches had to use safes. She had no idea what she was going to do if she had break into a safe.

Tara saw a hallway open around each side of the altar. She went to her left and found a closed door. As she opened the handle, she realized she'd found what she was looking for—the Sacristy. Not a large room, rectangular in shape and rather crowded, with one long wall fully devoted to cabinets. She opened one of the long doors to find it filled with altar server robes. A smaller cabinet held a shelf full of purificators. But one cabinet stood floor to ceiling.

Thank God, she thought. A cabinet with a lock, a small lock. Tara looked around. The church was too silent. She could smell the faint smoke from candles that had been lit in prayer. She didn't like being a thief. Stealing went against every moral teaching she'd been given. She told herself she had no choice.

With her extra strength, the metal was easy to pry apart. Opening the cabinet doors, she fully expected to see the Chalice sitting on a shelf. Not here? She knew what the piece looked like from her dream.

Now what? Without thinking, Tara put her hand on a shelf to wipe some dust away. Her hand tingled as her fingers touched the wood. *Hide* in plain sight, dummy. She looked up, seeing several chalices on the top shelf. She had to rise up on her toes to get to there, but she felt around, moving other chalices out of the way until she reached the prize.

A sound from inside the church startled the hell out of her. Caught. With her hand in the cookie jar. She didn't move, barely breathed. The seconds that passed seemed eternal. When she finally had the nerve to continue, she made the mistake of looking at her watch. Damn. She didn't have enough time to steal the Chalice and go to the school. Should she take the Chalice now or wait for Nicholai? A voice from what sounded like the inside of the church made up her mind. Now was not the time.

Putting the items she'd moved back to their respective places, Tara pushed the lock back together but not all the way, and left the room. She walked across the altar and headed towards the front of the church. She'd nearly reached the doors when a man rose from a pew to step in front of her. Not just a man; Gunner Manneheim.

Her heart nearly stopped beating again.

"You have something my Master wants very badly."

Sheer terror locked up her throat. She needed to stall. Sooner than later someone would start looking for her. "Sorry," she finally told him. "Good idea that didn't pan out right."

"You will tell me now or I will force the information out of you."

Tara didn't like the way his eyes lit up as he said those words. Definitely an uh-oh but to show fear at this point would only give him an edge. How brazen could she be when her knees threatened to buckle?

"Read my lips, OK? Not here. Nada. Zip. Got it?"

"I do not believe you. Nor does my Master."

Well now, that was just wonderful. Mister Purely Evil couldn't come out in daylight, so he had minions to do his dirty work for him. Locking her knees so she'd continue to stand up she said, "Look, I'm going to repeat myself one last time. You, too," she called, raising her voice as if talking to someone else that was listening. "The Chalice is not here. We have the wrong church. It's over at St. Stephens."

"You are lying."

That pissed her off. "And you're starting to sound like a broken record. Read my lips," she repeated. "I'm gonna do this once. Real slow. Not here. Wrong church. Do you think your pea-sized brain can handle that?"

Oops, she thought as his hands closed around her throat. Guess he couldn't take a joke.

She kicked out as hard as she could and caught a solid blow to his shin. That *had* to hurt. Still, his fingers only tightened.

I think I'm in trouble, she said to herself. She brought her fists down on his forearms. No luck. She tried to knee him in the groin, but he turned just at the last minute and she got mostly his hip.

Definitely in trouble now, she realized as black spots started to swim across her vision.

Don't panic, she told herself. Go for his eyes.

Instead the room started to darken. Don't panic, she repeated. She tried to play act and go limp. Part of the moment wasn't an act though. The room had begun to spin. And he just let her down slow as he choked the life out of her.

Nico. Help me.

****

Nicholai was on his way to her when she screamed for help. Thank God he didn't have far to go. He pulled up in front of St. Francis, his heart in his throat and beating so hard he could barely breathe. He burst into the church and found Charles Rhys-Jones bending over in the center aisle, holding onto his side with one hand, a pew with the other.

Nicholai raced up the aisle ready to kill Rhys-Jones when he saw a man lying on the floor, a knife in his heart. Gunner Manneheim? Then he looked further away.

"Tara," he cried, skidding to a stop next to his mate.

"She's alive," Charles told him.

After feeling her pulse, strong and steady, Nicholai was able to swallow. "What happened? What are you doing here?"

"Not sure," came the man's rueful smile.

"Your side—"

Charles lifted a hand that came away full of blood. "Thanks for noticing. But it's a flesh wound. Nothing more."

"My mate?"

"Too damn close, Valentin. Too damn close. What the hell were you thinking, leaving her alone like that?"

Bewildered, Nicholai didn't know what to say. "You saved Tara?" Rhys-Jones nodded. "Why?"

He shook his head again. “Damned if I know. Curiosity, I guess. Maybe a part of me can’t accept my sentence. I honestly don’t know.”

“And him?”

“He was trying to kill the lady when I walked in. I had a feeling he’d show up to cause trouble, although a church would have been the last place I expected to find your mate or him. Anyway, I’ve been following our friend here since he left the High Council.”

“And he was following us.”

“Looks like it. Anyway, when I walked in I figured I had to do something. I didn’t feel like having to face you if I didn’t.”

“You owed me nothing.”

“You’re right,” Charles nodded. “I didn’t. But I owed your mate a debt I didn’t think I’d ever get the chance to repay.”

Nicholai stood up. “Now you have.” He held out his hand in friendship. Charles accepted the gesture.

“I’m still an outcast.”

“When this is over, I will, no, we will, fight for you in any way we can.”

“Thanks.” Charles straightened his shoulders, wincing in pain. “What about him?”

Nicholai thought a moment. “Do you have a car?” Charles nodded yes.

Nicholai shrugged off his jacket and lifted Manneheim’s body to an upright position. When he saw the thin stiletto sticking out of the man’s chest he said, “Nasty piece.”

“Served its purpose,” Charles replied.

He put the jacket on the man and zipped the zipper. The jacket covered the wound and the knife. Then he lifted the man and sat him in a pew. “He’s had too much to drink, don’t you think?”

Charles smiled. “Where should I dump him?”

“I counted about three hours worth of woods

along the Thruway. Take your pick."

"What about the blood?"

Nicholai paused. "I have an idea. Do you have a handkerchief?"

Charles did. Nicholai lifted Tara and moved her closer to the pool of blood left by their enemy. He lifted her legs apart and smeared blood on the insides. Then they lifted Manneheim's body and took it out to the vestibule of the church. Nicholai ran back and wiped up any blood with the handkerchief.

When he was done he helped arrange the dead body so Charles could look like he was helping a drunk out of the church.

"I'm glad we're not enemies anymore," Charles said with a salute. "You're one hell of an adversary."

"You as well. Good luck." They clasped hands as friends.

****

A frisson of fear ran through his bones as he recognized the caller on the other end of the line. "I was forced to make a withdrawal this morning."

"I see. Valentin's mate is here now," Father Jim replied. "What I can't understand is how they figured it out so quickly."

"Valentin is no fool." A short laugh followed. "A pity really. He would have made an excellent member of the High Council."

The priest didn't care about Council's and Houses. He had a debt to these people he could never repay. They'd saved his family from his past and the mistakes he'd made, so he did what they asked. Still, he was curious. "What will you do now?"

"That is not something you need to know."

"What should I do about the Valentin's? If they're as smart as you're implying, they'll be hard to deceive."

"True. But you've learned over the years. Just play the role we've given you, be Father Jim."

"But they're expecting to find the Water."

This time the laughter on the other end of the line grated on his ear. "Of course, they are. And as far as you're concerned, that's exactly what they're going to find. Holy Water. Nothing more. Do you understand?"

"Yes."

"Good. We'll be in touch."

"God go with you," Father Jim replied. His tone told the caller exactly how he felt.

A deep sigh reached his ear. "For your sake, you'd better hope He does."

****

Nicholai ran out of the church and into the rectory. "Call an ambulance. Quick. My wife. She's collapsed. She's bleeding. Oh my God, the babies."

The priest followed him into the church, carrying a blanket and muttering prayers, running as fast as he could. A woman the Father called Rita followed. Then she ran out again to call for an ambulance. Nicholai cradled Tara's head as they waited for an ambulance to come. He sat listening to the priest, part of him wishing the man wouldn't pray, part of him wishing he'd never stop.

On the way to the hospital, Nicholai agonized. He wanted Sergei with him. He didn't want to trust his mate to a human doctor. On the other hand, she should have healed by now. Why hadn't she come out of it yet?

Nicholai let them take her into the Emergency Room but did everything he could to stay near. They were busy so no one gave him a hard time. Soon, a nurse came over to him to ask him to go to the desk for his insurance and Tara's information. He had none, having no need for it, so he gave them a credit card then went right back to her side. When one of the nurses came to check her, she told him about the blood on Tara's legs. She also told him, Tara seemed not to be bleeding any longer. They were waiting for an order, then they were going to take her to x-ray for an ultrasound. Since Tara was stable, the nurse advised him, he'd better get ready for a long wait. The entire hospital was understaffed. "Tara, love?" he asked a couple of hours later as she stirred.

Stretching, she looked around. When she saw her surroundings, she panicked. "Oh God, no. I've lost the babies. I've lost the babies."

"No, love," Nicholai rushed to reassure her. "The babe, babes, are fine. You have been unconscious."

"Manneheim," she whispered, fear flooding her gaze.

"Will no longer trouble anyone, love. He is dead."

"Dead? You killed him?"

"No, Tara. Not me. Charles Rhys-Jones, of all people." Nicholai told her the story as fast as he could. Then he parked his mouth on hers until he was certain she was all right.

"We have to get out of here," she said, once he let her up for air.

"I know. It is getting dark."

Being taken into a hospital for a legitimate reason was infinitely easier than trying to sneak out. But they managed. When a car accident took the attention of most of the Emergency Room staff, they made their move. They found her clothes, and by moving as fast as they dared past Security, they left the building the same way they entered.

"Come on," Nicholai urged, taking her hand and leading her back around to the front entrance of the hospital. She gave him a quizzical stare as he said, "Wait here."

He returned a few minutes later with a bit of a sheepish grin. "In all the excitement, I forgot to take the car. I left it at the church. I just called for a taxi to take us back."

She laughed at him. "I'll forgive you if you

never, ever, leave me alone again."

"I promise. As God is my witness, I promise. I am so sorry. If it had not been for Charles, if he hadn't been following you—"

She put a finger on his lips. "Don't punish yourself, Nico. Let's be grateful we're still alive and that everyone's unharmed. OK?"

"All of me wants to take you back to the hotel, call Sergei and Alexi, gather our House, and leave you surrounded." He held onto her for dear life.

"Shhh," she whispered, her hands running down his face as if to embed every line, every crease into her fingertips. "We're alive. That's all that matters."

In the cab, he tucked her next to him, unwilling to let her go for even a second. "I take it you know where the Chalice is."

She smiled. "Of course."

"I think he does too. He will try to destroy it."

"Not if we get to it first."

A thousand fears poked knives into his stomach. "Time is running out. The Sun has nearly set." Oh those insidious tools of destruction. "Maybe we should leave, let the rest of the Houses help us handle this."

She shook her head. "We can't."

"Today when I thought you dead I felt a need to pray. Then I realized that prayer is belief. But I am not certain even prayer is going to help us now."

"Neither am I."

Chapter Twenty-four

Why did the silence have to be so…silent? Why did the church seem so cold to her, so austere? Why did none of this feel right?

"How do we get in without being seen?" Tara asked. All right, she felt guilty about breaking into a church. She couldn't help it. She'd been raised by nuns.

"There is a side door over here."

"It's locked."

"Not anymore." Nicholai grinned, bending the lock with his fingers then prying the metal open. "Remind me to send a check for damages."

She would have laughed if she could. Had they been anywhere else and on any other mission— Tara shivered. The chilly air in the church increased her sense of foreboding. The evil one's presence seemed to permeate everywhere. Still, they had no choice.

Tara led Nicholai through the church. As they approached the altar she asked for aid. The prayer seemed to fall on deaf ears. God wasn't listening, perhaps to show them the error of their way that they needed to regain their Nobility? Or perhaps because the evil they now tried to fight had invaded the church. How she wished she knew.

She took Nicholai to the Sacristy and to the cabinet; opening the lock she'd never really closed. She began setting pieces on the floor to get them out of the way.

"Up in the corner," she told him, stepping out of the way so Nicholai could reach in. He seemed to stop and she covered her nervousness with words. "Do you feel the vibrations? Even the wood feels alive."

With his arm all the way inside and his head in between shelves she was unable to hear his answer.

"Alive?" Nicholai said, pulling back. "Not really. But I do feel a bit of a vibration."

That surprised her. Why did she feel the Chalice more than Nicholai? Nicholai had been a Noble far longer than she had been.

"Strange, I wouldn't have thought I would have more of a connection."

Nicholai cupped her face with his hands. "You had the dream, not I. Remember?"

He turned and pulled other pieces off the wood and out of the cabinet. As he did a chalice slid off the shelf and fell to the floor before she could catch it. They both froze at the sound. When she finally got her heart to stop pounding, Nicholai quipped, "Oops."

How she wanted to laugh. How incredibly strong Nicholai was to be joking at a time like this. He started to reach in and she grabbed his arm. "No. Wait."

He frowned. "Why?"

She didn't dare let him know how she was feeling. But caution never hurt anyone. "You saw what a simple wooden case did to me."

"I'm already a Noble," he countered. Then he shook his head. "All right. If it will make you feel better."

In the end she couldn't find anything else to use

and had to hand him a purificator. He wrapped his hand in the white cloth and reached into the cabinet again. As he pulled out the Chalice even she could feel its power.

"Wow," she breathed.

She'd seen the Chalice in her dream state, but the reality was so much more beautiful. The silver gleamed right through a fine layer of dust. The detail on the inlays were incredibly hard to describe, but she could tell what kind of painstaking work went into making the Chalice. The power of the piece awed her but so did the workmanship.

The strength and breadth of the Nobility rested in her mate's hands. She watched Nicholai stare at the Chalice, transfixed.

"Stunning. I had no idea. I would never have believed. Such power—"

Darkness descended upon them as if it had been cloaked. All her misgivings made sense now. Their enemy had been waiting for them.

"All mine," came a voice from behind them.

Tara whirled to see her brother standing there, a look she'd never seen before on his face. Feral, she'd tell herself later. Almost maniacal. A sinking feeling spread to her toes. The church seemed to laugh at her, laugh at her audacity. Since when did she think she could be more important than God?

No, Lord, she wanted to cry out. Not more important. Important to you. In the beginning, you created the Nobility to be just that. Somewhere along the way we forgot our purpose, that's true. But not our faith. Not our belief. Don't punish us.

Eerie laughter rang inside her head. A picture formed, one of her brother and her mate. Fighting. To the death. "Don't let him win, Morgan," she pleaded. "Please, brother."

A voice not his own answered. "He's no match for me and neither are you, child."

"You'll never get near her," Nicholai warned his adversary. He turned to her, shoving the Chalice into her hands. "Go. Run. Now."

She hesitated. This was wrong. The whole scene was wrong. Life didn't make sense without her mate. Life didn't make sense without honor, without wanting to sacrifice. "He'll kill you."

"He'll kill us all if you don't get out of here. Now go!"

She started backing out of the Sacristy and around the corner. She stepped up onto the altar of the church, feeling her way, trying not to take her eyes off her brother who followed. Nicholai followed them both, standing by the edge of the altar, waiting to see the next move.

Too late, she thought as doors slammed and windows sealed shut. It was like something out of a bad horror movie.

Had God abandoned her or simply proven to her that she had the courage to fight on her own? Maybe it was the power of the Chalice. Maybe it was the souls of her ancestors. She would never know exactly where the courage to answer came from. "You can do better than that, can't you?" she sneered.

"Tara, don't," Nicholai cried.

"Yes, little one. Goading your enemy at a time like this can be very detrimental to your health. And the babe's."

A second or two passed as she swallowed. Funny but the church didn't seem so foreboding now. And yes, she was stealing, but was taking back that which was originally yours a sin? She didn't think so.

"You didn't plan on that, did you? A child," she reminded their nemesis.

Morgan, but not Morgan, laughed. The sound sent shivers down her back. "No, brazen one, I did not. I never expected you to live."

Tara had no idea where the words kept coming from. Perhaps her own strength. Or maybe she was tired of being a puppet on someone else's string. Or perhaps this was God's way of giving sanction.

"Two mistakes. Let me see…just coincidence?"

A sliver of doubt skated across her brother's features. "Plans are meant to be changed. Like the path of a brook around stones in its bed. The path changes, but the destination is always the same."

Something inside told her now was the time to hammer away at its doubts. "What if you read the brook the wrong way? What if the paths around the stones lead you in the wrong direction? What happens to your plan then?"

That angered their nemesis for he barked out a command in a voice much older, much colder than Morgan's. "Kill them."

Morgan attacked and Nicholai leaped to defend her.

"Don't hurt him, Nico," she begged, knowing full well her mate might not have a choice.

"How touching." Tara whirled around as the air around them dropped thirty degrees. *The oldest of the old.* He stepped out of the shadows too beautiful to behold, too perfect to be real. Where she got the courage she would never know. Really never know. She lifted her eyes, straightened her shoulders, and caught his gaze.

For a moment the ancient one seemed stunned as if such a thing had never happened before. Then he tried to kill her by invading her mind. It was like sitting in a pit of slithering snakes, like being trapped in the smallest of spaces, like not being able to take back the one act that destroyed the one you loved. He tried to destroy her heart. Not the physical organ, but the part of her that made her who she was. Only Tara wasn't going to let him hurt her. She wrenched away before he finished its plan only to see her mate and her brother locked in mortal combat. If he couldn't destroy her, he was going to destroy the ones she loved.

"Hail Mary Full of Grace," she prayed.

"A human deity? How plebeian."

Plebeian or not, the words were a comfort. "The Lord is With Thee."

Nicholai tried to hold onto Morgan, but her brother kept breaking away. Morgan aimed blow after blow, yet Nicholai took each one and never aimed one back. Instead Nicholai wrestled, he sidestepped and tried to stay out of harm's way.

"I think I'll have him snap your mate's neck. That's the phrase you use, isn't it? Yes, your mate's neck. That would please me very much."

Forgive this poor sinner, Lord. And do not let others take my sins upon them. "Blessed Art Thou Among Women."

Morgan rained punch after punch onto, into, anywhere he could hit Nicholai. Finally one caught her mate square on the jaw and he fell backwards through the doorway and into the Sacristy, into the cabinet that held the other chalices. Nicholai fell to the floor on one knee and seemed too stunned to move. Several cups fell with him and banged onto the floor, startling her.

Her enemy was powerful. But wasn't God even more powerful? "And Blessed is the Fruit of Thy Womb, Jesus."

As Morgan charged, Nicholai grabbed hold of a chalice that had fallen to the floor.

"Forgive me, Tara," he cried, swinging the metal up into Morgan's chin. Her brother fell to the floor and never moved again. He was out cold.

"Pity," their nemesis said, dusting off his hands as if Morgan were yesterday's garbage. "I'll have to find another minion now."

Tara fought to keep the frown off her face.

Morgan wasn't dead. His jaw was probably broken and he was going to have the dental bill from hell, but he wasn't dead. Why didn't their adversary know that? Because he *was* fallible. She backed away again and stepped up onto the altar.

"Your minions are sadly lacking, oh great one."

"And you need to have that tongue of yours removed."

If Tara had thought the darkness dark before, sheer black greeted her eyes now. The air swirled around her, but her mouth remained intact. How could that be? The Water? The Chalice? The altar? Maybe just her own faith. Tara laughed, her tone full of disdain.

"Is that the best you can do?" she mocked. "My God."

"There is no such thing."

"Perhaps not for you but some of us do believe in Him."

"A Church will not stop me. Your belief will not stop me. Only that overgrown piece of silver protects you. Since it does, I think I'll play with him."

Windows rattled as a fierce wind began to whip all around them. The black darkness disappeared leaving only the shadows of a church at rest. Obviously their enemy wanted her to watch as Nicholai rose off the ground. That eerie laughter turned heartier. The old one was having fun. He started twirling Nicholai like the wheel on a casino gaming table, faster and faster, then up, down, all around.

"Stop," she cried. "It's me you want. And this—," she added holding up the Chalice. "Let him go, out of this Church, without harm. You can have the Chalice, the babies, and me."

The church rafters shook with his cry. "No!" Nicholai screamed from his airborne flight.

The wind stopped as suddenly as it started.

Nicholai fell hard but was on his feet a moment later.

"No, my love. Don't," he pleaded. He tried to run towards her, but the evil one would not let him.

That hurt. She would not be able to put her arms around him one last time.

"I love you, Nicholai. By all that is holy and good, our love will last forever. Now Go!"

"I cannot. If you die, I must die also."

"How touching," the eldest sneered. "Such sacrifice. Spare me the drivel."

The truth hit her so suddenly she almost didn't listen. She'd been so worried about sinning and hurting everyone else that she forgot to listen. The greatest gift from God was forgiveness. The greatest gift of all was Love. There was only one way to fight total evil. With total love.

"Nico, come here." As soon as she said the words, Nicholai was able to move. He crossed the room and took her in his arms. "One last kiss," she begged. "Please."

That seemed to amuse her enemy, but a frown of doubt crossed its features. Then she focused her entire being on her mate. Nicholai simply looked at her with a tender gaze. "You need to ask?"

He wrapped his arms around her, but she never let go of the Chalice. Their kiss was sweet and would endure any evil, or so she hoped. When at last her mate let her go she said, "Here. Come and get it."

As she stepped back to let the evil one approach, she pushed the top of the Chalice off. "We will never submit to your evil. What was done, was done, and cannot be undone. And with good reason." So saying, she threw the water that rested inside the Chalice all over its body. "Go back to the chasm that spawned you. I've had enough of you, your spite, your ugliness, your fun and games."

A screech split the air. The entire church shook

with the unearthly sound. She dropped the Chalice onto the floor, so she could cover her ears with her hands. She never wanted to hear a scream like that again. Foul smoke filled the air and she found she couldn't breathe. Next to her Nicholai coughed and choked. The rafters seemed to take the brunt of the abuse, but the windows creaked and trembled too. Then, as if someone had flipped a switch, the air cleared and silence reigned.

"Nico?" She found herself on all fours and crawled over to him, her hands touching him everywhere in an attempt at reassurance.

"I am all right, love," he replied, wonder in his tone as he tried to sit up. "Sore but all in one piece."

He stood, swayed, righted himself then reached out to help her stand. "Oh my God, Nico. I was so scared."

He laughed, a huge, belly-burst of a laugh. "Woman, if that is what you are like when you are scared, I cannot wait to see you when you are terrified."

She lifted her gaze towards the altar. *Thank you, God. Thank you.* "Do you think he's dead?"

Nicholai shook his head. "I have no idea."

"How will we ever be sure?"

"I do not know, sweetness. I do not know."

A moan brought their attention to the Sacristy. "Morgan. Oh my God, Morgan. He's alive, you know."

A huge smile broke out on Nicholai's face. "He is?"

They ran to her brother and Tara kneeled next to him.

"Tara," he said. He looked at her as he always had, slightly confused but no longer vacant and certainly not evil. His hand reached up to his jaw. "Hurt."

She bent down and kissed the injured area.

Funny, but it took her brother to tell her how to destroy their enemy. With faith and with belief in each other. Most of all, with love.

Nicholai helped him to his feet and they led him to a pew so he could sit down. Then she kneeled in front of him so he could see her. "Morgan, you must leave now."

Damned delayed relay switch. Precious moments passed as he tried to process her words.

"We have to get you out of here. Do you understand?"

He nodded a minute later. A desire to shout for joy warred with her frustration at not being able to communicate. "Go to my townhouse. You know where that is?"

He nodded, this time almost immediately. "Yes."

"Sergei is there. He'll take care of you until I get home. And you're going to do something very important, Morgan. Do you understand? Very important."

"Very important," he repeated.

"Good." Nicholai had gone and retrieved the Chalice. He handed the piece to her. "Take this to Sergei, Morgan. All right?"

"I can…do this."

Tara handed the Chalice to Morgan, making sure his hand covered the purificator. A part of her wished he'd slip. Maybe the power of the Chalice—

Some things were just meant to be. Morgan ran out of the Church as if the devil were after him. Maybe it was. But she didn't care.

"I love you, brother," she whispered at his retreating back.

Nicholai wrapped his arms around her and spread light kisses all over her face. "Are you OK?"

"I think so."

He kissed her soundly. "Now?"

"Better," she hemmed and hawed.

"I wouldn't be alive without you," he said, once he let them both come up for air. "I love you, Tara."

She gave him a shaky laugh and a look that said, "You've got to be kidding."

They were walking towards the front of the church when the door flew open. Father Jim ran to them, concern etched in his kindly features.

"My goodness. Are you both all right? What a storm. Seemed to blow up out of nowhere then was gone just as quick. I was on my way over here and I heard shouting."

Tara let Nicholai answer. All she could manage was to lay her head on his chest.

"We came back to thank you, Father. For your help today." Nicholai kissed the top of Tara's head. "My...wife only knew where the church entrance was. We thought there might be an entrance or a way to get back to the rectory from here. We were just about to leave when we heard a noise. I'm afraid we ran into a thief. I tried to stop him, I really did. But I think the burglar got away with something expensive looking. I think it was made of silver. And, to top it all off when we struggled, we made quite a mess all over the place."

Father Jim just stood there looking horrified. And grateful at the same time.

"That's going to be some shiner by the looks of it," the priest finally answered. "Lord have mercy, son. I would never have wanted to you be hurt, not for anything in the world." He walked back with them to the Sacristy and peered around to survey the damage. "All right, the thief knew what he was doing, the piece was our most expensive. But a Chalice can be replaced. People can't. So all I can say is thank you."

"I wonder how he knew where it was hidden," Nicholai said.

"I have no idea. But a few people besides myself

know its whereabouts. I guess nothing is sacred," the priest answered, his tone sad.

"What a shame," Tara commiserated, coming out of her state of shock. After all the acting she'd done, she could act again. "I mean, you must have treasured the piece to have hidden it."

The priest shook his head. "I told you, it doesn't matter. We'll replace it. Don't worry. Nothing is worth a human life."

Nicholai exchanged a look with her. "You are absolutely right. We are both safe and unharmed. That's all that matters. Still, it is a shame when people steal from a church."

They walked across the altar and Tara looked down at the carpeting. The water had created a stain. "I'm afraid we've ruined the carpeting on the altar, Father. I wonder if the stain will ever go away." Tara exchanged a look with her mate knowing the priest would never get her hidden meaning.

Father Jim didn't seem bothered by that either. "Oh, that? I'll have someone clean up. After all, it was only Holy Water."

****

They reached Tara's townhouse late the next evening. Tara asked Nicholai to stay over in the hotel. She was in no shape to put up with an eight-hour drive home. She told Nicholai, though, that she wouldn't be able to rest until she knew both Jeri and Morgan were safe.

As always, opening the door to her townhouse helped calm her down.

As she did, she saw Jeri standing by the window.

"Jeri," she cried, incredibly happy to see her friend standing there. Alive, well, in one piece and not prone in a bed anymore.

The elder woman turned very slowly as if

delaying the moment. Delaying the moment? What the hell was going on?

"Damn, child. I always knew you were pretty. Always knew that from the inside. But I never knew you were gorgeous."

Gorgeous? What the devil?...oh no. Tara wasn't ever saying that word to herself again. She'd had all the evil she could handle.

Where was Jeri's cane? Where was old Sam? The dog trotted in as Sergei entered the room. "Jeri?"

She still didn't get it. Jeri crossed the room looking straight at her. *Looking straight at her*. "Yes, child. Sometimes the Lord works in mysterious ways."

Tara's heart leaped in her chest. "You can see? Really see?"

"Sure enough. And like I said—"

"Don't," Nicholai admonished. "You'll give her a swelled head.

Tara cried out and threw her arms around her best bud. They laughed, they cried; better than that night she remembered with the movies. Sergei knew when to stay out of the way and went back to the kitchen to get everyone something to eat. Nicholai hovered and who could blame him. She couldn't. Even if she did need a little woman-to-woman time.

When Sergei returned, they all noshed on cheese, crackers, mini quiches—munch food.

"You should have seen her in action, Jeri," Nicholai praised. "I have never seen such courage."

Jeri simply nodded. "Knew it all along."

"Both of you stop. I told you before, it was the Chalice. I don't know how to explain, but it gave me the courage. Honest."

Both her mate and her best friend looked skeptical. But Sergei was the one who surprised her the most. She'd never received a look of fatherly pride from anyone in her life before. All of a sudden she felt humble.

After they ate, the mood turned serious and Tara asked the question that had haunted her since they walked out of the church. "Do you think he's gone?"

Nicholai sighed. "I'm not sure we will really ever know."

"What do you think they'll do with the Chalice?" she asked Nicholai.

He shrugged. "I spoke to Ariel. The High Council is being very cagey about that. What gets me is that we have absolutely no idea if the Water still exists or not."

"Holy water. You sure the priest said that?" Jeri asked.

Tara and Nicholai both nodded.

"I believe," Sergei told them, "that if it had been the Water of Change, we would have known. My guess is that someone got to the Water first."

Tara looked over at her mate. He gave her an imperceptible wink. They were both thinking the same thing. Han-Sing had never been accounted for.

"Maybe it's better this way," she replied. "I'm just glad Morgan is safe and sound.

Morgan had gotten to the townhouse ahead of them, though Tara had no idea how, and done exactly as she'd instructed. Then Sergei had taken both Morgan and the Chalice to the Retreat, asking the Sisters to watch over them. They needed a handyman, it seemed, so for now both would be taken care of.

"Frankly," Nicholai added. "I've had enough intrigue for one lifetime. Hopefully, we'll never have to find out."

"Ditto," she added.

Jeri rose and looked over at her with a smile. Tara still couldn't get used to that.

"All right," Jeri laughed. "I can take a hint. Sergei's gonna help these old bones get back home where they belong. Isn't that right, Sergei?"

"I see I have no choice," he chuckled.

"As a matter of fact, you're gonna watch a movie with me, isn't that right?

The elder man simply sighed as if the end of the world had come. They all knew how close a call it really had been.

Tara gave her friend a hug and a kiss goodbye and watched her leave.

"Could we take a walk?" she asked Nicholai.

"If you like."

She took his hand and led him out to the ocean. As they walked along the beach, she let their hands swing, as she would have done so many years ago on a date. They could date now. Maybe. Or just love each other until the end of their years and beyond.

Right now, though, only the moment mattered and she was content to listen to the ocean's song.

"I can't imagine what we'll do for excitement from here on in."

Nicholai stopped dead in his tracks. "*That's* not funny."

She laughed anyway. Thinking out loud she said, "I'll need to catch up on some work. And I'd like to make sure Morgan is settled. Can we stay a few days before we leave?"

"Of course. Alexi should be home by now. He will take care of things until we return."

"Nico, promise me something."

"Anything, love."

"I want this to be our home also."

Swinging her into his arms, his mouth devoured hers. "Anywhere you are is home, sweetness. You are my heart, my breath, my soul."

"And you're mine."

"Any regrets?"

"None." She returned the kiss with a slow sensual touch. "Morgan has a home, Jeri has her eyesight, and I have a family. What more could I ask for?"

Nicholai smiled wickedly. "This?"

"Well," she laughed. "There's always *that*."

They started walking again and he laughed with her. All of a sudden he stopped and lifted her high to the sky. As he let her slide down to the ground he told her, "And don't you forget it, *Buster*."

"*Buster?*" The rest of her words were swallowed by his kiss, a kiss signaling a new beginning for them all.

A word about the author...

Linda J. Parisi has been a member of New Jersey Romance Writers and RWA since 1993. In that time, she has served in numerous capacities on the NJRW Board of Directors and was Conference Chair for the 1999 NJRW Conference "That Touch of Magic." She has served RWA as a Golden Heart Coordinator, a Golden Heart judge, and as a Workshop Moderator. She has spent the last 14 years learning the craft of writing and was a RWA Pro long before the idea came about. And throughout her writing career, the best part of all has been the friends she has made. In her "other life," Linda works in new product development for a diagnostic technologies company. She has been married for thirty years; has one son, a junior at Rutgers, who is better at chemistry than she'll ever be. But she's got him beat when it comes to English 101.

www.ingramcontent.com/pod-product-compliance
Lightning Source LLC
Chambersburg PA
CBHW070219260626
47160CB00002B/600

9781601544889